To Rachel
Best wishe
Rica

RELUCTANT COURAGE

*A Family's Fight for Survival
in Nazi Occupied Oslo*

RICA NEWBERY

BookVenture Publishing LLC
1000 Country Lane Ste 300
Ishpeming MI 49849
www.bookventure.com
Hotline: 1(877) 276-9751
Fax: 1(877) 864-1686

Ordering Information:
Quantity sales. Special discounts are available on quantity purchases by corporations, associations, and others. For details, contact the publisher at the address above.

Printed in the United States of America.

Library of Congress Control Number	2017958636
ISBN-13: Softcover	978-1-64069-972-4
Hardback	978-1-64069-973-1
Pdf	978-1-64069-974-8
ePub	978-1-64069-975-5
Kindle	978-1-64069-976-2

Rev. date: 10/25/2017

Dedication/Acknowledgements

T his book could not have been written without the support and encouragement of my friends and family. My husband has offered much constructive feedback and supported me on the days when I have despaired. The Resistance Museum in Oslo and Falstad Museum, north of Trondheim, demonstrate many stories of local heroism, as Norwegians resisted Nazism on all fronts. I owe the most to my mother, Brit, who told humorous and heart-breaking stories from her childhood in Oslo in the war, and who is the inspiration for this book.

CHAPTER 1

Flat 7, 24 Kristian IV Gate, Oslo

September 25th, 1942

War entered Norway by stealth on April 9*th*, 1940. Norwegians were taken unawares and apart from the explosion of the Blucher on Oslo Fjord, they were taken without a fight. The people of Oslo just stared as German troops marched in and took over.

Soon everywhere you looked there were red flags with swastikas, soldiers with rifles, motorbikes, women in long queues for food, and posters full of Nazi propaganda. Maria faced each day with resignation and resentment, not wanting to think too far ahead, and not wanting to know too much. She had problems of her own and three daughters to feed.

She heard rumors of men and women dragged out of their beds in the middle of the night by the Gestapo, people shot in the streets, boys running off to join the resistance, and bombing raids up north. The last two years of life under the Nazi occupation had been one long cycle of survival, with dull routine punctuated by brief interludes of terror.

On the day that this story starts, September 25th, 1942, she had no idea how much worse things were yet to become.

＊　＊　＊　＊

It was three in the morning when Maria was woken by a pounding on the door. She groaned and propped herself up on her elbow. She opened one swollen eye and slurred, 'Go away.'

A familiar wail filled the street and there was more pounding on the door.

'Go back to bed. It'll be over in a minute.' Maria turned her back and pulled her pillow over her head. The banging increased and her daughters' cries became louder. Maria threw her pillow and blankets to one side, marched to the door, and unlocked it.

'My God, are you trying to break my door down? Go back to bed and stop panicking.'

'We're going to be bombed,' cried Eva. 'We've got to go down to the cellar now.'

'It's just another false alarm. If we keep rushing down to the cellar every time it goes off, we'll die of exhaustion anyway,' said Maria, returning to her bed.

'Mama, didn't you hear the explosion? We're all going to be killed,' shouted Eva. Maria screwed her eyes shut and drew her blankets up over her.

Solveig started crying, 'I don't want to be killed. Mama, please come, please.' She went back to her mother and shook her shoulders.

'There's nothing to worry about. Stop this rubbish now.'

'But Mama—'

'I said stop.'

'I don't want to go without Mama,' said Solveig as she sat on the floor and rocked backward and forward. 'Where's Papa?' She sniffed, crying and sucking her thumb.

'It's okay,' said Inger, bending down and putting her arm around her. 'We'll be all right. You can come into my bed.'

'Come on,' said Eva. 'For God's sake, the house could be on fire, but if *Mama* said it was okay you would just sit and be burned. You are so stupid.'

There was another wail of the air raid siren. Eva covered her ears and ran out of the flat.

Maria lay awake and listened as the wailing died down. She mused about her three daughters. She must have loved them once. She closed her eyes and felt the familiar knot of anger in the center of her chest. She tried to remember a time when she had been able to feel what she knew a mother should feel. Had she always been like this? Had it ever been possible to move without feeling as if she had lead weights crushing down on her? She sighed and returned her thoughts to her daughters.

Eva had just turned sixteen and was already considered a classic beauty with her long blond hair, intelligent blue eyes, and slim form. People said she was cold but Maria knew it was just that she was wary of people she did not know. Inger, less than a year younger than Eva, was quite different with her halo of red hair, green eyes, and freckles on her upturned nose. She had a large gap between her front teeth and a smile no one could resist.

As for little Solveig, just ten years old, with her straight, mousy hair and face always full of worry, what was to become of her? She was always asking why and never satisfied with the answers. She had to be the plainest and most irritating child of all time. Maybe if, if only . . . Maria shut her eyes. She could not let herself think about the past.

She could hear Inger and Solveig laughing next door. What could they find to laugh about at this time of night? But then they were just children. Where indeed was Johannes? Solveig might miss him, but what did she know?

He had not been back for over two weeks now. Last time he came back he was preoccupied and she was sure she could small perfume on him. She had started to check his pockets and shirts again. No lipstick like the last time this happened, but still, she could tell. He was in a good mood for no apparent reason and was called out on 'late night duty' more often than usual. She knew he was lying. Some big murder case apparently. She could show him some murder. Just because he looked so handsome in his police uniform, tall and powerfully built, with dark hair and dark eyes, didn't mean he could keep going off and just come home when it was over and ask for forgiveness. This time, this time, she would be strong. For once, just let him show his face.

She sat up and went to fill her wine glass. The bottle was by her bed, next to an ashtray which was spilling its contents over her lace mat and onto the cream carpet. She tipped the bottle upward. Empty. *Probably just as well,* she thought as she felt her head float and a wave of nausea come over her. Surely she hadn't just opened it this evening. She sank back into her pillow and closed her eyes.

* * * *

That morning Maria's high heels clicked toward the kitchen and she appeared in the doorway, wrapping her silk negligee around herself and shivering.

'Why isn't the fire lit?'

'There's no coal,' replied Eva.

'Go and get some then.'

'But I've been in the cellar all night. Anyway, it's Inger's turn.'

'Go down and get the coal at once.'

'But I've just got dressed. I don't want to get coal dust on me again.'

'You should have thought of that before.'

Eva glared at her mother, grabbed the coal scuttle, and stamped out of the kitchen, slamming the door as she went. As she tramped downstairs, her steps echoed menacingly all over the building. Maria swore under her breath, lit a cigarette, closed her eyes, and inhaled deeply. Why was it always such a battle with Eva?

Solveig and Inger carried on in silence while Maria ground her wartime 'coffee beans' and went through her morning ritual of brewing coffee in a small brass saucepan used solely for this purpose. It was a long time since she could get real coffee, even on the black market. The burnt ground peas gave an acrid smell, more of a reek than an aroma, and the taste was bitter enough to jolt the senses. For the rest of it, imagination had to suffice.

A stamping and clanking noise echoed up the stairs until Eva's angry face appeared back in the kitchen. Inger and Solveig kept as quiet as possible, bracing themselves for another row. Eva started to light the fire, making as much noise and fuss as she possibly could. Maria sat with her back to her, looking out of the window and sipping her coffee. Solveig sneaked her thumb in her mouth.

'I thought you had stopped that,' said Eva as she turned to rinse her hands. 'You're ten years old now. I'll tell your friends at school that you are a baby-baby-suck-a-thumb.'

'That's not fair. Please don't,' said Solveig, slurring her voice before she took her thumb out.

'I will,' said Eva, waving her thumb in front of her mouth and making sucking noises in the air.

Solveig started to cry. 'Please don't, I'll give you all my pocket money.'

'Ooh, a whole twenty-five cents. I'll be *so* rich.'

'I hate you,' shouted Solveig, running out of the kitchen to her room. Inger cleared up the plates and scowled at Eva.

'Why do you have to be so mean?' she said. 'She's only little.'

Before Eva could answer, Inger went out and headed toward Solveig's room at the end of the long corridor that ran through the center of their spacious town flat. Eva raised her eyes upward and shouted after her.

'She'll never learn to grow up if you keep babying her like that.'

Maria turned around and glared at Eva.

'For heaven's sake. I've got a bad enough headache already without all this. Go and get them, apologize, and have your breakfast before you are all late for school.'

'Or what?' said Eva.

'Just do it,' said Maria in a low voice. Eva sighed and went to Solveig's room. Maria turned back to the window and lit another cigarette.

Just as the girls returned to the kitchen, there were whining noises from the sky, faint at first then becoming gradually louder. Several sounds mixed together, shriller than the siren, like giant dentist's drills getting higher and higher, sharper and sharper, and then winding down as if exhausted. Then a moment's pause in which low engine sounds could be heard before the next wail, then so loud . . .

'They're going to bomb us!' shouted Eva running to the door, *'Come on!'*

This time they all followed her, even Maria. The girls ran downstairs joining the neighbors. Everyone in the eight flats at 24 Kristian IV Gate crowded down the staircase as they went down to the cellar. When they squeezed in the door, Maria could not see anything at first. She heard people whispering and smelled damp sackcloth and coal. Someone lit a candle and people's faces came into view.

The cellar was lit up by a several candles brought in by an elderly couple who had sheltered there last night. Some of the neighbors were wrapped in blankets, some looked dressed for work or school, and some were wearing pajamas with coats and gloves.

Maria shivered as she wrapped her arms around herself. She wished she had more on than her silk negligee and high heels, but what she regretted most was leaving her cigarettes behind. When a lady next to her offered a blanket, Maria shook her head. She was absolutely fine, thank you. She did not want to be beholden to anyone for anything. Her pride would have to keep her warm.

Maria looked for the Baumans from the flat next door but could not see them. She recognized the Andresens, the ones from the flat below, whose baby was always crying. He had just started to crawl now and was heading toward a candle. He cried when his mother stopped him, and he struggled to leave his mother's arms. Their daughter was jumping on a pile of sack cloths from which emanated clouds of black soot. Old Mrs. Hagen, the busybody from the ground floor, shouted at her to stop; she could not breathe with all the dust. Other families that Maria vaguely recognized but never spoke to if she could avoid it, were huddled together sitting on sacks of coal, wooden crates, or blankets they had brought down with them.

The howling of the airplanes got louder. People lowered their heads and hunched their shoulders, bracing as if a plane might crash through the ceiling. The Stutts from the ground floor held their hands over their ears and Mrs. Hagen knelt on the rough concrete floor and prayed.

Eventually, the sounds of aircraft became fainter and less frequent until they might have been thunder a long way away, or maybe just the wind. There was a pause. People instinctively looked up, although there was only candlelight flickering on the ceiling black with coal dust. Solveig unfurled herself and reached out for Inger's hand.

Ragnar Andresen opened the door to let in the morning light. People got up, brushed the black dust and cobwebs off them, and started blowing out the candles. The Stutts laughed and shook hands, the Andresens hugged each other, and old Mrs. Hagen crossed herself and cried. Maria shrugged and clicked her way upstairs as her daughters followed.

CHAPTER 2

Later that day, after the girls returned from school, Maria was busy cooking supper. Solveig was trying to tell her the tale of her lost homework. She had spent days writing a story then dropped her schoolbag in a puddle on the way to school. The ink on the paper had blurred and the pages had become a soggy mess. She had been severely reprimanded by her teacher and told she had to write it all out again that evening. While Solveig was recounting this, Maria was preoccupied with converting a whole swede into fine slices which she could deep-fry in the last of the bit of butter she had managed to save.

'Here, Solveig, you just have to stop being so clumsy and careless. Stop crying and give me a hand. Your father will be home soon and supper is going to be late.'

She called Eva and Inger and gave instructions. Inger went next door to the dining area of the large living room and laid the table with lace mats, silver cutlery, and crystal glasses. She would also put out the silver candlesticks. Even though they had little else but swedes and potatoes to eat, standards still had to be kept up. Maria could make anything look special and on a good day there would be some delicacy bought from the black market at an enormous price. Tonight, she had two pork chops. She had cut them finely, made crackling from the rind and gravy from the juice.

Solveig spent ages shredding some cabbage and then presented it to her mother. Maria scowled, took the knife from her, and went over it again. Solveig slumped herself on a chair and, covering her hand, put her thumb into her mouth. She put her finger in some spilt gravy on the table and made a star with eight long lines.

'Clear that up at once!' shouted Maria.

When they had finished their chores, Maria sent the girls away to get changed for supper and went into the main bedroom.

She sat down at her art deco dressing table and looked at herself in the mirror. Her makeup was smudged and her lipstick worn off. Her shoulder-length hair looked greasy and hung limply behind her ears. She looked at her watch and frowned. With deft hands, she brushed her hair back, smoothed it down, pinned it at the back of her head, and fixed it with hair spray. She took out her deep red lipstick and retouched her lips, then applied mascara to her eyelashes. She put on her black high heels and reached down for her perfume. As she sprayed behind her ears and on the inside of her wrists, the room filled with the heavy aroma of Arpège.

She stood up and looked at herself sideways in the ornately framed full-length mirror and held her stomach in. With one last pat of her hair and inspection of her face, she walked down the corridor to the sitting room to wait for Johannes. After their last quarrel, he had told her he could not stand it anymore.

She poured herself some brandy and paced up and down, checking her face in the mirror and fiddling with her hair. She picked up a magazine, turned the pages while barely glancing at the pictures, then got up to refill her glass and resume her pacing.

Eventually, the front door opened and Johannes came in. He was an imposing figure in his policeman's uniform with his heavy black jacket and black cap. His hair was black and his dark brown eyes contrasted with his pale skin. He took his coat off with one arm as he held a huge bouquet of orange lilies, Maria's favorite, in the other.

'Hello, I'm here!'

'Papa,' shouted the girls as they ran up the corridor. Inger got to him first and threw her arms around him, kissing him three times on each cheek. Solveig got to him just afterward and hugged his legs while Eva walked nonchalantly toward him, flicking her hair and giving one of her brief waves.

'Hey, steady on,' he said, laughing and lifting up the bunch of flowers, 'I've only got two arms and these will get squashed. Inger and Solveig, have a look in my coat pockets and, Eva, here's something for you.' He took a silk scarf out of his jacket and handed it to her.

'Oooh,' shouted Inger and Solveig as they fished out several wrapped chocolates and an assortment of sweets.

Maria emerged from the living room holding a cigarette which she inhaled and blew out with pursed lips, sending the smoke upward in a thin stream.

'Kind of you to come home, or had you forgotten where we lived?'

'Maria, how could I forget where the most beautiful woman in the world lives? I have counted the days and now I am home with my four favorite girls,' he said, swinging Inger and Solveig around with the flowers squashed in one hand, and Inger and Solveig laughing and stumbling as they danced around him. Eva folded her arms and could not help laughing as well.

'The flowers, careful!' said Maria as she grabbed the bouquet. She held them at arm's length with her head on one side, then took them into the kitchen and took out her largest porcelain vase. While she was arranging them, Johannes came in and went up behind her, putting his arms around her waist. He leant his head on top of hers and inhaled. 'Mmmm, Arpêge. Smells divine.'

'I'll give you "divine," you old snake charmer. Think you can "divine" your way into my good books with your wily words?'

She tried to suppress a smile and frowned. He drew her closer and kissed her behind her ear.

'Just stop it,' she said, 'and get the girls to sit down at the table. Tell Eva to come and help me serve up.' She leant back into him for a moment then quickly moved over to the cooker where the fried swede slices and pork were keeping warm. She shouted out of the door.

Soon they were all seated and Johannes picked up his knife and fork.

'Please start,' said Maria.

Before she had barely taken a mouthful, Solveig started up.

'Mr. Gulbrand threw a piece of chalk at Ivar in math today,' Solveig said. 'He was drawing a picture of Hitler on his exercise book—you know, with a moustache—then he drew a machine gun with lots of bullets going to his head and a big spurt of blood coming out.'

'How *absolutely* fascinating,' said Eva as she mimed a massive yawn and rolled her eyes upward. The chattering continued as they emptied their plates while Johannes concentrated on his Aquavit more than his food, refilling his glass several times. The girls finished their first course and left their plates so well scraped they could almost see their own reflections in them.

'Eva, can you help me get the cake out?' shouted Maria. Eva followed her into the kitchen.

'Who wants some chocolate cake?' said Maria as she came back in. Eva was behind her with a crystal bowl full of whipped cream. Maria had queued for six hours to buy that.

'Ooh yes, me,' said Inger.

'And me,' said Solveig, clapping her hands and bouncing in her chair.

Maria sat down and took out a silver cake slicer, looking at Johannes questioningly. Inger and Solveig were laughing about Mr. Gulbrand, who apparently had holes in his jacket elbows and was wearing odd socks that day.

'*I can't hear myself think,*' shouted Eva. 'Little girls like to chatter; big girls know better.' Solveig stuck her tongue out at Eva and Inger laughed.

'I saw that Solveig,' said Maria, 'I will not have this at the dinner table. Go to your room!'

'But Mama, I haven't had my cake.'

'Well, you should learn better manners and remember next time. Go on.'

'Maria, she didn't mean it. I'm sure she is sorry,' said Johannes.

'Yes, I'm sorry. I'm sorry, Eva,' said Solveig as her face crumpled into tears.

'Johannes, you can't just turn up after weeks away and tell me Solveig doesn't mean it. You don't know what I have to put up with. I would have thought you could support me for once.'

Then turning to Solveig, she stared at her and pointed to the door. Solveig got up slowly and dragged herself to the door. Silence descended on the family group. Eva ate her cake, taking second helpings of cream despite protesting she did not want any. Inger ate her cake very slowly. Maria pushed her plate away, having only taken a bite while Johannes stared morosely at his glass, which he filled with Aquavit yet again and drank down in one go.

Solveig trudged down the long, dark corridor to her room. She had the small room at the end with its tiny window. If she stood up on her bed, she could see down to the wide street below and to the block of flats across. Her room was bare apart from a few books on her shelf, and her small wardrobe contained only four dresses: one was for school, two were for play, and one was for best. Three of them were her sister's cast-offs, two were made in the same design and same dark green color. Her mother used to make Eva and Inger's dresses match as if they were twins.

She had a small writing desk and wooden chair where she was supposed to do her homework every night. Under her bed, she had a baby-size wooden stool with a green peasant design which she liked to sit on when she played with her dolls. Her three dolls were now kept hidden as Eva called her a 'big baby' for still having them now that she was ten.

The fireplace was never used. Her mother would not allow coal in their bedrooms as it 'just made a lot of dust and all the ashes have to be cleared out.' She was already busy enough. Solveig was accustomed to her bedroom being cold in the winter, but she would snuggle under her thick duvet and wrap her hot water bottle up in her moth-eaten lilac shawl and soon feel warm.

This evening her room was cold again and, still hungry, she climbed into her bed and pulled her duvet up over her ears. She leant down under her bed and took out the library book she was reading, *Hans Christian Andersen's Fairy Tales,* and turned to 'The Little Match Girl,' her favorite. She sniffed and wiped her eyes, which were now swollen and dry as she had no more tears left for that day.

She was just finding her place when she heard a familiar knock on the door. Inger came in with something hidden under her cardigan, which she had draped over her shoulders. 'Shush, quickly, before Mother hears me,' whispered Inger as she brought out a plate with the piece of cake her mother had left and a spoon.

'How did you get this?'

'Shush, never mind. She'll just think that Father ate it. You know what he's like.'

'What are they doing?'

'Just talking.'

'Inger, I'm, er, I'm so scared, and I'm scared all the time.'

'You'll be safe here. Papa won't let anything happen to you.' Inger stepped across the room and gave her a kiss on her cheek and a quick hug. She then put the cake on the stool beside the bed and hurried out closing the door carefully behind her. Solveig came out of bed, wrapped her soft shawl around her, took out her dolls, and sat them around her while she sat on the stool.

'If you are good, I'll let you have some of my cake,' she said 'You'll be safe now. Papa is here.'

Inger walked back unnoticed. They had moved to the comfort of the settee and arm chairs in the lounge area. Maria was fiddling with her necklace and Johannes was staring out of the window, seemingly oblivious to his surroundings.

As soon as Maria saw Inger, she told her and Eva to go to bed.

'But it's only quarter to nine,' cried Inger.

'Can't we stay up and chat? We haven't seen Papa for ages,' said Eva.

'Go on, your father and I have to talk,' said Maria.

'Please can we stay,' began Inger, but she stopped as her mother sent her a stony glare.

'Okay, okay, off you go,' said Maria, flinching as Inger kissed her goodnight.

Eva flicked her hair back and scowled as she moved to the door without saying good night. Johannes nodded at them and went back into his reverie.

*   *   *   *

When they had left, Johannes walked over to the mantelpiece, took another cigarette out of the silver case, and lit it.

'There's something I need to tell you, Maria.'

Maria walked over to the gramophone. The moment she had been dreading was coming, but she was not ready to hear it spoken. She wanted to obliterate her dread and anger just to feel close to him for a moment. She put on a record and turned up the volume as a heavy beat and sultry voice sang out. She paced in long, slow strides to the center of the room, closed her eyes, and swayed slowly with one hand on her hip and the other held out. As her head lifted, Johannes walked over and took hold of her waist. He placed his face close to hers and inhaled the musky scent of the Arpêge.

They danced close together, spinning occasionally until the record was played out and they danced some more without it. Maria disentangled herself and looked at him intently. She went over to the cocktail cabinet and took out two crystal glasses and a bottle of brandy.

'There's some of the Remy Martin left. Here, let's have a toast,' said Maria as she poured out two large shots. 'Here's to us.'

'Skal,' said Johannes as he drank down the brandy in one draft.

'Hey, that's our best brandy! It's supposed to be savored, not gulped down.'

'Savored slowly, like savoring a beautiful woman?' He got up and pulled her toward him, kissing her full on the lips. She pushed him away momentarily then returned the kiss. She closed her eyes, which were suffused with a longing that washed away all her anger as if the last ten years had never happened.

'Hey, stop! One of the children might come in,' said Maria.

'No, they won't,' said Johannes. Maria pushed him away properly this time.

'Yes, they might. It's bedtime for the grown-ups now, isn't it?'

'Now that's the best thing anyone has said to me all day.'

★   ★   ★   ★

In the early hours of the morning, Johannes disentangled himself from Maria who was fast asleep. He looked at her for a long time and moved a strand of hair from her forehead. As he was getting dressed, Maria woke up.

'Why are you getting up so early?'

'I have to go.'

'Stay. Come back home, Johannes. You've been away for long enough. I need you. The girls need you.'

Johannes sat on the edge of the bed and looked down at the floor. 'I came here to tell you last night, but . . . you're so beautiful, Maria,' said Johannes quietly. 'I'm sorry, but I can't live here anymore.' He paused and stared at her, then wrenched himself away.

Maria wrapped her silk negligee around herself and followed him down the long, dark corridor. 'What's her name, Johannes? What's the name of your whore? Do you think I'm stupid? Just a stupid, little wife who can't smell perfume on her husband's shirt, who hasn't seen lipstick on his collar, damp from where someone has tried to remove it? You just get back to her and I hope you rot in hell, you bastard!'

'I'm so sorry.' Johannes went to the front door and as he put his coat on, Maria slapped him across the face.

'If you walk out that door, don't bother to come back, *ever!*' she yelled. She slapped him again and pummeled both her fists on his chest, blocking the front door as she did so. He grabbed hold of both her arms, his knuckles turning white and his teeth clenching together.

'Ow, you are hurting me. Why don't you just kill me and get it over with?'

'For God's sake, pull yourself together.'

'Huh? Such a big strong man you are, you creep.' She flew at him again. This time he pushed her back with such force that she fell and hit her head on the wall.

'*Bastard!*' she shouted.

Johannes stepped toward Maria. 'I'm really sorry, oh God, I'm sorry. What have I done?' He bent down to lift her up. But Maria pushed him away, stood up, and folded her arms. 'I love you,' he continued, 'but I can't bear this anymore. I've got to leave. I'm so sorry.'

Maria glared at him. 'Go to hell and don't ever come back.' Johannes adjusted his black uniform coat, put on his police hat, and left the house without another word.

Maria went into the lounge, walked toward the gramophone, took the record out, and smashed it on the mantelpiece. She filled one of the empty glasses from last night with brandy, took the bottle in her other hand, walked back to the bedroom, and locked the door.

CHAPTER 3

The Next Day

Eva got up first as usual. She washed herself thoroughly with the bathroom sink filled to the top with hot water as the windowless bathroom filled with steam. A loud knocking came on the door. 'Eva, hurry up I need the loo!' Inger sounded frantic.

'I'm coming. Can't I have a moment to myself without someone battering the door down?'

'You've been in there for hours Eva,' shouted Inger.

'I've only been in here for five minutes. Why do you always make such a fuss?'

Eva came out smelling of soap and toothpaste and Inger ran to the toilet, not stopping to lock the door. She splashed her face with cold water and brushed her teeth in less than a minute. She dressed quickly and joined Eva in the kitchen where she was putting out bread and some smoked herring with a paste of carrot and swede to moisturize it. She turned to Inger. 'Did you hear them last night? It was worse than the row they had last year. Last time she stayed in her bedroom for three days and Aunt Else had to come and help. I better go and get Solveig.'

Eva ran down the corridor and knocked on Solveig's door. After several knocks, she opened the door and went in. There was a large mound of duvet and Solveig was completely hidden inside. The only evidence of her being in there was her feet, still in yesterday's socks, sticking out of the other end. Eva shook the mound, which started to move, and Solveig's face emerged, pale with swollen eyes and knotted hair, resembling a hamster that had been hibernating for a year.

'Time to get dressed and have breakfast. Mr. Gulbrand has already warned you about being late.'

'But you and Inger were late as well.'

'Yes, but we are older and he didn't notice.'

'It's not fair,' said Solveig, pulling on her crumpled green dress over yesterday's underwear.

'Life's not fair, so get used to it,' replied Eva. 'Now come on get dressed.'

Solveig joined her sisters for breakfast, appearing in her baggy dress, odd socks, and her shoes unlaced as usual. Tufts of hair stuck out at the back of her head.

'Ah, here she is,' said Inger.

'What a mess,' said Eva laughing.

Solveig stuck her tongue out at Eva and sat down. 'Where's Mama?'

'She's not well,' said Inger.

'I heard them last night,' said Solveig. 'She told Papa never to come back again. What if we never see him again?' She started to cry.

'Just another of their stupid rows,' said Eva.

'Do you remember when this happened before?' said Inger, 'She and Papa had a really bad row, but he still came back. He'll come back, you see. They have quarrels just like we do, but they always make friends again.'

'I want to see her!' Solveig ran down the corridor and knocked on the main bedroom door. 'Mama, are you all right?' She tried to open the door but it was locked. She banged again and cried. Eva went after her.

'Shush, don't make her angry. Stop being such a big baby and leave her alone!' Eva grabbed Solveig's hand and pulled her roughly back to the kitchen.

'I hate you, Eva, you are horrible.'

'Solveig, that's not fair,' said Inger, 'Eva has got breakfast ready for us and is only trying to help. Do you want to help Mama?'

'Yes,' said Solveig.

'Well, let her sleep. Do you remember what the doctor said when you were ill over Christmas? He said, "Bed rest and sleep are the best healers," yes?'

'I like Doctor Tellefsen. He gave me some candy and he's funny. Should we get him to come and see Mama today?'

'Let's see how she is later. Come on, let's finish breakfast and then see if we can sort out your hair.'

Solveig took a huge mouthful of bread and jam, getting dark purple all round her mouth and cheeks. Inger laughed and rolled her eyes up. After she had finished eating and been sent by Inger to the bathroom to wash her face and hands, Eva called them back into the kitchen.

'Inger, we're already late. I can't leave Mama like this. Can you take Solveig to school?'

'I don't want to go to school. What if Mama tries to, er, you know, tries again?' replied Inger.

'She promised us she would never do that again and that she would never leave us.' Eva looked out of the door and shook her head. 'I don't know.'

'Can't I just take Solveig to the park and come back a bit later?' said Inger.

'Yeah, maybe that's the best idea. Okay. Be careful of the soldiers. Just ignore them if they try to talk to you.'

'Don't worry, I never even look at them.'

'I'll ring Aunt Else. She'll know what to do.'

Solveig and Inger put their coats on.

'I don't want to go if Mama is ill,' said Solveig.

'Eva is going to ask Aunty Else to come and make sure she is all right. She'll be fine, don't worry,' said Inger, tying up the tangled mess of laces on Solveig's shoes.

'What about school?'

'Eva says it is okay to stay off today.'

'Won't we get into trouble?'

'No, not if it's an emergency.'

'Wheee, no school!' shouted Solveig, clapping her hands then remembering herself. 'But what if Mama has to go to hospital again?'

'I'm sure she will be all right. Really,' said Inger, putting her arm around her and giving her a kiss. 'Come on. Last one downstairs is a dummy.' They set off with a big clatter of shoes and laughter echoing all the way down the three flights of stairs.

*   *   *   *

After they had gone, Eva went down to her mother's door and knocked softly. Silence. She knocked more loudly and still more loudly as she shouted, *Mother! Wake up!* She waited for a few minutes, then knocked and shouted once more, but still there was no answer. She paced up and down outside, tugging her hair then walking into the living room. She picked up the phone and dialed.

'Hello, Aunt Else?'

'Hello, is that you, Eva? How lovely to hear from you. Is everything all right?'

'Mother hasn't got up yet. She isn't answering her door and it's locked. She and father had a huge row last night.'

'Not another row. Are Solveig and Inger all right?'

'Inger has taken Solveig to the park.'

'Okay, I'm coming straight over. I'll take my bike so I'll be there in about half an hour.'

After a short time, during which Eva tried her mother's door a few more times, Elsa arrived breathless at the door. Eva opened it and hugged her.

'Is she up yet?'

'No.'

'Right, action stations,' said Else as she hung her coat up. She was taller than Maria and although she was unmistakably her sister, she had a wider mouth and gentle hazel eyes. Else knocked on the door and shouted. After there was no answer, she shouted even more loudly, 'Maria, if you don't come out now I will knock the door down and drag you out of bed myself.'

From the bedroom, a faint voice said, 'Go away!'

'What's that?'

'Go away and just leave me alone,' said the voice slightly more loudly.

'There's no way I'm going to leave you alone. Everyone is worried sick about you. The children are frightened for you and you are being really selfish. My God, you're just like our mother.'

'I'm not like our mother!'

'Oh yes?'

'All right, just stop shouting and banging so much and I'll let you in. Bloody hell.'

A moment later there was a click as the bolt was drawn across, and the door opened a crack. They heard Maria sigh as she pushed the door open and went back to bed.

Maria sat up on the bed. Her hair was flattened on one side, her eyes were smeared with black, and there were black smudges on her pillow. She sat with her head hung down and rubbed her fingers over her forehead, wincing as Else drew the curtains.

'What time it?'

'Eleven o'clock,' replied Else, returning to sit next to Maria.

'Oh my god.' Her voice was hoarse and her speech faintly slurred.

'What happened? Did he hit you?'

'No, I hit him. I hit him really hard and slapped his face.'

'Then what are the bruises on your arms?'

Maria looked at the thick red and brown marks around her upper arms, touched one, and winced in pain. 'He just got hold of me to stop me hitting him. He looked so angry I thought he would kill me. I wish he had!' She screwed her face up and started to cry. Else put her arm around her.

'You don't mean that,' she said, then after a moment, 'your breath smells like an ashtray filled with gone-off brandy. How much did you drink last night?'

'I don't know. Johannes and I had a few, and there was a bit left after he went.' Else picked up the bottle of Remy Martin on the bedside table and peered at it.

'Mmm, empty. I have to say you can certainly get drunk in style. No ordinary booze for my sister!'

Maria smiled. 'That's better,' said Else, 'I'll get you a glass of water.'

Maria stood up shakily and frowned at herself in the mirror. When Else came back with a large glass filled to the brim, she sat down and began to sip slowly.

'Doctor Else's orders, cheers,' said Maria.

'Wait while I run you a bath. Eva, can you go and put the kettle on. Oh yes, and brew some of your mother's evil coffee, I could do with some.'

Else ran the bath. The water was lukewarm and ran slowly, making frequent spluttering noises while the pipes clanked behind the walls. Eventually the kettle boiled and was poured into the bath so that there were now a good twelve inches of steaming water. Else took a bath towel out of the airing cupboard and went down for Maria. She helped her in and stayed with her until Maria had washed herself thoroughly and rinsed her hair. She helped Maria out of the bath, wrapped her in the towel, walked her down to her room, and took some clothes out for her. 'Here, Maria, it's cold today. Your special coffee will be ready in a couple of minutes. I'm dying for a cup.'

'I think I'm just dying,' said Maria.

When Maria came into the kitchen, Eva walked over to her. 'Are you all right now, Mother?' she asked in a quiet but angry voice.

'Yes, I'm fine, thank you. Just a bit tired.'

'You're always "tired." Why couldn't you answer your door, or at least speak to us? You don't care about any of us.'

'Of course I care about you,' said Maria.

'Oh, really, do you *really*?' Eva glared at her.

'Hey, Eva, that's no way to talk to your mother. Say sorry at once,' said Else.

'Sorr-*eee!*' said Eva.

'*Eva!*'

'Just as well your father isn't here. See what I have to put up with Else,' said Maria.

'Well, whose fault is that?' shouted Eva. Else sprang out of her chair and ran after Eva.

'Your mother loves you very much and works really hard to look after you every day. You of all people know how hard things have been for her these last few years.'

'Yes, that's what everyone says, but what about me?'

'I know it hasn't been easy for you,' said Else, putting her arm around her. 'So, where did Inger and Solveig go?'

'They went to Palace Park.'

'I don't know if it's safe out there. You better go and get them.'

'All right, Auntie.'

Else gave her a kiss. 'There, you're a good girl, really.'

They went back into the kitchen. 'I am sorry, Mama,' said Eva, staring at the floor. Maria nodded briefly and Eva grabbed her coat and ran from the flat.

*   *   *   *

In the street that led to the park were several large blocks of flats surrounded by gardens, some with fences and some with walls. On several walls, words were painted in red or white paint, with letters half a meter high. The paint on many of the letters had run down in thin streaks. The words FREEDOM, GOD SAVE OUR KING, NORWAY WILL NEVER SURRENDER were written on sides of buildings and walls right down the street. There were roughly drawn symbols of King Haakon everywhere.

Just as she was coming into Palace Park, she saw three German soldiers on the corner busy talking and smoking. She crossed the road to avoid them. One of them looked up and shouted, *'Guten Morgen, Fraulein,'* and gave a low whistle. She frowned and looked away as she walked even faster with her shoulders hunched up, holding her arms across her chest, and pulling her coat over her shoulders. The soldiers laughed and one of them cupped his hands over his chest and raised his eyebrows. Eva blushed deep red and ran into the park.

She went toward the palace, a low oblong with long rows of windows and an ornate porch of columns and arches at the entrance. It was an imposing sight softened by its pale-yellow ocher paint. It was prominent at the top of a gentle hill so it overlooked Karl Johannes Gate. There were five soldiers standing guard in front of the palace and on the flagpole outside was a German flag. Above the arches and hanging down in front of the entrance were long flags, deep red with black swastikas in white circles on them. These red flags were everywhere and Eva barely remembered what the palace had looked like without them.

She ran toward the small fenced-off area in the park which had some swings and a slide and called for Inger and Solveig. She turned away from the soldiers and went toward the swings at the outer edge.

'Eva!' shouted Inger and Solveig.

'Hi,' said Eva as she ran over to them.

'Is Mama all right?' said Inger.

'Yes, Aunt Else came over.'

Solveig came running up breathlessly. 'Eva, are you going to play with us?'

'No, Aunt Else is with us and has told me to come and get you.'

'Auntie's here! *Goodeee,*' shouted Solveig. Inger took her hand and they set off home.

'Don't look at the soldiers,' said Eva sternly as they passed the side of the palace. The soldiers on the corner waved and shouted 'Cheer up!' in German but the three girls ignored them as they hurried past.

*   *   *   *

When the girls arrived home, Aunt Else and Maria were talking in the kitchen. There was a large saucepan of potatoes simmering next to them. The two younger girls greeted their aunt excitedly.

Maria's eyes were pink; her forehead was swollen with a livid red mark just on the hairline. Bruising had tracked down over one of her eyes, making a purple and blue pattern contrasting with the pallor of the rest of her face. She leant back in her chair, holding her real black-market coffee and smoking. She barely acknowledged the girls apart from telling them that she had been very ill with an upset stomach but was getting better now.

'Will Papa come back and see us soon?' said Solveig. But Maria did not answer. She stared out of the window and took a deep drag of her cigarette.

'I want Papa!' shouted Solveig, starting to cry.

'Of course he'll come back,' said Inger. 'Here, let's go and tidy your room. I've never seen such a mess in my life. And then let's see if we can remember that story you wrote. It was one of my favorites.'

CHAPTER 4

Wednesday

September 29th, 1942

A few days later, as Maria and Else were drinking coffee after breakfast and the children were getting ready to go to school, there was a loud knock. Maria went out and opened the door.

There were two German soldiers in full uniform with swastikas on their cuffs, guns in leather holsters, and well-tailored gray jackets full of pockets and silver buttons. Their trousers were tucked into long, highly polished brown boots and they had flat caps each with a silver eagle on the front. One of them held a large board with a list of names and addresses showing on the top one.

'*Guten Morgen,* Frau Halversen.' The first soldier clicked his heels together, bent over in a half bow with one arm behind his back, and quickly returned to his very upright posture.

'Hello?' said Maria.

With them was a middle-aged man with glasses wearing a baggy jacket, hat, brown shirt, and a dull green tie. His shoes were muddy and scuffed. The first officer spoke in German and the man with glasses translated into Norwegian:

'Soldaten Lehman and Kraus want me to introduce them. They have come to check out your home.'

'Why?'

'Warum?' said the interpreter to the officers. They spoke and he translated.

'It is procedure. Please let them pass.' Maria just stared at them and stood back to let them through. They marched into the kitchen and nodded to Else.

'Guten Morgen, Fraulein,' said Lehman.

Else could speak German but remained silent.

'They will inspect the rooms now, Madam.'

'But my children are in there,' said Maria.

'Tell them to go into the kitchen,' said Lehman, the one who did most of the talking while the other took notes. Maria called the girls. Eva and Inger came into the corridor first and with some more stifled shouts of 'Hurry up!' from Maria, Solveig appeared clutching a large book and pillow case with her dolls. They slid past the soldiers going as close to the wall opposite as they could, all looking terrified.

'Why are those horrible soldiers here?' Solveig's voice echoed down the corridor, followed by several frantic shushes and a bang as the door was hastily slammed shut.

The soldiers marched into each room talking to each other, pointing, and nodding over various items of furniture. When they had finished, the soldiers gathered in the living room and remained standing. They looked through the papers they had and discussed some more points.

'Frau Halversen, from six o'clock tomorrow evening, Officer Wolff will be living here. You are to leave before he comes.'

'What? This is my family's house and we live here. There's been a mistake,' shouted Maria.

'Police Inspector Halversen does not live here.'

'My husband *does* live here, officer.'

'He has not given his address as here. Don't lie to us, Frau Halversen.'

'I am not lying. How dare you. I am not going anywhere. Tell your boss to find somewhere else. I live here and have nowhere to go. Do you want to send us out onto the street?' The translator looked at her with irritation and spoke in German to the soldiers.

'Obstructing the war effort is a criminal offence and crimes against the Fuhrer will not go unpunished. Where you go does not concern us, but you must leave,' delivered the translator, echoing the officious tone of the soldiers.

'We will still be here. You will have to arrest me before I let any German soldier live in my home.'

'We will report your uncooperative behavior to Herr Wolff at once,' said Lehman.

They walked out and when they got to the door, the main officer clipped his heels and bowed again. As he did so, he raised his right arm diagonally forward and clipping his heels said, *'Heil Hitler.'* As the interpreter followed behind them, Maria gripped his sleeve.

'Call yourself a Norwegian?' She spat on the floor by his feet and stared at him, eyes hard with contempt. He pulled his sleeve free and without looking back at her followed after the officers, their boots resounding loudly down the three flights of stairs.

Maria hurried into her bedroom and changed into a fashionably tailored suit of fine gray and white checks with a flare under the waist of her jacket, which accentuated her slim figure. She put on her ivory blouse, red amber beads, and pearl earrings. She pinned her hair back, put on her black high heels, and left the house.

'Where are you going?' said Eva.

'I have to sort something out,' said Maria and rushed off.

*   *   *   *

Maria walked briskly along Kristian IV Gate, straight on through Grensen, and then turned left toward the police headquarters at 19 Mollergata. She crossed the road several times to avoid the groups of soldiers that seemed to be everywhere. She was almost running despite her tight skirt and high heels.

As she approached the police headquarters, she stopped. Outside were three soldiers heavy with guns and on either side of the door were the usual red flags with swastikas. These contrasted with the dull gray building with its three long rows of arched windows and square tower. The Norwegian flag at the top had been replaced by a German one as elsewhere. Maria shuddered. The place was like a cross between a castle and a warehouse, massive and ominous.

Under the tower was a large central archway through which was the entrance. She marched across the road and, staring defiantly at the soldiers, walked past them to the door. She entered a large hallway, dark brown, the only relief being the noticeboards which were filled with scraps of paper and official notices. The dim lights high up near the ceiling only exacerbated the gloom.

Just inside the entrance was a queue in front of the reception desk. She walked straight to the front and, oblivious to the furious looks of the crowd, rang the bell repeatedly until the elderly officer turned around.

'I'm not deaf. Now you, madam, you better just go back to the queue or I'll have you taken out of the building.'

'This is an emergency. I demand to see my husband, Police Inspector Halversen, right now. Right away.'

'And what is this emergency?'

'There's no time to explain. I'm not going until I see my husband.' The police officer started to speak, but Maria gave him such a fierce look that he put his pen down and picked up the phone.

'Okay, Mrs. Halversen, someone is coming.'

In a moment, an office assistant came out and took Maria down the corridor a short way and stopped outside a large open door. Through it could be seen an office with twelve desks, most of which were occupied by young women, all busy typing. On a couple of desks were young police officers writing by hand.

'Does anyone know where Police Inspector Halversen is?' shouted the assistant.

No one heard him above the clicking of the typewriters and frequent whirrs followed by pinging noises. He shouted this out again and there was a lull as they all stopped. A secretary sitting at the back stopped and stared intently at Mrs. Halversen. She adjusted her glasses and patted a stray lock of hair back into a tight bun set just clear of the collar of her crisp white blouse. She got up, went across the room to speak to them, and then went to fetch a policeman from next door.

'Well?' said Maria when he arrived.

'Hello, Mrs. Halversen,' said the young policeman. 'Yes, Jo is out on a homicide. He won't be back for hours yet.'

'I have got to see him now.'

'That's not possible.'

'Do you know where he is?' The police officer nodded. 'Well, then tell someone to go and get him at once.'

'I can't do that.'

'Oh, really? Then take me to someone who can. Who is your commanding officer?' She said this with such authority that the young officer jumped to attention and walked briskly down the corridor. She followed him, her high heels outdoing his boots in the noise echoing from the high walls. He came to the door of the chief police inspector, knocked, and at the reply walked in. Just as he was apologizing for the disturbance, Maria pushed her way past him and strode right up to the inspector's desk.

'This young officer is not letting me see my husband, but it is a family emergency and I have to see Police Inspector Halversen right away.'

'Hello, Mrs. Halversen,' said the police chief, heaving his bulk out of his chair and walking over to shake hands. 'I never forget a beautiful face. Remember last May? How are your little girls?'

'Not so little now, sir,' said Maria looking briefly at him then looking down with a faint smile.

'What can I do for the wife of my most respected and esteemed colleague?'

Maria explained. The police chief smiled and said he would arrange for her husband to be fetched down to see her immediately.

'Detective Ersad,' he said, drawing himself up to his full height again, 'Tell Detective Marthinssen to drive up to Grefsen and bring Inspector Halversen here at once.'

'Yes sir!' said the young police officer.

'And make sure Mrs. Halversen is given a chair so she can wait in the main office.'

'Yes sir!'

'When you have done that, come back to see me.'

With one more nod and 'Yes Sir,' the police officer accompanied Maria to the main office. He took a chair from an empty desk nearby and put it near the filing cabinet inside the door indicating for her to sit down. He then made a couple of brief phone calls, repeating what he had said twice and insisting that the police chief inspector had given these instructions. He said to Maria that her husband should be with her in about half an hour and left the office.

The young officer hurried back to the chief inspector and knocked on his door. He was called in and, as soon as he reached the desk, saluted.

'What do you mean by bringing that woman in here like that?' said the chief inspector.

'I am sorry, sir. I thought you were pleased to help her, with respect, sir.'

'Huh? Respect? For your information, officer, I have more important things to do than play nursemaid every time some hysterical woman turns up wanting to see her husband.'

'But sir—'

'Sort it out next time. Just in case you haven't noticed, officer, we have a war on our hands here and Prime Minister Quisling is coming to HQ tomorrow, so we better not have a whole line of women sobbing on the floor then.'

'Yes sir,' said the officer, saluting again and marching stiffly out of the office. He walked quickly down the large corridor and, without looking at the woman who had made such a fool of him, returned to his work.

Maria sat down bolt upright in the hard chair, folding her arms and crossing her legs. She swung the foot of her upper leg up and down continuously as if doing so would bring her husband to her sooner. The secretaries carried on apparently oblivious; all except the one at the back, who had spoken to her before. She stopped typing, paused then gathered up some files and walked over to the filing cabinet where Maria was sitting.

Maria looked up as a plump young woman with glasses, a tight bun at the nape of her neck, and a white shirt started placing files in the cabinet. Maria looked through her, through the window and through the dark gray buildings opposite. Half the shops were boarded up and everyone looked tired and dreary. The secretary looked intently at Maria again and cleared her throat.

'Mrs. Halversen? I couldn't help overhearing you when you came in. Can I get you a hot drink or some water while you wait? I hope you are all right.' Maria glared at her.

'Thank you, miss, but I am perfectly okay. I can just wait here.'

'Are you sure I can't get you anything?'

'As I said, I'm just fine. Thank you.' Maria turned her head away.

'Sorry, I did not mean to trouble you,' said the secretary in a very soft voice. Maria appeared not to hear her as she looked out of the window again.

★　★　★　★

After a while, Johannes appeared in the door and walked up to Maria. He was wearing his coat over his uniform and his usually immaculate boots were covered with mud and pine needles. He looked pale and had dark circles under his eyes. The cleft in his chin stood out more than usual and his face was expressionless.

'What's wrong? What's happened?' Maria just stared at him. 'Oh my god, are the girls all right?'

'Yes, the girls are all right. I don't suppose you care whether *I'm* all right? Because of you, we're having a bloody Nazi taking over our house. Apparently, you no longer live at Kristian IV Gate.'

'I can explain that.'

'I have to be told by two of your German soldier friends that you have a new address?'

'I moved out after you told me never to come back, or have you forgotten?'

'I want you to come home. I don't want a bloody German living in our house.'

'It's always the same with you, Maria. I move back in and you just attack me all the time. I, er, well, I've moved in with someone.'

'Really? So you're all happy in your love nest now? It's not enough that you are a liar, a gambler, and a cheat. I hope you and your little whore will be very happy together, you selfish bastard.'

'I was going to tell you, but, er...' Johannes stuttered, avoiding her eyes, 'But I'll make sure you get enough money each month and will come and see the girls whenever I can.'

'If there's any money left after you've spent it all on your lady friend, or is it lady *friends*? How many young women have you got now? I bet they are all so pretty, no stretch marks on their pretty young figures, eh?'

'Please, Maria, please stop shouting. The whole building will hear you.'

'What do I care? If you come anywhere near the house, I'll, I'll . . .' Maria stopped and burst into tears. Johannes walked up to her, brought her close to him, and kissed her on the lips. For a moment, she slumped into him and returned the kiss, then pushed him away.

'I still love you, Maria.'

'Then come home and leave your lady friend.'

'It's too late. I'm sorry.' They stood in silence for a moment. Maria wiped her tears and hung her head. 'I can't do anything about the German officer. I'm really sorry, Maria.'

'They've told me to leave the house by six o'clock tomorrow evening. But I am not moving out so some damn Nazi can move in.'

'I had no idea. I'm really sorry. Are you going to go up to Bronnoysund then?'

'What? Stay with my parents? Stay with my mother? I'd rather live on the street with the sewer rats than ask her for any favors.'

'What about the girls then?'

'You really don't know what she's like. They would be better off anywhere, *anywhere* at all, than with her.'

'But your father is good to them and to you, isn't he?'

'If only it was just my father. Poor Papa. He's the kindest man in the world, but he just lives in her shadow—if you can call it living. No, I'm not going to go there. I'd rather go to jail.'

'I'm really sorry, Maria.'

'Is that all you can do? Drop me in it and then keep saying you're sorry?

Sorry isn't enough. Go and have a lovely time with your lady friend and don't worry about us. I hope you rot in hell, you bastard.'

Johannes tried to reply, but Maria turned her back and clattered her way down the corridor. She strode past the office, past the young officer who was in trouble on her behalf, and past the soldiers at the entrance. If any of them had looked at her, they would surely have turned to stone.

CHAPTER 5

The Same Day

When Maria came back, Else and the girls were busy in the kitchen preparing supper. Solveig was laying the table in the kitchen and Inger was in charge of slowly frying the sausages: a few bits of ground pork mixed with minced dried herring, turnip puree, and a spoon of flour.

'Hello, I'm back,' called Maria from the hallway.

'Mama!' shouted Inger and Solveig, rushing out to meet her. Eva looked expectantly. Inger gave her mother the usual huge hug and Solveig flung her arms around her. Maria braced herself, gave Inger a quick kiss on her head and patted Solveig lightly on her shoulders.

'For goodness sake, anyone would think I had been away for a year.'

'It's been ages. What were you doing?' said Eva.

'I went to speak to your father.'

'Is he coming home tonight?' said Solveig.

'No, he has to work. Now that the Germans are here, he is having to work extra hard.'

'Oh,' said Solveig, 'He never comes home. Doesn't he love us anymore?'

Before Maria could answer, Else stepped out of the kitchen.

'Of course he loves you, Solveig. He loves all his girls. But like Mama says, it is a terrible time for policemen at the moment. They have to keep us safe like before and now keep us safe from all the Germans as well.' Maria pursed her lips and nodded wearily.

'We've made a nice supper for you,' said Solveig, 'and I laid the table all by myself.'

'Good girl,' said Maria absently. She went into the kitchen but did not look at the table. Instead she rummaged in a drawer and took out a packet of cigarettes and a box of matches. Supper was a quiet event that afternoon.

* * * *

At precisely six o'clock the next day, there was a loud knocking at the door. Maria stood up, patted her hair, smoothed down her skirt, and braced her shoulders back. Else stood up apprehensively. The girls, whose chatter and bickering had become mere background noise, emerged from Inger's room in complete silence. Else beckoned to them to go into the kitchen.

When Maria opened the door, three men in military uniform could be seen. They had guns in holsters round their waists and caps with metal eagles and wings on the front. They had red arm bands with white discs containing black swastikas over their dark gray uniforms. The two younger ones were carrying two suitcases each, and the older one carried a briefcase and held a piece of blue paper with various black and green marks. His black collar had two dark silver bands on each side and from the central button of the collar hung a heavy square cross, black with thick silver edging.

'Frau Halversen?' said the older man.

Maria nodded. 'Officer Wolff?'

He bowed slightly, clipped his heels and straightened up immediately. He held out his hand, but Maria kept her arms folded and stared stonily at him. *'Sprechen Sie Deutsch?'* Maria remained silent. 'Do you speak English?'

'A little. Do you speak Norwegian?'

'No, but I learn and soon can speak it,' he said in Norwegian, *'Snakke Norsk, Ja?* And in fluent English: 'Here is my permit. I am here by order of the Fuhrer.' He handed her the blue document, which she simply stared at. 'You were ordered to leave the house.'

'I live here. I not go,' she said slowly in English.

'It is the law of the Nasjonal Samling government. I am an officer of the Wehrmacht and am here on duty.' He folded the permit and put it in his pocket.

Maria folded her arms and took a step toward him and repeated, 'I live here. I not go. *Jeg vill ikke ga.* You have to arrest me before I go. I *not* go.' She glared at him.

Herr Wolff turned to the officers who accompanied him and spoke to them in German.

'I need to be near the palace and near my office. Are there any other flats near here I can use?'

'No. The only ones left are too small. This is the only flat which fits your requirements, sir.'

'I'll check it over.'

Herr Wolff turned to Maria. 'I need to see the rooms.'

'Not understand.'

Herr Wolff indicated that he wanted to come in and pointed to his eyes and the rooms.

'No,' said Maria, blocking the doorway.

Herr Wolff nodded to his soldiers, who then walked in and pushed Maria aside.

'Carefully,' said Herr Wolff as he nodded to Maria and followed the soldiers in.

'I am sorry, Frau Halversen.'

Maria backed away and said to herself in Norwegian, 'That's all anyone ever says to me these days.' She pointed to the rooms, nodded, then went into the kitchen to join Else and her daughters who were huddled together next to their aunt, their faces pale and eyes dilated with fear.

'It's all right,' said Maria. 'They are just having a look around. They'll be gone in a minute.' She took a deep breath, squared her shoulders, and went back out.

As the soldiers came toward her along the corridor, she pointed to the bedrooms on her left. 'These bedrooms are my daughters"—and pointing to her bedroom on the right—'that is my bedroom. Not room for anyone else.'

Herr Wolff looked into the girls' bedrooms and nodded.

'You must leave this flat in one week. While you are looking for somewhere to stay, you will have to share these bedrooms. I will be in the large bedroom,' he said in a gentle but authoritative voice. You must move your things out now and I will return at ten.'

'*Nei!*' shouted Maria. '*Du kan* ikke *gjore det.*'

'Again, I am sorry, Mrs. Halversen, but I must have proper lodgings. You must do as I order or my men will arrest you now.'

Maria pulled herself up to her full height and, ignoring the tears on her cheek, narrowed her eyes. 'Take my room then. I not forget this.'

'You must introduce me to your family,' said Herr Wolff.

Maria glared at him then slumped her shoulders. 'Yes, but you not tell them. I tell them myself.' Herr Wolff nodded.

He followed Maria into the kitchen.

'Here are my daughters and my sister who, er, live here *noen dage* . . . some days.'

Officer Wolff bowed curtly to them all. His movements were quick and precise. He stood rigidly and looked at each of the family members. He was short and lean with elegant long fingers and perfectly manicured nails. On his right hand was a large silver ring with an eagle's head and wings. When he took his cap off, he had shortly cropped white hair, which was unexpected on a man who looked to be about forty-five years old. His black eyebrows were perfectly trimmed. He had a fine nose and his pale lips were as delicate as a woman's. The only clue that he might have been a soldier, apart from his uniform, was his weather-beaten and tanned skin. This contrasted with his eyes, which were pale gray.

Maria introduced Else and each of her girls and he repeated their names.

'You have a fine family. Eva reminds me of my eldest daughter. A beautiful young woman, like her mother.' Eva squirmed and blushed deep red.

'Do not take that look at my daughter,' said Maria.

'*Es tut mir Leid*—I mean, sorry, Frau Halversen, I meant no disrespect.' He turned toward Maria and bowed courteously. He left the kitchen and Maria followed him as he went into the sitting room and sat down at the table.

'Please, come and sit down.'

'I better to stand, thank you,' said Maria, struggling with her English.

'Well, then I will stand too. An officer cannot sit in the presence of a lady.'

'I will not agree that my girls will speak to you.'

'Then I will not speak to them, it will be as you ask. Now, we must agree. First, I will use the sitting room.' He indicated to the room as Maria looked blank. 'This room, on Sunday and Wednesday evening. You can use the room the rest of the time, but you must not disturb me when I am sleeping.'

'When do you sleep?'

'I go to bed at ten o'clock and read for half an hour. Then there must be total silence. I get up at five thirty and have my morning bath, so I will not be in your way when you get up. I always go out for a walk at six and have my breakfast at seven.'

'Breakfast here?' said Maria, scowling.

'No. I will have breakfast on my way to my office. I shall not trouble you for food. Once a week I will need my laundry done.' Maria looked blank. Herr Wolff mimed washing with his hands. 'Wash clothes?'

'Ah, vaske klieg. Nei, Jeg vil ikke vaske noen soldater klaer,' said Maria.

The officer paused, walked a couple of paces studying the floor, then turned back to her with a wry smile. He had not understood her but knew perfectly well what *nei* meant and could see from her angry expressions and the shaking of her head that there was no way she was going to go near any of his laundry.

'Very well. I shall make other arrangements. No washing. No,' he said, shaking his head and waving his hand back and forth. He looked over to the large desk by the window. 'That needs to be moved into my bedroom. I will need that for my work,' he said in English.

Maria folded her arms and hunched her shoulders. Shaking her head, she said, 'Officer, how many soldiers are here in Oslo?'

'There are very many soldiers.'

'Think you any of them strong enough to move a table or must a poor weak woman do *alt* . . . um, everything here?'

Officer Wolff paused again and looked at her reflectively. His mouth turned up slightly and his eyebrows lifted.

'On the contrary, madam, I think you are a very strong woman, a true Aryan. I will get the desk moved by my men. Until then I will have to use this room to work in.'

'*Er det alt?*'

'Also, you can have visitors as long as they do not interrupt my work, and no Jews will be allowed in here.'

'No Jews? But—'

'That's enough. There will be no Jews here.'

'Or what?'

'You will not disobey my orders in this respect, *Gnadige Frau*.'

'I think that is clear, officer,' said Maria, holding her chin up and holding his gaze steadily.

'I hope that we can be, *freundlich*. I wish you no harm.'

Maria did not conceal her hostility in the silence that followed. 'Can I go now?'

'Yes, thank you, *Takk*. I will come back at ten.'

Maria showed him to the door and noticed that the two younger soldiers were waiting outside for him.

'*Auf Wiedersehen*,' said Officer Wolff with a short bow.

Maria just folded her arms and stared back at him.

* * * *

She took a deep breath and, drawing herself up tall, walked into the kitchen.

In a moment, the silence of the flat was filled with three voices all going '*No!*' and Maria's voice speaking sternly and then shouting as the protests from the girls got even louder. Else's soft conciliatory voice was barely audible above the din.

The kitchen door was flung open and the racket continued down the corridor. Solveig, who was sobbing loudly, ran into her own room, moved her desk in front of the door, and wrapped herself up in her duvet.

Eva marched into Inger's room and cried out, 'I am not going to sleep in this pigsty!'

'You're a pig yourself,' said Inger making a loud grunting noise as she pushed her nose up with her index finger and bared her upper teeth.

'Mama, you can't make me go in that room.'

'Well, what if Inger goes into your room?'

'And turn my room into a disgusting tramp's den?' cried Eva.

Inger shouted back, *I'm not a disgusting tramp!* Just because you are such a goody-goody tidy little "Miss Perfect" who is so very superior to everybody—'

'*Stop it both of you!* One more word and I'll wring your necks, I swear I will,' screamed Maria, grabbing hold of both of them by their shoulders and shaking them several times.

'It's not your mother's fault. She didn't ask for the war and she didn't ask to have an officer to stay,' said Else.

Maria took some deep breaths then indicated for them all to go into the living room. She hid her hands behind her back so no one would see them shaking. She explained the rules but made no mention of the fact that Officer Wolff had told her she would have to move out in a week. There was no way she was going to move out of her own home. She would make him so unwelcome he would be sure to leave. The girls protested but simmered down with more threats from their mother.

Else looked around. 'Where's Solveig?' She went to Solveig's room and knocked.

'Go away,' cried a muffled voice.

'Solveig, can't you let your Aunty Else in?

There was a pause while the desk was moved back. Solveig opened the door a crack then went back to her bed and under her duvet. Her dolls were sitting beside her and she had the edge of the lilac shawl wrapped around her right hand with her thumb in her mouth. She was tapping her left hand over it and rocking herself very gently.

Else pulled on the duvet. 'Come on, little one. Mama is waiting.' Solveig's face emerged. She was pale and her eyes were still wide with fright.

'Come on, sweetie.' They were met by cigarette smoke as they came down the long corridor. Solveig pulled a face.

When they were all seated, Maria, cigarette in hand, explained the situation again and this time they sat motionless and speechless.

'I will take my dressing table into Eva's room. Eva, take your desk into Inger's room. There is just enough room for them both. Inger, pick up all your clothes and hang them in your wardrobe and tidy your schoolbooks up. Else, I am sorry but you can't stay on the settee because Officer Wolff will need access to the living room at all times.'

'I will have to go back home,' said Else.

'Don't go, aunty,' said Solveig, snuggling up to her. Her hand was still wrapped in the lilac shawl, which was draped around her shoulders.

'Else, you don't have to stay, but you could sleep in Solveig's room. There's room for you on the bed,' said Maria.

'Oh, *please* stay,' said Solveig

'Well, I can stay for a few more days.'

'*Goodeee!*' Solveig freed her hand from the lilac shawl and clapped her hands.

'I hope you don't snore, Solveig,' said Else.

Eva, who had been scowling throughout, jumped up as if startled. 'What about my bed?'

Maria gasped and put both her hands over her mouth. 'Oh damn. I didn't think about that.'

'See, I'll have to stay in my own room after all. Ha-ha, saved from the animal den, saved from the rat hole,' sang Eva while Inger started to do her pig's face at her.

'Shush. Eva, you can't do that because I have to sleep somewhere. You and Inger will have to share her bed.'

'No!'

'No!'

'You can have your pillow at each end, and there'll be enough room.'

'Yuck. I don't want to sleep next to Inger's smelly old feet.'

'My feet are not smelly.'

'Inger can come into my bed,' said Solveig.

'Oh, what about me?' said Else, pulling a face of mock hurt and taking her left index finger to her left eye and pulling it out as if it were a stream of tears.

'We can all sleep together!' said Solveig, laughing.

'Hmmm. Let me think.' Maria paused and frowned. 'Eva and Inger, you will have to share the bed until I can work something out. Maybe we can get a spare mattress from somewhere and put it on the floor.'

'But there's no room,' said Inger.

'There'll be enough room,' said Maria. She stood up and clapped her hands together. 'Right, no more arguing. Officer Wolff will be here at ten and there's a lot of work to do before he gets back. Solveig, your room isn't exactly tidy either, and if you want aunty to stay you better tidy it up.'

'I'll make it so tidy she'll stay forever.' Solveig skipped excitedly down to her room.

While the girls were tidying and moving their things, Maria took armfuls of clothes and dumped them on Eva's bed. She scooped all her makeup and perfumes into a clothes basket and squeezed past Eva, carrying the last of her clothes out of the room. There was much grumbling and bickering coming from Inger and Eva, and laughter from Solveig and Else. Eventually, the rooms were sorted out.

Maria went to give the rooms one last check. She paused in her bedroom, now devoid of her dressing table, chair, and photos. Then she took a sharp intake of breath and looked at the top of the wardrobe. She dragged a second art nouveau chair over, took off her shoes, and standing up on tiptoe reached through cobwebs and dust to get an old shoe box. She shook the box, blew off some more dust, and put it under her arm. She went into Eva's room, now her room, placed it under the bed, and returned to the kitchen.

She sent the girls to their rooms and listened to Inger and Eva as they continued to argue. She and Else sat in silence, glancing every few seconds at the kitchen clock, wishing that time would move faster to get it over with, and wishing also that that time would stand still so that it would never happen. Neither of them would sleep much tonight.

CHAPTER 6

Evening of the Same Day

Herr Wolff waited in the back of the car while his two soldiers carried his suitcases up the three flights of stairs to his allotted flat. He emerged reluctantly and slowly ascended the staircase. At the door he paused, sighed, and squared his shoulders. He had no wish to encounter Mrs. Halversen again, and yet he felt something like excitement at the prospect. He gritted his teeth and rang the doorbell.

Maria answered and after allowing the two soldiers in with the luggage before taking their leave, she nodded at Herr Wolff. She looked weary. Her eyes were dull and cold, a blank resignation replacing the flashes of anger from the previous day. Herr Wolff tried to shake her hand but she kept her distance, simply pointing to the bedroom and handing him a clean towel. He nodded a thank-you and after saying "Good Night" in the Norwegian he had already practiced, he watched her turn her back and walk into the kitchen, closing the door behind her.

He went into the main bedroom and unpacked three uniform suits, seven white shirts, two pairs of blue pajamas, a drawer full of socks and underwear, and a bag with his shaving equipment and other items for his personal hygiene. He took out two pictures in ornate silver frames and a wad of letters held together with an elastic band. One was of a woman and three children of similar ages to the Halversen girls, except the youngest was a boy. The other was a picture of Hitler. He put them both by the bed, sat down, and picked up the photo of his family again. He took the most recent letter from the wad and read it, although he knew every word by heart.

Her letters came every week and were a lifeline to him. News of his family was one of the few joys he allowed himself. He had missed so much of the children's lives posted in different parts of the world and his periods of leave were never long enough. Katherina was close friends with many of the military wives, and like them she had had to learn to be independent.

She ran the house efficiently, was devoted to her children, and prided herself on being a good citizen and member of the Nazi party. She was happy for her children to be fully committed members of the Hitler Youth, and even if it had not been compulsory, she would have supported it. She loved the healthy approach to life, with plenty of physical exercise, adventures camping in the wild, and even the chance to have military training. Her son, who had just joined, loved the rifle practice although he was less keen on the lessons they had to attend. Katherina was pleased that her children were being taught the virtues of obedience, self-sacrifice, and race-consciousness.

Her daughters had been members of the League of Girls for some time. They enjoyed their evenings at the local Nazi Party premises, singing songs which glorified the Fatherland, and working for the war effort by singing for soldiers or making presents for them., They would also go out on long hikes when they might collect herbs. Katherina was proud of her daughters who were glowing with health and purpose, and Herr Wolff was proud of all of them. He resumed reading the letter.

24th September 1942

Dearest Leo,

I have not had a letter from you for a long time and hope and pray you are all right.

Lisa has not been herself recently. One of her best friends has disappeared with her family. She is really upset as she knows her friend is Jewish and she should not have anything to do with her, but she says that her friend was a really lovely person, not like a Jewish person at all. She says there must be a mistake. She dare not tell anyone else about it as she knows they will not understand her. Amelie is fine. She is doing really well at school and says she is just as good as the boys at math. I do not know if that is much use to her, but it makes her happy. Liam is thriving. It is really good for him to be out on all these activities. He is too tired to be naughty when he gets home! As for me, I have never been so busy, what with raising money for the war effort and keeping things together for the children. I do not know how I ever managed my job before. I am sure Hitler is right when he says that there is more than enough for a woman to do at home.

I miss you so much. I dream of you every night and long to feel your arms around me again.

All my love my dearest one,
Katherina

Herr Wolff folded the letter up, replaced it into the wad, and placed the wad under his pillow. He must write soon, but he had so much work to catch up on. He sighed, then picked up a bundle of files, pens, and a notebook and went into the living room.

He opened the heavy suitcase by the bookshelf, moved the few books and ornaments that were already there to one side of the top shelf, and started loading his own books. Most of them were military and German history books. There were several books on theories of race and eugenics, *Mein Kampf,* a German-Norwegian dictionary, and a white leather-bound Bible. He sat down at the large desk, and without even looking out of the window, opened the top file and started making notes.

He could not have imagined that these arrangements would last more than a week. However, when that passed, Maria carried on as normal and observing that she had no intention of leaving, he carried on as normal as well. This new normal. He found himself looking forward to their brief encounters, despite her coldness, and so nothing more was said about it.

★   ★   ★   ★

At midnight the flat was quiet. Inger and Eva had finally managed to sort out their sleeping arrangements after Eva took some cushions from the lounge padded out with some towels and extra blankets from the airing cupboard as a makeshift bed. After playing cards and talking in whispers for over an hour, they fell asleep. Solveig was snugly wrapped up in her lilac shawl at the end of her bed and sleeping soundly. Elsa, with her head on Solveig's pillow and feet diagonally off the bed so they did not touch Solveig's head, shifted from one side to another, slowly, so as not to wake her niece. For someone who was so good at comforting other people, she had few thoughts of solace for herself.

Maria sat on Eva's bed going over the events of the day. *How dare they? All of them. How dare they do this to her?* Eventually, she went into the kitchen searching for a drink and poured the remains of some cooking brandy into a mug. She saw that the light was now on in Herr Wolff's room, *her* room, and went into the living room. She went over to the book shelf where volumes of dull books had replaced her magazines, noted the lack of cushions on the sofa, and frowned. She sat down by the phone, picked up the receiver, and dialed zero.

'Operator,' said a brisk voice after a few rings.

'Bronnoysund three-seven-three please,' she said. She let the phone ring and after it had rung some twenty times, there was a reply.

'Hello, who is this?' said Maria's mother.

'It's Maria. I am sorry to call so late.'

'Has something happened? What's wrong?'

'He's left me, Mother.'

'That no-good, womanizing, drunken bastard! What did I always say? Has he gone to one of his whores? But then you always let him back. Poor little doormat Maria.'

'No, it's different this time. He has told the Germans that he doesn't live here and now I've got a Nazi officer taking over the flat.'

'The bastard!' Maria's mother repeated a whole litany of insults with her voice getting louder and louder. Then she paused and gasped. 'My dear sweet God, you can't live in the flat with a German soldier. What if he rapes you or murders all of you? God help us.' She was shouting so loudly by this time that Maria moved the receiver a good ten inches from her ear.

'He's under orders, Mother. He's a high-ranking army officer and will be out most of the day.'

'You must come home at once, and take the children here where it is safe.'

'I want to stay here.'

'Oh yes? You just want to wait by the door for your beloved Johannes to come home and spend time with you in between his nights with his whores.'

'The girls have their friends here. Else and Torhild are here and we'll be okay'—she paused—'but I need some money.'

'Yes, of course, I might have known you were calling to ask for money'

'Can I speak to Father?'

'Oh, here we go, still Papa's little girl. Well, he's gone to bed and I'm not getting him up.'

'Please, Mama.'

'I will tell him you phoned and that rather than come home, you prefer to put your own daughters at risk with a Nazi in the house.'

'Please ask him to phone me tomorrow.'

'Yes, and I'll tell him you are asking for money again.'

'As you please. Good night, Mother.'

'Good night, darling.'

Maria slammed the phone down and cursed at it. She paced up and down the living room and smoked a cigarette. After a brief visit to the bathroom, she tiptoed into her room, Eva's room, which was now crammed with her dressing table, washing basin and jug, all the photos from the living room, and her clothes still piled up over the chair. She threw her clothes on top of the pile and rummaged around until she found her nightie. It was a cold night, so she wrapped herself up in a knitted blanket from the top of the bed. As she did so, she caught sight of the shoe box protruding from under the bed.

She pulled it out from under the bed, sat down, and slowly removed the lid. Inside was a pair of pale blue bootees and a lacy cardigan to match. Beside them was a photo, black-and-white, of her younger self holding a baby, her face lit up with joy. She stroked the booties and raised them to her nose, trying for a last scent of her baby boy, but it had long faded. Even the memory of the scent had faded. She stroked her cheeks with them, then carefully replaced them in the tissue and smoothed down the lid. She sat on the bed holding the box, rocking gently backward and forward, until she fell asleep.

*　*　*　*

In the rambling country house in Vik, near Bronnoysund, halfway up the coast of Norway, Maria's mother put down the phone. She was tall and slender, wearing a demure silk dressing gown with an oriental pattern. Her long white hair was swept up and held in place with a bejeweled hair slide, which she had applied hastily as she rose out of bed. It was easy to imagine how beautiful she had been when she was young. She walked with poise and elegance, with every little gesture and expression studied to perfection.

As she left the room, Maria's father came downstairs from his bedroom.

'Hello? Ruth? Who was calling so late? Is everything okay?'

'That was Maria. She's waking us up at this time of night asking for money. I told her it was too late to speak to you. Johannes has left her again. He must have left her ten times already and he just goes off gambling and losing all his money—and ours too.'

'I think it was just the three times.'

'I'm sure it was more. It wears me out. Why Maria keeps taking him back, I really don't know. And you, you've been too generous to her. She knew what he was like when she married him. I warned her, but would she listen to me? Well, she made her own choice and now we are expected to go on supporting her and the girls.'

'What else can we do? Do you want Maria to work in a factory and take your granddaughters to an orphanage?'

'Of course not. She could get a perfectly good job as a secretary and the girls are practically grown up. When I was Eva's age, I took care of all my brothers and sisters while my mother was ill. I never went to school like they do now. What does a girl need to go to school for anyway? She's only going to get married and have children.'

'If Maria hadn't been to school, she wouldn't be able to get a job as a secretary, would she?'

'Oh, you always twist what I say. Obviously, girls should be able to read and write, but they can learn all that before they are ten. They have it so easy these days.'

'Don't you want your children and grandchildren to be happier than you were?'

'Sometimes I think you care more about your precious Maria and her children than you do about me.'

'You know that's not true, Ruth. But Maria has had a lot of problems. First Olav, then Johannes and his gambling, then the miscarriages, and she nearly died when Solveig was born.'

Ruth was not listening to him. She carried on talking as he spoke. 'There's Else who hasn't married yet, Torhild who'll never be able to marry with her weak heart, Helga who has gone to America, Lars and Nils who never come and visit us with their children, and Olav, my only grandson, dead.'

'You have your three beautiful granddaughters in Oslo.'

'Really? Eva is a cheeky rude girl, Inger is untidy and careless, and Solveig, well, she is lazy and really plain. I cried so much when Olav died, but you had to go to Oslo and be with your lovely Maria, didn't you?'

'She was ill and Johannes nearly let the doctors take her to an asylum. There's no way my daughter was going to go to a mental hospital. She wasn't insane; she was just ill with exhaustion and grief.'

'And so was I, Jorgen, your own wife. And was there anyone to take care of me when Kristian and Erik fell off the ice floes and drowned? No, I had to carry on taking care of all the children. And you, working all the hours God gave us and never talking to me. What use were you to me then?'

'I know. I should have been there for you. I only wish I could make it up to you, but that was a long time ago and we have five wonderful grown children, which is more than a lot of people have.'

'Well, I am glad Maria has you there when she needs you, because I certainly don't.'

'She was in a terrible state when Olav died. Surely you can understand that now?'

'And my heart was really bad then with the strain of it all. I was on my own for months. I could have died for all you cared.'

'It was only a few weeks. I am here now and always will be here for you.'

'Except when you drop everything to go to your darling daughter.'

'Sometimes I wonder at you. Don't you care about your daughter at all?'

'Oh, you are going to start that again, are you? Maria was always such a difficult child, but I still looked after her, which is more than you did. You always spoilt her and now look at the result.'

'What do you mean?'

'Selfish, weak-minded, and money-grabbing.'

'How can you say that about your own daughter? She's no better and no worse than anyone else trying to survive in this world. We all have our faults, even you, Ruth.'

'You just don't want to face the truth. At least I'm honest.'

'That's not honesty. For God's sake, how can you be so petty-minded and malicious?'

'Me? Petty-minded and malicious? That is such a vicious and cruel thing to say. If you want to delude yourself about Maria, that is your problem. You should at least be honest with yourself, not hurl insults at me. That's all I get around here, and you so high and mighty.'

'Enough! That's enough. Stop talking. For God's sake, shut up. I'm going to bed.'

'Please don't shout, it scares me, and—' She clutched her chest and sat down heavily on the settee, lying down and fanning herself with her other hand. 'Call. Kari. Please.'

Jorgen called Kari, who was already hovering around outside the door and asked her to help him take her upstairs. Kari escorted her into her bedroom and after a great deal of pillow plumping and fluffing up her duvet, Kari helped her take off her dressing gown and get into bed. Ruth sank into the pillows and made Kari give her another couple of pills before leaning back to sleep. Kari waited outside until she was sure she was asleep before going to her room at the end of the landing. Ruth had a bell and Kari slept lightly as the bell rang often.

Jorgen left the room but did not go to bed. As he passed the hallway, he glanced, as he always did, at their wedding photo in its ornate silver frame on a table next to their grandfather clock. The groom stood tall and proud and the bride smiled exultantly, full of hope and beauty. How lovely Ruth had been then, and how happy he had been.

He walked into the garden and lit a cigarette, exhaling invisibly in the heavy mist; black apart from a slither of moon and a chink of light from the window. He already felt guilty for insulting her. He rarely lost control of his feelings and when he did he always regretted it. Ruth was fragile and had never fully recovered from the grief and hardship of her earlier life. Sometimes, she would forget herself, and her face would light up into a smile of such beauty it hurt him. It was these moments he lived for, these glimpses of a happier time, that he yearned for.

CHAPTER 7

Johannes

Later That Evening

Later that evening a police car drove up to a small flat on the outskirts of Oslo. A stocky man in a black police uniform heaved himself out and walked slowly to the door. Just as he took out his key, a young woman flung back the door.

'Johannes, I thought you would never come!' She threw her arms around him and kissed his cheeks. She had long, wavy blond hair and a pink wool dress that emphasized her generous proportions. Johannes smiled as he disentangled himself.

'Sorry, Klara, we're working on that case, you know, the woman who was stabbed out by the woods near Grefsen.'

'Uh-huh. Come and eat. I've got pork chops and *surkal*, and some red wine.'

'Red wine? What are we celebrating?'

'It's a year since we first got together. I have something else for us to celebrate tonight Johannes—but later.'

'Oh yes? What could that be?' he said as he slipped his hands behind her and pulled her into him. She pulled his face to hers and they kissed slowly, drawing apart to smile then kiss again. Eventually, Klara pulled herself away and straightened her hair.

'I said later. You're always in such a rush!'

'Can you blame me?'

They went into the kitchen where a small table was laid with two red candles, serviettes, and wine glasses. She sat him down and poured out some red wine, then put the chops on to fry with the onions, adding extra butter and a sprinkle of sugar to caramelize them. The small kitchen was soon full of the aroma of onions and burnt sugar.

She placed the chops on a warmed-up serving dish with the fried onion, potatoes, and *surkal*. She filled Johannes's glass with more wine and picked up her own.

'*Skal,*' said Klara.

'*Skal,*' said Johannes. They both took a long draft.

'I saw Maria today in the office. I'm sorry, but I couldn't help overhearing Gustav calling out that she had to see you urgently. I know I shouldn't have, but I couldn't help going over to her and asking if I could help.'

'And?'

'She looked really angry. She just ignored me as if I didn't exist.'

Johannes laughed. 'That sounds like Maria all right.'

'What was wrong?'

'Nothing terrible, but they have just had an officer billeted to the flat, and Maria blames me. She's furious.'

'Well, I don't blame her. Some families have had to move out of Oslo completely because the soldiers have taken over their whole house or flat. My friend's parents had to have three junior soldiers staying. Can you imagine? They decided to move in with her sister in Trondheim. They weren't allowed to take their belongings with them either.' Klara paused. 'You didn't tell me how beautiful she is, Johannes. I feel like a great sack of potatoes compared to her. I can't believe how you could want to leave her.'

'Mmm, the more the better, come here,' he said, sliding his hand over the curve of her thigh under the table.

Klara ignored him. 'Have you told her you are coming to live with me yet?'

'Mmm, yes,' he replied, hunching his shoulders and looking down at his glass.

'At last. Wonderful.' Klara held up her glass. '*Skal.*'

Johannes poured out another glass of red wine and lit a cigarette.

'Tell me what happened with Maria, why she made you so unhappy,' said Klara.

'We were happy once, I suppose,' he said, still staring at his wine glass. 'It was all a long time ago now.' He picked up his knife and fork and dug into his pork.

'Go on, tell me. I want to know everything about you.'

*   *   *   *

Johannes could remember it all so vividly. After Inger was born, Maria had three miscarriages, one of them quite late. She lost a lot of blood. When the doctor told them that they should not risk any more pregnancies, she refused to listen. When she became pregnant again, her father paid for a nurse and Maria spent her entire pregnancy in bed. Her mother refused to speak to her, although it was not clear whether it was because of Maria's 'selfishness putting them all through that worry' or whether it was because of the expense.

When Olav was born, it was a miracle. Maria had never looked more radiant and Johannes had never felt so proud. But Olav vomited all his feeds, whimpered continuously, and screamed when he was held. He became jaundiced and died when he was three days old.

Maria cried for days and became like an old woman sitting still all day, not eating and not even having a bath. She would not open the curtains and just stared at the walls day after day. She lost so much weight she was barely recognizable and her hair started to fall out. They paid a nurse to take care of her and the two girls.

The nurse packed her bags after Maria had thrown some specially prepared soup over her. The nurse had tried to feed her, but Maria turned her head away and when she persisted, she slapped her across the face. The nurse would have left before if it had not been for her generous pay packet from Maria's father. After the maid left, Johannes asked if Eva and Inger, who were just five and four, could stay with Maria's mother and father in Bronnoysund

Maria's mother complained nonstop about their presence and only ever spoke to the girls to tell them off. Maria's father tried to speak to them, but they were distant and more like little ghosts than children. Johannes phoned soon after their arrival, but his voice was so slurred Maria's mother refused to let him speak to them. After that she put the phone down on him whenever he called, which was usually at an unreasonably late hour anyway. The girls never asked when they would be able to go home—they were too scared of what the answer might be.

Back in Oslo there was no one to notice if Maria ate or dressed. Johannes was seldom home and it was not until Maria cut her wrists that her father came back to Oslo with the girls. The first thing he did was discharge her from Gaustad Hospital against medical advice and send the girls to stay with their aunts Else and Torhild in Blommenholm. He then looked after Maria at home. He made her get up, made her wash, made her eat, and took her for walks every day. He was gentle but refused to take no for an answer. In the end Maria started to move around without prompting and to open the curtains before he asked.

He stayed for a month and although Maria was still depressed, she could now get up, get dressed, and do the housework. She took her two girls back from her sisters as the summer holidays were over. Else had to go back to her work as a teacher and Torhild had to avoid any strain because of a heart problem. Maria's father wanted to stay but was no longer able to resist the entreaties of his wife or the demands of his business and had to return to Bronnoysund. Maria was still prone to sitting and staring into space and seldom spoke, but she could at least do enough to give the essential care needed to her two girls.

Johannes remembered how he had continued to stay away from home. He had felt as if he no longer existed for Maria and he had lost touch with his daughters. When he was not at work, he was drunk or gambling at the casino. He lost all their savings and started selling Maria's jewelry to pay his debts. Despite this, Maria begged Johannes to have one more go at having a baby. The doctor said another pregnancy would kill her, but Maria had made up her mind. She wanted to have a son. She kept on trying despite several more miscarriages.

When she finally took a pregnancy beyond the first three months, she was happy again just like her old self. She would chat and laugh with Johannes and flirt with him as if he were a new lover. But then she went into premature labor. The doctor said it was just as well because her blood pressure was so high it could have given her a stroke. When she was told that her new baby was a girl, she shrieked out *"No!"* and had a fit. The doctor said she was lucky to survive and so was the little girl.

After a few days, she got up and carried on as normal. She did everything she had to do as before, looking after the girls as well as the new baby, even when the baby cried day and night for four months. But Maria never cried and never complained. She was efficient, but never once did she stop to smile or play with her little baby daughter, little Solveig.

★   ★   ★   ★

Johannes ate silently, lost in his thoughts.

He sighed and put his hand over hers. Klara was so young. What would she know about a baby who died, a woman who wanted to die and then became like the walking dead? When Maria was recovering, she started putting on her makeup and high heels again, but he never heard her laugh after that.

'There's nothing to tell,' he replied. 'I'd much rather hear more about you.'

After they finished eating, Johannes went outside. It was claustrophobic in the small kitchen with its blackout curtains obscuring the view. It was dark and the row of modern flats with their dark bricks and black roofs made it seem even darker. Further along there were gardens and white wooden houses softening the skyline, and over the top of the trees was a thin white moon. He breathed in the cool air and went back in.

He reached for her hand and kissed it. Klara wrapped her arms around him, enveloping him in soft wool and perfume.

'Darling Johannes, I love you so much,' she said as she pulled him up and led him by the hand into the bedroom.

CHAPTER 8

Johannes

Police Headquarters

Tuesday

November 24th, 1942

A couple of months later, in the police headquarters, Klara was sitting at her desk typing. A senior police officer walked in with the office manager, a tall woman with short graying hair, a plain black dress with a high collar, and a silver cross prominently displayed on a heavy silver chain. She had a calm, authoritative manner, and after a brief conversation with the officer took a file and walked over to Klara in the back.

'We need twenty copies typed up immediately,' she said, handing her the file.

'Yes.'

'And it is top secret. I have told the superintendent that you are my most trusted member of staff.'

'Thank you. Shall I bring them to you when I have finished?' Miss Rygg nodded.

'I shall expect them within the hour.'

Klara put her glasses on, got some supplies of paper and carbon sheets, and took the file to her desk. As she read, she looked shaken. Her fingers clattered over the keys and her bell rang loudly every time she got to the end of the line. Her speed of typing was legendary, and she had been told that she sounded like a machine gun when she got going. Very soon she had gathered the original file and her copies and taken them to Miss Rygg's office. She kept one extra copy hidden inside another file.

When she came out, instead of going straight back to the office, she went into the room where the police officers wrote their reports. The room was crowded as it often was at the end of the day as policemen smoked and chatted over the day's events. She looked over the heads of several officers bent over desks and several sitting on desks laughing together, and in the corner she saw Johannes. He did not see her as he was looking intensely at a young woman in an exceedingly tight sweater standing right in front of him. They were both smiling and as they did so, they moved almost imperceptibly closer to each other. Johannes laughed again and she lifted her arm in a mock slap to his face and wagged her finger at him. He carried on smiling and all through this, neither of them had stopped gazing at each other and neither had moved back.

Johannes looked up, his eyes bright, and saw Klara across the room. He looked startled for an instant, then quickly stepped back from the new secretary and said something briefly to her. She looked across the room with the same bright eyes that Johannes had just showed. He walked over to Klara, weaving his way through his fellow officers lolling about on various chairs and desks and greeted her with a huge smile, put his arm around her waist, and kissed her on the cheek.

'Here, none of that!' said one of his junior colleagues.

'Klara, you're too good for him, take me!' said another.

'No, take me!'

Klara smiled at them. 'Promise?'

'You bet!'

She turned to Johannes and said quietly, 'I need to talk to you urgently.'

'Can't it wait until tonight? I still have to do my report.'

'Pretend it's a lover's row, Johannes,' she said very softly, then raised her voice so everyone could hear. 'Where have you been for the last three nights? Who are you seeing?' Johannes went bright red and the room went quiet. The woman with the bright eyes looked startled and turned her back toward them, picking up a book from the nearest desk and turning the pages as if fascinated.

'Not here,' he said, regaining his composure. He pulled her by the arm and walked down the corridor with her. He opened a senior officer's door and peered in. Seeing it was empty, he drew her in and closed the door.

'Are you trying to make a fool of me in front of my men?'

'I said the first thing that came into my head, which just happened to be the truth. But that's not why I'm here. I've just typed a top-secret notice, which is coming out tonight.' She explained hurriedly and handed him a piece of paper with a list of names and addresses. His face went white.

There was a list of over fifty Jewish families with addresses and orders for police to arrest them, and take them to the harbor outside the army base. They were to be deported to Germany in the *SS Donau* on the twenty-sixth of November.

'Go back to the office, and pretend to cry so no one suspects anything.'

'That won't be difficult.'

'I won't be back tonight.'

'I'll expect you when I see you,' muttered Klara as she wiped her eyes with her hanky.

Johannes sighed. He had a long night ahead of him and even then, he would not be able to reach all the families in time. He would start with his, or rather Maria's neighbors, on the third floor at Kristian IV Gate. Their daughters had played together ever since they were old enough to climb up and down the stairs and play in the courtyard.

CHAPTER 9

Johannes

Later That Day

J ohannes drove near to his old flat and parked in the main street by a general store. Policemen and officials were allowed to skip the usual queues and he squeezed through the doorway, ignoring the glares of women who had been waiting hours already. He asked for a slab of cheese, four slices of raisin cake, and the last of some faded roses. He walked slowly toward the flat, trying to appear as if he was off-duty and just making a visit home.

He climbed up the stairs, half hoping and half dreading that Maria might appear and, at the same time, ready to give his excuses if it should be Herr Wolff. He rang the Bauman's doorbell, waited for a couple of minutes, then rang again. After repeating this for about ten minutes, an anxious face appeared at the door. When Gila Bauman saw it was Johannes, she looked relieved. He put his fingers to his lips and gestured for her to let him in.

'I have to be very quick,' he explained. 'The Gestapo and our own police are arresting all the remaining Jews in Oslo and taking them to Germany. You have no time to pack. You must leave immediately. Are you all here?'

Gila let out a muted scream and rushed back into the kitchen. 'Jacob, you were right, we've got to get out of here. I thought we had more time. The children, oh no, I can't believe this is happening.'

Their daughter and two sons stood up and rushed to their rooms. They understood all too well. They had heard the rumors. They were used to being scared, but now they were terrified.

Jacob went to the door. Johannes spoke urgently.

'Don't take anything more than you would normally carry, and don't run. Go by the backstreets and find your way to this address.' He handed Jacob a piece of paper. 'Both of you read it, then destroy it in case the Gestapo find it. Quick now.'

'Thank you,' said Jacob, 'You better go. Some of our neighbors are spies and I know how dangerous it is for you. God bless you.'

Johannes embraced him and, after checking that no one was outside the door, slipped back into the corridor.

Jacob gathered the family, telling them to whisper, to stop panicking and to concentrate. They had to leave the flat without being seen. If anyone did see them, they would have to appear as if they were going out to see friends. Jacob rushed to his study, rolled back the carpet, lifted a floorboard, and took out a wad of cash that he had accumulated over the last year. He had hoped this day would never come but had known that it would.

* * * *

Johannes was about to leave the building when he heard footsteps coming up the stairs. He held his breath as they got nearer.

There was Officer Wolff in full uniform. Johannes saluted him.

'What is your business here, police inspector?'

'I am Police Inspector Halversen, and I have come to see my wife.'

Herr Wolff looked intently at him.

'I see. It's been a long time, yah?'

'And you are Officer Wolff?' Johannes clipped his heels and stood at attention. 'I need to see my wife.'

'Ah, I wish you good luck.' Officer Wolff smiled knowingly. He produced his key and let himself into the flat. 'I won't disturb you,' he said with a curt nod as he disappeared into the sitting room.

Johannes scowled as he waited outside the door. He had to watch a Nazi walk into his own home while he had to ring the doorbell. But he reminded himself that he was the one who had left. He took a deep breath and pulled his shoulders back.

Maria opened the door and on seeing Johannes tried to close it again. Johannes put his boot in the door and kept it there.

'I thought you didn't live here anymore.'

'Maria, just give me five minutes. I need to see you.'

'Oh, really? It's a bit late for that now don't you think?'

'Please, Maria.'

Maria shrugged and rolled her eyes up. 'Whatever it is, it better be good,' she said as she let him in.

They went into the living room and sat down. Maria took the cigarette box out and offered him one.

'There's only a few left.' He took one anyway.

'How are you, Maria?'

'How do you think? I have a Nazi living in the house and the girls are so rude, they just quarrel all the time and complain that they are hungry. I have chilblains from queuing outside in the freezing cold, and there's nothing to eat, just rubbish.'

'I'm sorry.'

'What's the use of that?'

Johannes inhaled his cigarette deeply and looked out of the window.

'How are your parents?' he said.

'Just the same as ever. How my father puts up with Mother I don't know. Anyway, what is it to you? You, who are so busy that you have no time to see your own daughters.'

'I love them. I really wish I could see them more often.'

'Oh really? Or are you too busy having fun with your live-in lady friend?'

Johannes sighed. 'I still love you, Maria. I think about you all the time.'

'What use is that to me when you're not here?'

Johannes sighed and got up from the chair. He handed her the paper bag containing the food and flowers. Maria took it and peered in.

'Still trying to make up for everything with flowers? Lucky me, I get some cheese and wilted flowers.'

Johannes stepped toward her in an attempt to embrace her, but she pushed him away. He paused and looked at her with sadness and longing. 'I have to go.'

Johannes hurried down the three flights of stairs. He had many more houses to visit and no certainty of getting to them before the Gestapo.

★　★　★　★

Out on the street it was getting dark. The pavements were frosty and yesterday's snow lay in a translucent layer over the gray cobblestones and window ledges. The road was busy with pedestrians, crowded trams, and bicycles. Occasionally a black car or a group of soldiers on motorbikes would drive past. Johannes in his black uniform merged in. There were a lot of policemen around at the moment.

CHAPTER 10

The Next Day, Wednesday

September 25th

Back at Kristian IV Gate

Mrs. Ostby told her class that school would be held at Mr. Bronstad's the next day because her mother was ill. The pupils had been to Mr. Bronstad many times before and all knew their way there. It was a large house on the corner, where he lived with his married daughter and grandchildren, all of whom were out at work during the day. They liked going there because he had two dogs who would greet them like long lost friends and a huge fireplace which he kept well stocked with logs. He was pretty deaf, so they could whisper to their heart's content and he never seemed to notice when they laughed.

That afternoon Mrs. Ostby called Eva over before all the pupils left. 'I hope Inger is all right. She hasn't been her normal self at all this morning.'

'Inger?'

'Yes, she hasn't said a word all morning, and you know how chatty she normally is. I haven't had to tell off at all today. Most unusual.' Mrs. Ostby smiled and shook her head. There was a brief hubbub in the hall as everyone gathered their things, followed by silence as the children ran off in different directions.

As they left, Eva put her arm into Inger's and Solveig came running up behind and grabbed hold of her other hand. Inger, who had not said a word, let go of their hands and clutched her stomach. She bent over and moaned. When she looked up, her face was pale and there were deep shadows under her eyes.

'What's wrong?' said Eva

'I couldn't sleep last night because of a stomachache. I thought it was better this morning, but now it's getting worse and I think I'm going to be sick.'

'Take some deep breaths. Come on, sit down here and put your head down between your legs.' Eva pulled her to a wall. Inger took some deep breaths then vomited on the pavement. The yellow fluid made rivulets in the snow. She heaved a few more times but nothing more came. Eva looked at the fluid.

'Didn't you have any breakfast this morning?'

'No, I wasn't hungry. Actually, I was feeling a bit sick, but then I felt better.' She got up and Eva put her arm around her. Solveig took hold of her other hand carefully and kept looking up at her as they walked on.

As they came past the gate to Palace Park, a group of soldiers were looking at them. One of them shouted out, 'Halt!'

'Oh no, what do they want now?' said Eva under her breath. They stopped and waited. The soldier, who was a different one from the one who spoke to them the previous day, marched over, looking angry.

'No. Red. Hats,' he said in broken Norwegian. *'Das ist verboten!'*

'Why?'

'Students are forbidden to wear red. Give it to me.'

'But I'm at school, I'm not a student, and it's the only hat I have got.'

'I don't understand what you say.'

'Ich bin nicht eine student. Das ist mein einste hat,' said Eva.

'Give it to me,' said the soldier, holding his hand out. Eva took it off and clasped it tight as he tried to pull it out of her hand. 'Give it to me,' he repeated. Eva drew breath ready for a fight, then seeing some other soldiers coming over toward them, she sighed and let go.

As the girls were about to set off, Inger suddenly leaned forward and vomited green fluid all over the soldier's boots. He went red with fury, then shouted at them in German. The three girls walked away as fast as they could, stopping every now and again as Inger bent double. Finally, they reached the flat, but it took ages for them to climb up the three flights of stairs.

'Mother, quick! Inger is fainting,' said Eva as soon as they got in the door.

'Mama, Inger was sick on the pavement,' said Solveig at the same time.

Maria came out of the kitchen, wiping her flour-covered hands on her apron. A cloud of steam followed her and filled the hallway with the smell of cabbage mingled with cod liver oil.

'I'm all right, Mama,' said Inger smiling. 'It's just a stomach bug. Arne was sick last week and he was better the next day.'

'You look very pale. Go and lie down. Take your boots off!' Inger bent over to take them off, then sank onto the floor and clasped her stomach.

'Ow, sorry, another bad pain, but it will pass in a minute,' said Inger, still holding her stomach. Solveig went up to her and started pulling off one of her boots. Eva pulled the other one off and Inger's socks came off with them, leaving her woolen tights.

'Hey, give me my socks back,' said Inger, leaning over to put them back on.

'You've got odd socks,' said Solveig, laughing. Inger smiled.

'They're both Norway's colors, so I wear one of each, red and blue for King Haakon.'

'King Haakon is it? Who will it be for tomorrow then?' said Maria from the bathroom as she rummaged around in the cabinet for a thermometer.

'I want to wear socks for King Haakon too.'

'Solveig, do you think the color of your socks would make any difference to anyone?' said Eva.

'*I* would know. We could be sisters of Norway together!' said Inger, looking more cheerful.

'For heaven's sake, "sisters of Norway,"' said Eva, mimicking their enthusiasm with a sneer on every syllable. 'Do you think that's going to help the men and women who are really doing something for the country? Grow up.' Solveig stuck her tongue out at Eva.

'Sisters of Norway, together forever and ever,' said Solveig, repeating this in a singsong voice until Eva went to slap her. Solveig ran to her room laughing and slammed the door. Eva started to run after her, then sang out:

'Little baby sucks her thumb, little baby stupid and dumb, stupid and so dumb, dumb dumb.'

A voice shouted out of Solveig's room: *'I hate you!'*

Another voice screamed out of the bathroom: 'Stop fighting or I swear there'll be nothing to eat tonight.'

Inger had now got up and, laughing and shaking her head, went to lie down. Maria came in after her with the thermometer. Eva followed.

Maria helped Inger out of her sweater and trousers, put her pajama top over her vest, and let her keep her tights on. She felt Inger's forehead and shook down the thermometer.

'Here, keep this under your tongue and don't breathe through your mouth.' She pulled Inger's duvet over her and smoothed down her hair. A few moments later, she took out the thermometer and stared at it.

'Is it okay, Mama?' said Inger.

'It's thirty-nine degrees,' said Maria, still checking the thermometer. 'You have a really high fever.' She paused and thought. 'You're too hot. We'll have to cool you down . . . um, yes, we did this before when Solveig had measles. I'll get some water.'

'I'm so thirsty.'

'Eva, go and get Inger a glass of water.'

A few minutes later, Solveig came out of her room wearing a red hand-me-down sweater that was far too large for her, hanging over blue tights. She had her old lilac shawl around her shoulders and unwrapped it from her right hand as she came out. She walked up to Inger and Eva's bedroom. Inger was wearing just her underwear and sitting on a towel on the edge of the bed while Maria was dipping a flannel in a large bowl of lukewarm water and dabbing her arms, legs, and face repeatedly, careful not to allow water on the bed. Inger was drinking her water in large gulps.

'What's wrong with Inger?' said Solveig.

'She has a high fever,' said Eva.

'I want to help,' said Solveig. Eva looked at her and put her finger to her lips.

'Shush.'

'Eva, take Solveig and help her get started on her homework,' said Maria, still not looking up. 'Check the vegetables. I think they'll be cooked by now. Just take them off the heat and there's some meatball mixture. There's one onion left. Chop it up and fry it beside the meatballs.' She carried on dabbing Inger's limbs and felt her forehead as she spoke.

'Can I help cook the meatballs?' asked Solveig.

'No, Mrs. Ostby says you haven't been doing your homework properly. And I don't want you to burn your fingers again,' replied Maria.

'Come on, Solveig,' said Eva. 'We need to let Inger rest.'

Inger waved at them then shuddered. 'I feel cold now, Mama. Can I put the duvet over me?' Maria nodded and set about drying her.

'Leave your pajamas here by the bed. I don't want you to get overheated again.' Inger nodded, sank back onto her pillow, and closed her eyes. Maria straightened the duvet and felt her forehead again. She sat there for another ten minutes, occasionally stroking Inger's hair and feeling her forehead. Inger fell asleep.

When Maria returned to the kitchen, Solveig was seated in front of her exercise book and math text book. She had rubbed out the sums she was working on so many times that alongside a smudged area there was a hole in the page.

'I *hate* arithmetic.'

'Solveig, your teacher says you are top of the class in Norwegian and write really good stories, so you should be able to do math. She thinks you are just being lazy.'

'I'm *not* being lazy! Sums are really difficult.'

'They look easy to me,' said Eva, turning around from the cooker where she was frying the meatballs and onion.

'You always say that.'

'Mother, what is in these meatballs? They smell disgusting,' said Eva.

'It's the fish oil.'

'No, it isn't just that. Really, what's in them?'

'I went to the new butcher this morning and this was all he had left.

He says it is "war mince." It's made from finely chopped herring and beef heart.'

'Yuck!' said Eva and Solveig together.

'Well, if you don't like it, see if you can do any better. Solveig, you can finish your homework now because I want you to lay the table.'

'Goody! Can I put the yellow candles on the table?'

'No, we need to keep all our candles for the blackouts,' said Maria.

'Aw, please?'

'Solveig, has anyone told you there's—' said Eva.

'Has any one told you there's a war going on?' said Solveig, mimicking her in a high, shrill voice.

'Solveig, if you can't just do one simple thing without a huge fuss, I will send you to your room with no supper. And Eva, do you think that just this once you could lay off Solveig? Is it too much to ask while Inger is so ill?'

'Sorry, Mother.'

Solveig cleared her books up and took them down to her room. On her way back, she peeped into Inger and Eva's bedroom. Inger was lying back with her eyes closed, holding her stomach and moaning so softly that she could not be heard from the corridor.

'Mama, Inger's not well,' shouted Solveig.

Maria went to her and stood in the doorway. She was tossing and turning, clutching her stomach.

'I'm going to be sick!' Maria grabbed the basin and placed it under Inger's chin. She writhed and twisted her head forward but missed the bowl. She vomited a pale yellow fluid all over the duvet, sheets, and carpet. Maria sat down beside her, put her arm around her, and rocked her back and forth. Solveig sat on the other side and held her hand. Maria lay Inger down and started peeling off the soiled duvet and sheets while Solveig helped.

'You better go and eat with Eva,' said Maria. 'I'll stay here.'

'But I don't want to leave Inger. Please, can I help?'

'Shush, she's is nearly asleep,' said Maria.

Inger opened her eyes and smiled softly at Solveig. 'I'm okay, just a bit tired. Come and see me after you have eaten.'

Maria got clean sheets and duvet covers and scrubbed the carpet. In the kitchen Solveig and Eva wolfed down their potato and meatballs despite the 'war mince,' but neither spoke, not even to tease or complain.

Solveig went into Inger's room after they finished, but by now she was asleep again. When she went to her room, Solveig sat down at the end of the bed and rocked herself.

'Dear God,' she said, 'I'm sorry that I don't really believe in you, but if you are true, please can you make Inger better. Please, I will be so good and kind to everyone, even Eva, if you make her better. And please let Papa come back soon as well. Amen.'

*   *   *   *

The evening passed quietly. Officer Wolff was out and Maria was in the bathroom washing a pile of sheets and clothes. Solveig and Eva had called a truce and were playing cards in the kitchen. Every now and again Maria popped in to see Inger who had been asleep most of the evening. Occasionally she would be in pain, but in between times she was able to rest.

Maria was up most of the night as Inger vomited twice more, although she barely brought anything up either time. Every now and again, she groaned and started crying with pain. Her fever returned and Maria gave her some aspirin ground between two teaspoons with a little sugar and a drop of water. She bathed Inger's face in water and several times pulled the duvet down to her waist. Inger would start shaking again and pull it back up. Eva was sleeping in Maria's bed and Maria was on the make-do mattress they had put on the floor as a temporary measure, but which had somehow become permanent.

Solveig had wanted to sleep with them, but with some brisk words from her mother, she gave up and settled down in her own bed. It had been ages since she had stopped playing with her dolls, but that night she had taken out the smallest one, her little rag doll, Topsy, and tucked her in beside her.

Eva stared at herself in front of her mother's mirror, combing her hair in different directions and posing to see how she could look more grown up. After this she started exploring her mother's makeup drawer and jewelry box. When she had finished putting mascara around her eyes and applied a thick layer of deep red lipstick, she pouted at herself in the mirror.

*   *   *   *

Officer Wolff came in later than usual and after a short visit to the bathroom took his briefcase into his room. He sat at the desk, took out a pile of files and after putting on a pair of reading glasses started to peruse them, marking occasional words with a red pen. He smiled as he read a letter from his wife and heard how well they were doing. He was proud to hear that his son had been awarded a prize for his athletics with the local Hitler Youth. But the person he thought about when he went to bed was not his wife; it was Maria. He paced the room at night, tormented with desire and guilt.

CHAPTER 11

Maria

Thursday

November 26th, 1942

Maria had been up all night and had smudged makeup under her eyes on a colorless face. Her hair was greasy and pulled back behind her ears. She had a blanket on over her silk dressing gown and was walking around in Eva's knitted socks. On hearing the door click, she checked the time and looked over to Inger. Inger had finally fallen asleep in the early hours of the morning.

Eva and Solveig came into the kitchen. Solveig had the same red sweater she had worn the previous night over some trousers and Eva had her mother's spare cardigan.

'It's freezing in here,' said Solveig. Eva walked over to the stove and felt it.

'Oh, it's not on.' She looked in the cupboard and went into the pantry. 'There's no bread left, no cheese. All I can find is this can of cod roe.'

'Isn't there any salami?'

'No,' replied Eva, standing on a chair to reach into the cupboard.

'I'm hungry. I want Mama.'

'She said to leave her alone with Inger.'

'I want to see her.' Solveig went to their bedroom with Eva in full pursuit.

Solveig stopped in the doorway. Inger had hollows in her cheeks and her lips were swollen and chapped. She was lying motionless on her back with her eyes shut and breathing fast. There was a faint smell like pear drops in the room. Maria was sitting on the mattress on the floor, staring at her.

'Shush, Solveig, Inger is sleeping.'

'Is she all right?' said Solveig in a loud whisper.

'I'm going to phone Dr. Tellefsen when surgery opens at eight. What time is it now?'

'Ten to eight,' said Eva. Maria got up and followed the girls into the kitchen.

'It's freezing in here. Eva, get the stove going.'

'All right, mother. I'll have to get some logs first because we've run out,' said Eva, picking up the log basket and heading out.

'Thank you, Eva,' said Maria. Then she turned to Solveig. 'Have you had breakfast yet?'

'There's nothing to eat,' said Solveig.

Maria went over to the cupboards. 'Here's some flour and'—rummaging at the back—'here's a bit of butter I've saved. I'll make some velvet porridge. Maybe Inger will have some.'

'Goody, can I stir in the milk?'

'Oh, no more milk powder. We'll have to make it with water and a pinch of salt.'

'Can we have extra sugar instead then, like last time?'

'I've only got a teaspoon left, but we have a bit of honey.' She took a saucepan and melted the butter in it. Then she stirred in some flour until it had cooked, then stirred in some water with a dash of salt. Instead of a creamy white, the porridge looked like soggy newspaper. Eva came in with the logs and busied herself with paper and matches.

At precisely eight o' clock Maria instructed Eva to finish making the 'velvet porridge' and went to the phone in the living room.

'Dr. Tellefsen, please.' She waited for a moment, then said, 'But my daughter is very ill; she can't wait until then.' Another pause. 'No, she's too ill to move.' And after another pause, she said, 'Let me speak to Dr.

Tellefsen now, or I'm going to come down to the surgery and drag him out myself!' After a few seconds, Dr. Tellefsen came onto the phone.

'There is no call for speaking like that to my receptionist. I have a waiting room full of people. Do you want me to leave them all here to traipse out to your daughter?'

'Yes, she's sick!'

'What's wrong then?' He listened as Maria explained the situation, then cutting her short, he continued, 'Mmm, yes, yes, but, look, there are so many kids with stomachache at the moment. It's the stuff these shopkeepers put in the bread, not to mention all that cabbage and swede. It's practically indigestible.'

'I'm not stupid, doctor. I know when a child is ill.'

'Yes, yes. Have you got any syrup of figs?'

'What? Didn't you hear me?'

'Give her two teaspoons of that or cascara if you have it, give her two aspirins and sips of water every ten minutes. I will come around on my way back from surgery. I'm sure it's nothing to worry about. Give your address to my receptionist.'

'But . . . but . . .' Maria gave the details to the receptionist who spoke to her coldly and put the phone down on her when Maria swore at her. Solveig and Eva had come into the living room and were staring at her.

'Isn't the doctor going to come?' said Solveig

'Yes, but he's got a surgery full of people he has to see first.'

'We should take her to hospital. It can't wait,' said Eva.

'And how am I going to get her there?'

'Father's police car?'

'He's not there. I've tried. He's never there when you need him.'

'Mr. Trelstad downstairs has a car.'

'Yes, but he doesn't have any fuel.'

'Mrs. Ostby's mother has a wheelchair. Maybe we could borrow that,' said Solveig.

'I'll wait until Dr. Tellefsen comes. She's too ill to move. Now, you two must get off to school.'

'I want to stay here with Inger,' said Solveig.

'It would be better for her if it is really quiet here, and I'd like to see the day you can keep quiet.'

'The day that hell freezes over,' said Eva.

'You're a fine one to talk,' said Maria. 'Maybe you two could be civil to each other for once. Eva, make sure Solveig gets to school safely. Hurry up now or you'll be late. Anna will be calling any minute.'

Solveig put her boots on and she and Eva went into Inger's room to say goodbye. Inger was awake now and smiled as they came in.

'Good morning.'

'Are you feeling better?' said Solveig.

'Yes, I think so. My tummy ache is a bit better. I am sure I'll be better tonight, and then we can finish that story.'

'Yes please,' said Solveig.

'Make sure you tell Dr. Tellefsen everything so he can find out what's wrong and give you the right medicine. You look very ill.' Eva bent down and gave her a hug.

'Ow!' said Inger, laughing. 'Ow! I mustn't laugh; it hurts too much.' She folded her arms over her stomach and smiled.

Solveig and Eva set off from the flat with their boots, scarves, and schoolbags. Eva was wearing Maria's blue wool hat with a large multicolored pompom on top.

'Hurry up, you're late!' shouted Maria after them. Eva stopped at the top of the stairs.

'Funny Anna hasn't been round. Maybe she called and we didn't hear her. She must have gone on ahead.' Eva rang on the door but there was no answer. As she knocked on the window panel, the door came open slightly and she noticed that the lock was broken.

'That's odd.' Eva pushed the door open and called out, 'Hello, Anna? Mrs. Bauman? It's Eva. Hello?' She went in and Solveig followed her. There were no lights on and the flat was cold. Eva called as she went to the kitchen, but the flat was silent.

'I don't think we should go in to their flat,' whispered Solveig as she was going back to the front door and ready to run away. Eva went into each room. Blankets were pulled off the beds, the settee was pulled from the wall, cupboard doors were open, a pile of papers from the writing desk had been scattered, and books which had been pulled out from the shelves were strewn on the floor. Eva came back to the hallway and checked the coat rack. Their coats and boots were gone.

'There's no one here.'

'Eva, I'm scared. Let's go and tell Mama.'

'No. Inger will want to know and she'll be really worried. Mother is in a terrible state already. No, we'll tell teacher at school. Now, be quiet so they don't hear us leaving.'

'Lots of people have gone to Sweden to get away from the war. Do you think that's where they've gone?'

'Just shush and come *on*.'

★   ★   ★   ★

Maria had called police HQ so many times that morning that the receptionist just put the receiver straight down when she heard her voice. Threatening to have her arrested for wasting police time had not worked. Maria had insisted that they could find Johannes and when they said he had not come into the office, she swore at them.

At about midday Dr. Tellefsen arrived. He was a tall man in his forties and looked exhausted. He carried a doctor's bag in one hand and overcoat over his other arm. His overcoat and hat were soaking wet despite the fact that he had brushed off as much snow as he could.

'It's terrible out there,' he said, stamping his feet and taking off his coat. 'Can I put this somewhere to dry while we see our young patient?' Maria took a clothes rack out of the cupboard and sorted his coat and hat out by the stove, then showed him into the bedroom.

'Inger, so you have a bit of a bad tummy then?'

'Hello, Dr. Tellefsen,' she said, smiling. 'It's been really sore all night, but I think it is a bit better now.'

'She's been sick three times in the night and her fever has come back, doctor. She is in a lot of pain.'

'Well, well, let's have a look. Can you sit up?' He helped her up as she winced. Maria placed the pillow behind her. He sat by the bed and took Inger's pulse. He took a torch out of his bag and looked in her throat. He took an auroscope and looked in both ears. 'Let's have a look at your tummy then.'

Inger moved down the bed, wincing with pain again and lifted her pajama top up. He pressed gently on one side of her abdomen and then the other, and then lower down on each side. Each time he pressed, Inger flinched with pain. 'Mmm, quite tender all over,' he said to himself.

'I'm no doctor, but it doesn't look "quite tender" to me. It looks as if she is in agony,' said Maria.

'Was it "agony"?' he said to Inger.

'It did hurt really badly.'

'Where in the tummy did it hurt the most?'

'Everywhere. It hurts all over, doctor, and it hurts every time I move.'

'Well, there are a lot of bad tummy aches going around at the moment. Take some of this medicine and it should be better in a couple of days.' He gave Maria a small bottle of syrup of figs from his bag and some aspirin.

'That's not just "tummy ache," doctor. She's got a really bad fever and she hasn't kept any fluids down all night.'

'Inger, I'm sure you'll be better tomorrow. Mother's, eh? Always making such a big fuss!' He winked at Inger who smiled back. Maria followed him into the hall.

'Doctor, she needs to go to hospital.'

'No, no, my dear. She's got a fever, but that will clear up in a couple of days. I've seen a lot of cases like this recently. I think it's related to malnutrition and going-off food.'

'I can assure you that my girls are fed properly and are not malnourished. There's no rotten food in *this* house. What about the pain, surely that's not right?'

'She has pain "everywhere." I think that is the "pain" of a young lady who wants to stay at home from school.'

'But she loves school. She wanted to go today because they are learning about China. She loves hearing about faraway countries. She wants to travel the world when she grows up. No, doctor, I know my daughter. If she says she has pain, she has pain.'

'And I know what a stomach bug looks like, Mrs. Halversen. Now, if you will excuse me, I have some more people to see, people with real illnesses, not schoolgirls with over-anxious mothers.'

'You better be right, doctor.'

'Or?' he said as Maria handed him his coat and hat. He put them on and picked up bag. 'Good day, Mrs. Halversen.'

Maria folded her arms and glared at him as he left.

CHAPTER 12

Later on Thursday

November 26th

After school was over Solveig and Eva set off home together. They were in a subdued mood and barely spoke. As they passed the palace gate, they kept their heads down, having no desire to interact with the soldiers. On cue, the soldiers ignored them. They were busy stamping their feet and clapping their hands together in a vain attempt to keep warm. More snow had settled overnight and frozen, so it was slippery and crunchy underfoot.

As the girls came around the corner, they saw a group of about ten women and children gathered on the pavement. They had suitcases and some carried blankets over their arms. There were four Norwegian policemen and one officer wearing the black uniform of the Gestapo. They were checking the members of the group into a van one by one as the Gestapo officer checked the list. On the other side of the road, a group of spectators looked on. Only the occasional crying of a child, mothers' pleas, and commands of officers were heard against the unnatural silence of the street.

Solveig held onto Eva's hand more tightly.

'Why are all those people being taken into the van?'

'Quisling is making it illegal for Jewish people to stay in Norway. They are being arrested.'

'Have they done something wrong?'

'No, they're just ordinary people.'

'Where are they going to?'

'Teacher said that some of them are being sent to labor camps. She thinks some of them have been sent to Germany.'

'Why do they have to do labor?'

'Teacher says that they treat them like slaves and make them build roads or make weapons.'

'Will they have to stay there until the war is over then?'

'I don't think the war is ever going to end,' said Eva wearily.

'But everyone keeps talking about what they are going to do when the war ends,' said Solveig, looking anxious.

'The Germans say they are going to make the world a huge Nazi state.'

'What's a Nazi state?'

'Some bloody awful place where a lot of fat, ugly Nazis parade the streets all day and kill anyone they don't like, so a few people they call "Aryans" can get fat feeding off the rest of the world.'

'That's horrible. That's what you said the soldier called you.'

'To hell with their "Aryan" shit. I'm a human being and a citizen of the world.'

'That's what I want to be.'

'Of course you are. Everyone is.'

'Mrs. Ostby says that the Germans arrested Mr. Reistad and Mr. Groven because they refused to say that Jewish people were bad.'

'Hundreds of teachers were arrested, but they had to let them all go again because Quisling couldn't find anyone to teach the children. But they will never teach us how to be Nazis. They would die first and so would I.'

'I don't want to be made into a Nazi and I don't want to die. I'm scared.'

'Come on, let's get a move on,' said Eva, increasing her pace while Solveig ran behind her to keep up.

* * * *

When they got back to the flat, they rushed in to check on Inger. It was early afternoon by now and usually supper would be cooking, but the kitchen was empty and the stove was unlit again. Maria was sitting on the mattress opposite Inger, who was awake but staring into space, her breathing now rapid and shallow. Maria went over to her to give her a few more sips of water, but it trickled down her chin. Inger's lips were cracked and her eyes sunken. She looked up at the girls and waved her hand.

Solveig ran in to kiss her and tell her all about her day but stopped and stared at her. Her smile and eagerness gave way to fear. 'Inger, are you all right?' Inger opened her eyes and smiled.

'Solveig, you're back already.' Her voice was almost inaudible. She leant her head on the pillow and closed her eyes.

'Mother, she should go to hospital at once,' said Eva sharply.

'Dr. Tellefsen says she's just got a stomach bug. He refused to send her to hospital.'

'That old bastard. He doesn't know what he's talking about. Ring him.'

'Yes, I keep trying and they keep saying he'll be back shortly. Stay with her and try to get her to take some sips of water.'

Maria rang the surgery yet again.

'Dr. Tellefsen won't be back today.'

'I need an ambulance, it's an emergency.'

'There are no ambulances at the moment. There's no petrol.'

'No petrol! Are you crazy?'

'It's not my fault, so don't shout. We are trying to do our best here. The nurse was crying yesterday because it's so bad and Dr. Tellefsen is really upset about it all.'

'Can the nurse come?'

'No, she has ten more people to see here, and then has to see some more people on the way home.'

'So, there's no emergency service.'

'We're hoping to get some fuel tomorrow.'

'Tomorrow is no good!'

'I know you are upset, but there's no need to shout,' said the receptionist.

Maria slammed the receiver down. Picking up the phone again, she asked the operator to put her through to Christiania Taxi, but there was no reply. After trying a few more taxi firms she finally managed to speak to someone.

'But my daughter's ill. It's an emergency,' she shouted. They had explained to her that they were waiting for a fuel delivery and had used their last supplies to help the ambulance service out.

She picked up the phone and asked the operator for police HQ.

'Inspector Halversen, please.' There was a pause. 'When will he be back?' Another pause. 'Tell him he has to come home right away. His daughter is ill and needs to go to hospital. Thank you.'

She went back into the bedroom. Inger was looking out of the window, smiling brightly. Her cheeks were two bright red spots and her eyes were deeply hollowed.

'Look Mama, Grandma is coming up the stairs. She's holding little baby Olav, he's so sweet.' She was laughing softly.

'Mama, is the ambulance on its way?' said Eva. Maria shook her head. Solveig went over to Inger and held her hand.

'Don't look so scared, Solveig, everything is going to be all right. Tomorrow I will finish the story. I am starting to feel better already,' said Inger faintly. She stared brightly out of the window and nodded and waved. Solveig looked out of the window but all she could see were the clouds, heavy and dull in the fading light.

Maria paced up and down the kitchen and kept rushing into the living room to stare at the phone, which remained silent. Eva was begging her to get some help from the neighbors downstairs, from Mr. Pettersen from the corner shop, down the street from Mr. Bronstad, and Maria was saying that she did not know anyone who had a car.

'You do, mother.' Eva stared hard at her.

'What?'

Eva nodded toward Herr Wolff's door. Maria took a deep breath and knocked on his door. There was no answer and when she tried his door it was locked. She headed back to the phone.

'German headquarters please, I need to speak to Officer Wolff.' The operator checked a few numbers then put her through. A woman's voice answered and Maria repeated her request.

'He's in a meeting, Mrs. Halversen. I'm sorry.'

'Tell him there's an emergency at his lodgings and I have to speak to him right away.'

'Very well, hold on.' Maria heard the click of high heels echoing over a hard floor. Very soon heavier footsteps accompanied them.

'Mrs. Halversen?' said Officer Wolff. Maria was crying and shouting by now, but managed to explain.

'I shall come round right away.' He instructed his secretary who busied herself with a number of phone calls and as he was putting on his jacket, he took the phone back from her. He spoke briskly ending with 'That's an order, Dr. Froberg.'

A few minutes later, Officer Wolff came up the stairs to Maria's flat, accompanied by two men in German uniforms carrying a stretcher. Maria let him in and motioned them in.

'Are they medically qualified?'

'No, but I have arranged for her to see Dr. Froberg on arrival at the hospital. He has been instructed to get a bed ready for her.' Maria showed them in and went to Inger's bed.

'Inger, these men have come to take you to hospital.'

'But I'm all right, Mama. I just want to sleep.'

'Inger, the doctor will make sure you get the best medicine. You have a high fever.'

'Okay, Mama.' She started to get up but then fell back again. 'I'm so tired. Please let me sleep, then I can go in the morning.'

'Inger, please, darling. These men will carry you downstairs. You *have* to go to hospital.' She took a blanket and wrapped it around her, and stepped back as the soldiers laid her on the stretcher. Maria then put the duvet over her and woolen socks on her feet.

'Ah, my special blue and red pair,' said Inger, smiling. Solveig ran to her room and came back with her lilac shawl.

'Take this to keep warm too.'

'Eva, look after Solveig while I go with Inger.'

'But I want to come too,' said Solveig.

'No.'

Solveig put her lilac shawl over Inger's duvet and kissed her on the cheek. Inger smiled at her and waved.

'See you soon,' said Inger, smiling for a moment before she closed her eyes.

*   *   *   *

After they left, Eva and Solveig went into the freezing kitchen and searched the cupboards for something to eat. There was some velvet porridge left over from the morning and a tin of peaches which Maria had been saving for a special occasion.

'I want to be with Inger and Mama,' said Solveig.

'So do I. But we can't, so we just have to manage. Come on, let's go and get some logs and make the stove warm. Then we can eat the peaches.'

'Mama will be cross.'

'No, she said I have to make sure you eat something. Come on, let's get this stove sorted out.' They went to the yard, got a basket of logs and some coal and dragged it up the three flights of stairs. Eva got the fire lit while Solveig stirred the velvet porridge until it was hot and opened the tin of peaches. When the stove was lit and Eva had served the porridge with the peaches, neither of them ate more than a couple of mouthfuls. Solveig went to her room and read her storybook out loud to her dolls while Eva paced up and down in the living room. Eventually they went to bed but neither slept.

*   *   *   *

At about three in the morning, their father came into the flat. He told them to get dressed quickly and come to the hospital with him.

'Can we see Inger and Mama?' said Solveig. He nodded.

'Dad, what's wrong?' said Eva.

'Come on. It's cold outside, so dress up warm.' They walked briskly downstairs and into his police car.

The hospital was only a couple of blocks away. Johannes walked so quickly down the corridors that Eva and Solveig had to run to keep up with him. Very soon they got to the ward where Inger was. They saw Maria standing inside a side ward. One of the nurses had her arm around her and the other was bending down straightening the sheets. As soon as she saw Johannes, she went out.

She just stood and stared at them.

'No!' screamed Eva before running into the side room. Solveig followed. There were clean sheets on the bed covering every part of Inger except her face. The top sheet was folded back. Inger was lying absolutely still with her face turned straight up and her eyes closed. The bright pink spots on her cheeks had vanished, and her face was completely white apart from the hollows of her cheeks and around her eyes. Solveig took her hand and shook it.

'Wake up, Inger,' she said urgently. 'Wake up.' She shook her hand again and put it to her cheek. It was cold. She stood on tiptoe and kissed her cheek. 'Inger, I missed you. I want to look after you and make sure you are better.' She pulled Inger's hand again, but her arm just drooped down.

Solveig's father came in and gently straightened Inger's arm.

'Come on, Solveig,' he said as he put his arm around her, 'we need to go back out.' Solveig stared at Inger; she looked so beautiful. The red lights of her hair contrasted with the whiteness of her face, interrupted only by a dusting of freckles across her nose.

Maria sat on the bench outside sobbing. Johannes sat Solveig down at the other end.

'Solveig, Inger has gone to heaven. She will be able to sing and laugh all day now.'

'But she said she was getting better,' said Solveig, tears rolling down her cheeks.

'There's no such place as heaven,' said Eva. 'Inger is dead, just dead. Can't anyone tell the truth around here?' She sat on the bench next to them and sobbed.

Maria went back into the room where the nurse had put the sheet over Inger's face and pulled it back. 'Give me some time with my daughter. Please leave.'

The nurse left her and went to the family group. She sat down beside them and waited. Maria sat by Inger's bed, holding her hand for a long time. She could not bear to let go.

*   *   *   *

After Maria came out of the side ward, the girls and Johannes went in to kiss Inger good night and sweet dreams. Solveig had to be dragged out.

'I don't want to leave her on her own. She needs more blankets. She's so cold.' Johannes picked her up as if she were a baby and carried her out, followed by Maria and Eva, their heads bowed and arms folded.

Officer Wolff came up the corridor and stopped in front of Johannes and his daughters. He bowed briefly and said, '*Es tut mir leid, Unschild . . .* I mean, I am very sorry for your loss,' then departed.

Johannes took Maria and the girls home in his police car. When they got back, Maria sent the girls to their bedrooms and pulled the blackout curtains together, checking if there were any cracks. Then she paused, turned off the lights, opened the curtains, and stared out of the window.

Johannes went over to her and tried to hug her, but she slapped him on the face and punched him over and over again until he clasped her so tight she had to stop. She then collapsed into him and he held her and rocked her until her crying subsided to voiceless sobs and her sobs subsided to silent heaves.

Finally, he took her to bed and both lay there fully clothed, holding on to each other until they were so cold they had to go under the duvet. Maria still heaved and sobbed between long silences and neither of them slept.

Eva sat on her mattress, pulling out the hair on the nape of her neck, several hairs at a time. The pain eased the tightness in her throat, and made her oblivious to everything else even when she was shivering with cold.

Solveig searched her room for her lilac shawl before she remembered where it had gone. She took all her dolls out and wrapped them up in an old sweater. She curled up with them into a tight ball, pulled the duvet over all their heads, and sucked her thumb.

The dawn was slow in coming and when it did come, it brought yet more snow and yet more cold.

*　　*　　*　　*

Officer Wolff spent the night in his office holding on to a photo of his wife and children smoking one cigarette after another. He then searched through some files his secretary had left on his desk at his request, and perused the one on Dr. Tellefsen. He wrote an entry and picked up the phone.

Later that morning a black car followed Dr. Tellefsen as he walked to work. Officer Wolff's two young bodyguards drove past, parked ahead of him, and waited for him on the pavement. Shortly after that a highly discontented Dr. Froberg arrived at the overflowing clinic. Dr. Tellefsen had been beaten up and arrested for crimes against the Third Reich.

CHAPTER 13

Friday

November 27th

The next morning Johannes tried to comfort Maria but was told to get back to his girlfriend or anything else that was more important to him than she and the girls. Johannes heaved on his coat and slipped out of the house without waking them.

Maria dragged herself out of bed and, without bothering to put on her dressing gown, went into Eva and Inger's bedroom. She sat on Inger's bed and smoothed down the sheets. She pulled a couple of stray hairs off the pillow and wound them into a curl. She picked up a photo of Inger and Eva leaning out of a train, laughing and waving goodbye as they set off to summer camp. She caressed Inger's face in the photo and kissed it.

When Maria returned to her room, she put the photo in her jewelry box and, finding a locket given to her by her grandmother, placed the curl of red hair in it. She put the locket around her neck, and that was where the locket stayed for many years to come.

*   *   *   *

After two days, they had the funeral. Maria's mother told them they must all come to live with them in Bronnoysund. Maria said no, but that Eva and Solveig could go. Eva said no, and Solveig begged to stay with Mama. Johannes came late to the funeral and, after enduring a stream of abuse from his mother-in-law, remained silent throughout the ceremony. Inger's teachers and friends came and a long queue filed past the open coffin to pay their last respects. Solveig looked in, screamed over and over again, and had to be taken home by Aunt Else, who had come to stay as soon as she was told.

The priest paid a tribute to a beautiful and lovely girl, a daughter, a sister, a niece, a granddaughter, a pupil, a friend, a young woman who made everyone laugh and wanted to travel the world if she did not lose her ticket, lose her passport, lose her socks. Everybody had loved Inger. He talked on, while everyone cried or choked back their tears. Everyone, that is, except Maria, who sat staring into space, like a statue carved from a block of ice.

When they came back to the flat, Else served dried biscuits and assorted snacks that people had salvaged from their own meager supplies. Johannes kissed the girls goodbye and spoke to Maria, who had just nodded absently as he left. Else told them that she had to go back up to Bronnoysund to look after their mother, whose heart was badly affected by the strain of the funeral and all the traveling.

Herr Wolff paid his respects and informed Maria that a new flat had become vacant and that he would be moving the next day. He gave his thanks and went to shake hands, but Maria just nodded and turned her back on him.

Eventually, everyone left and Maria went into her room and locked the door. Solveig and Eva did not even try to knock. When Solveig came to Eva's room, dragging her duvet and holding her smallest doll, Eva told her to go away. Solveig walked slowly back to her room, allowing plenty of time for someone to stop her, but nobody did. This was the first of many evenings of silence, with each of them wrapped in their own grief, and each one completely isolated from the other.

* * * *

After a while Maria put her makeup and high heels on again and was angrier and brisker than ever. She made the girls get up and get dressed properly again. She instructed Eva to go and queue for some fish and bread. She marched a reluctant Solveig to school. The teacher welcomed her back, but Solveig just stared out of the window, oblivious to her surroundings. Eva wanted her hair to be permed and dyed red like Inger's, but Maria refused. Where would she get the money from and why would Eva want to spoil her beautiful blond waves?

Over the next few months, Maria started cooking again and would swap suggestions with other housewives as they waited in the queues. They talked about their favorite recipes and conjured up the feasts that they would eat when the war was over: whipped cream, potatoes fried in butter, roast pork, steak, and real pineapple—not slices of turnip dyed yellow and soaked in pineapple essence. They talked about people who had disappeared, about rumors spread from underground newspapers, about the graffiti of the resistance, and the symbols of King Haakon. They talked about what they would do when the war was over, about the clothes they would wear, the shoes they would strap on, the real nylons they would wear—not streaky tea-stained legs, the parties they would go to, the furniture they would buy, the curtains, all the modern conveniences they would have. Life in the future became more and more glorious and exciting.

The women laughed and cracked jokes as they queued in the rain, the snow, the damp, and sometimes in the sun. Then they would raise their faces in total adoration in order to absorb every single ray. All this—the sunshine, the wonderful future, the jokes—were side by side with the swastikas, the military parades, and the Gestapo raids in the middle of the night.

Eva found her own way through her grief. At first it was unbearable and she wished that she had been the one to die so that she would not have to suffer anymore. Her guilt and sorrow soon turned to anger. She could not endure it, *would* not endure it. Oh no, Eva was going to have some fun. What did she have to lose?

She started to go out every night. She made new friends and they would meet in each other's houses and talk about boys, boys, and boys. They had crushes on their teachers, on older brothers, on boys they met when they went skiing, ice-skating, and boys who cycled past them and stopped to talk. They sewed borders on old jackets, took coats in at the waist, and wore them with tight belts to show off their figures. They heated up curling tongs on kitchen stoves and made fashionable waves in their hair. They plastered on their mothers' makeup and learned how to make carbon out of matchsticks or burnt cork and apply it as eyeliner. They used old paint brushes to salvage remnants of lipstick, and added charcoal to make their lips the darkest red, like the smoldering Gloria Swanson. They listened to records and secretly learned about jazz, which the Nazis had outlawed, but which continued to thrive if you went to the right places with the right boys. They went to the cinema and sat though the propaganda until the Hollywood films came on. They sighed at Clark Gable and swooned over Errol Flynn.

Solveig made a new friend, Ragnhild, as Anna had moved away a while ago. In fact, Solveig recalled, it was the day before Inger had died, when they had found the flat empty. Solveig had not stopped to wonder about this, determined to believe that they had escaped to Sweden, like so many other people had. She had not stopped hoping for a letter from Anna but searched the mail less often as time went on.

Solveig still struggled with her math but excelled at Norwegian. She and Ragnhild used to tell each other stories and go for long walks together. They were always talking and always getting told off at school. Solveig still sneaked one of her dolls from its hiding place in her cupboard when she went to bed but was careful not to get caught. Eva had lost interest even in teasing her, and her mother had taken to locking herself in the living room to smoke, sew, and listen to records.

Solveig discovered the library and, having read all the children's books, was working her way through shelf after shelf of adult books. She read everything: classic novels, romance, crime thrillers, travel books, and even psychology books. The librarian thought she was getting them for her mother and Solveig thought it was easiest to go along with this. In the evenings, she would curl up under her duvet and read and read. The books opened the door to the whole world as she searched to make sense of people, of good and evil, to make sense of life, of the world, of everything.

She was only ten.

CHAPTER 14

Five Months Later

April 1943

Eva and her friend Kari became inseparable partners in the classroom, both being cynical about and bored by their lessons. They sat at the back of the class, whispering to each other as usual.

The teacher told the class to open their books at the page they got to the day before and started to write on the board.

'I want to see him again,' said Kari.

'Who?' said Eva.

'You know, *him.*'

'That soldier?'

'Yes, I think he likes me.'

'He's not here on holiday, you know.'

'I know, there's a war on, he's the enemy, blah, blah, blah, but he's really nice.'

'For God's sake, don't tell me you've got a crush on him.'

'I think I'm in love.'

'Eva, Kari, shush. Any more from you and I shall give you extra work to do. Now Eva, tell me, what is the capital of America?' said the teacher, pulling herself up to her full height, putting her hands on her hips, and glaring at the two girls.

'New York,' said Eva.

'Anyone else?'

'Washington,' came several voices. Eva shrugged.

'Well, it's the biggest place there.'

'Eva, if you want to get your matriculation, you better start paying some attention. Okay, class, can anyone tell me what the capital of Russia is?'

Kari wrote in pencil in the margin of her notebook. 'Come for tea after school?'

Eva peered at the message and wrote in her book, 'I'll have to take Solveig home first.'

'Eva, Kari, I don't want to know what you are writing, but you are both to come and see me after class, and if I see you writing any more notes, I shall read them to the whole class. This is not infant school.'

Eva and her friend went back to their books, suppressing their laughter, and started copying down what their teacher had written on the blackboard. After a moment, Eva frowned, pushed her books away, leaned back in her chair, and stared out of the window. Who cared what the capital of America was? Washington, New York, what did it matter? The Nazis had taken over and the war was going to go on forever.

'Eva, if you are not going to even try to pretend to pay attention in class, you better leave the classroom, *right now!*' shouted her teacher.

Eva got up and picked up her bag, leaving her books on the table.

'I'm going, okay?'

'You better come back after the lesson and apologize to me. I am going to write a letter to your mother.'

'You can write whatever you like. I'm never coming back to this lousy classroom and your boring teaching ever again. I quit.'

'I shall have to report this to the headmaster.'

'What, the acting headmaster? That old man? He wouldn't even know who I am.'

'Eva, stop right now. How dare you talk to me like that!'

'Goodbye, Miss Ovstedal, Enjoy the rest of your life.' Eva marched out of the classroom and slammed the door. She walked home, oblivious to the wolf whistles of the German soldiers and to the graffiti on the garden walls which had sprung up overnight. King Haakon forever. We will win.

* * * *

Eva went to Kari's house later that afternoon. It was one of the huge houses in a quiet street off Kirkeveien near Frogner Park. Like most houses in the street, it was built from wood and painted white.

Eva wanted to go to a restaurant in the center of town, as one of her other friends had told her that a party was being held by German soldiers to celebrate one of their officer's birthdays.

'But they're Nazis,' said Kari.

'So what?' replied Eva.

'How can you say that? You of all people—you hate them.'

'I still hate them.'

'So how can you bear to spend time with them?'

'I'm just using them same as they use us. They buy us drinks and we can go out and have a good meal. And I love dancing. If we have to live in a Nazi state, we might as well have a good time,' said Eva.

'I don't know,' said Kari.

'Oh, come on. I just want to go and have some fun,' said Eva.

'I suppose it can't do any harm. We don't have to stay if we don't like it. Some of the soldiers just look like boys, and some of them are really good-looking. They can't all be bad, can they?' said Kari.

'Don't bet on it,' said Eva, 'even if they started off okay, they've all been stuffed full with Hitler's Third Reich rubbish. I mean, you only have to go to the cinema to see it all, how they go on and on about their "Glorious Fatherland," and all their posters and notices everywhere. You can't get away from it. I'm surprised we haven't *all* been brainwashed.'

'I think a lot of people have been. There are spies everywhere. Anyway, it can't go on forever.'

'Oh yes, and who told you that? The Christmas elf?'

'There's no need to be so sarcastic. The resistance is spreading leaflets and they say they are starting to make some ground. King Haakon says that the Nazis will never win. Churchill says they will never win. There's no way Hitler can win over the whole world,' said Kari.

'You can believe that if you want to,' said Eva, looking at her friend with pity.

'Anyway, do you really think being with a German soldier will make you feel better?' said Kari.

'I just want to have some fun. I never said I wanted to *be* with any of them.'

⋆ ⋆ ⋆ ⋆

Theatercafeen was in the Hotel Continental on Stortingsgata, on the other side of Karl Johannes Gate. The two girls were ushered in by a guard by the door, their only qualification for getting in being their female gender and glamorous appearance. There was a live band with several violinists, trumpeters, a double bass, and a drummer, all led by a conductor. A woman in a tight sequined dress showing a deep cleavage droned mournfully as she pouted her lips and poured soul into the microphone. The air was thick with smoke and humming with excitement.

The place was crowded with a mixture of young German soldiers, a few officers and some civilians, mainly young women. Some sparkled with jewelry, skimpy silk dresses, and furs as they linked arms with senior officers, and some were dressed more plainly with square-shouldered blouses and tight skirts, but they all had the same glow. There were tables where food and wine were served and a crowd of men was at the bar.

Eva and Kari had just walked in when two young soldiers came up and indicated for them to sit down. They got them some drinks and spent the next couple of hours chatting and filling the glasses of the girls, who become more relaxed, spoke more, and laughed more. The soldiers ordered some food, which Eva ate slowly, pretending she was not hungry, and dessert to which the girls had reluctantly agreed and then demolished. The soldiers took them to the dance floor, swirling them around and drawing them in close when the music became slow.

Kari went for a walk with one of them and Eva was left dancing with the other. At the end of the dance, instead of taking her to sit down, he took her to the side of the dance floor against the wall, ran his hand down her back, and nuzzled his face into her neck. Eva, who had been laughing, became serious and pushed him away. He pushed back into her and had her trapped against the wall. He pressed his whole body against hers and put one hand over her breast. She tried to push him away again, but he pushed even harder into her. He put his hand up her blouse at the back and fiddled with her bra. He slid his other hand under her bra at the front, clasping over her breast. He licked her neck, nuzzled in her ear, brought his lips around to hers, and put his tongue into her mouth. His saliva trickled down her cheek.

Eva was writhing, hitting him, and retching with disgust as his hand crept down from her breast toward the waistband of her slacks. His hand crept down to the top of her pants and edged down further. She wrenched her mouth away and screamed, but he planted his mouth over hers again and pressed his body into hers. He gripped both her wrists, holding them up against the wall. His breathing got louder and faster and she squirmed as she felt him pressing himself into her even harder.

Suddenly two men seized him, pulled him away, and lifted him for a moment before throwing him on the ground. An officer came up behind them.

'Leave that lady alone!' he said in German.

'She's just a Norwegian tart,' said the soldier, pulling himself up. The officer punched him in the face. When he fell to the floor, two men who had initially intervened heaved him up. One of them punched him in the stomach while the other forced him up and twisted his hand behind his back. The soldier had buckled, but they held him up and on the officer's instructions marched him out of the club.

Eva hurriedly straightened her blouse, wiped her face with the back of her hand, and looked up. 'Officer Wolff!'

Officer Wolff clicked his heels.

'Good evening, Miss Halversen,' he said in his perfect Norwegian. 'I am sorry this soldier was bothering you. If you will permit me to say, this club is not a suitable place for a young lady like you. Let me escort you home.' He put out his arm formally. Eva stepped forward and placed her arm in his equally, formally.

'Thank you, Officer Wolff. What about my friend?'

'Your friend?'

'She went for a walk with the other soldier.'

'Please wait here.' The officer strode out toward the door and found his bodyguards outside, locking arms with the offending soldier, whose lower lip was swollen and deeply cracked. His left cheek was purple and almost hid his eye, which was closed and puffy.

'What is your name?' said Officer Wolff

'Sergeant Mueller, sir,' he said, drawing himself up to his full height and wincing with pain as he did so.

'I will not report you this time, but if I find you treating any woman like that again, I shall have you arrested.'

'Yes, sir, it won't happen again, sir,' he said, slurring his words as the crack on his lip opened and some blood trickled out. He dragged himself along the pavement, clutching his stomach.

Eva's friend and the soldier were nearby. They had been smoking and laughing together but now were just standing, staring. Officer Wolff went up to them.

'Are you Miss Halversen's friend?'

'Yes. Why?'

'I am taking her home. She wanted to know where you were.'

'Well, here I am.'

'Do you want to come back with her?'

'No, I am busy.'

'Sergeant, what is your name?' he said in German. The soldier told him. 'We are here to serve Germany. We are to behave like soldiers and honor our Fatherland. If you do not look after this young lady and make sure she gets home safely, I will hear about it. You do not want to disobey my orders.' He saluted and the soldier stood up and saluted him fully. After Officer Wolff and his two accompanying soldiers turned back, the sergeant dropped his cigarette and stubbed it out with his shoe.

'Who's that?'

'That's my, er, what do you say, er, boss?' he said in English.

'Yes, big boss man,' she said and laughed again as she mimicked Officer Wolff's stern expression and rigid stature. But the soldier did not laugh. He looked up the street at his friend, who was still struggling to walk.

'Come, I take you home,' he said, 'You must show way.'

*   *   *   *

Officer Wolff returned to the club. Eva was now sitting at the table on her own, ignoring several men who were trying to catch her eye. She had refused two offers of drinks and refused a dance. She was frowning and looking at the door, tapping her fingers on the table. When Officer Wolff reappeared, she continued to frown.

'Miss Halversen, your friend says she is all right. I have made sure that she will be safely escorted home. Now, if you please . . .' he gestured to the door. Eva nodded and followed him out.

A black car drew up just as they came out of the restaurant. Officer Wolff opened the door for her and let himself in the other side. His two soldiers were in the front. A few minutes later, they arrived at Kristian IV Gate and he got out and opened the door for her.

'I will not expect to see you at Theatercafeen again. It is not safe for a young lady. If you were my daughter—'

'But I am *not* you daughter and I am old enough to decide where I go for myself, thank you.'

Officer Wolff smiled slightly and nodded. 'You are your mother's daughter, I see.'

'I am just myself. But I have to thank you for helping me tonight. Thank you. *Vielen Dank,*' said Eva staring at her feet. She then drew herself up to her full height and, staring straight at him, nodded.

'Good night.' He bowed his head in return and waited while she walked into the apartment block. He stood outside a little longer and looked up. He wondered what Maria was doing at the moment and if she was at home.

Eva took a hanky and powder compact out of her handbag and wiped off her lipstick and black smudges from under her eyes as she walked slowly upstairs. It was midnight. She let herself in and tiptoed to her room.

'Eva, where have you been?' shouted her mother from the sitting room. She had just taken off her high heels and poured herself a drink.

'I told you I was going to see Kari tonight. I've been at her house with some friends.'

'Oh yes, in that outfit? And don't think I can't tell that you've wiped off a whole load of lipstick—and I can smell cigarettes.

'Okay, we went out.'

'Where?'

'Does it matter? What difference does it make?'

'*Where?*'

'Just out.'

'I can stay up all night until you tell me,' said Maria as she walked up to the door of Eva's bedroom and glared at her.

Eva folded her arms and looked at the ceiling. 'I'm sixteen now, old enough to have the keys and old enough to go where I want.'

'Well, I've got the keys to the kitchen cupboard and you can be sure that you will have absolutely nothing to eat until you have told me, even if I have to follow you out of this house and take the food out of your mouth with my own bare hands.'

Eva stared ahead and braced her shoulders, folding her arms even tighter around her. They both stood there in complete silence for several minutes. Eva tried to push past her to get into her room, but Maria leaned against it and would not budge. Eventually, Eva went red in the face and tears came into her eyes.

'I went to Theatercafeen with Kari. Happy now?'

Maria slapped her across the face and shouted, '*Theatercafeen?* Where all the soldiers and their floozies go? That's just great! I've got one daughter dead and now one a Nazi whore. I'd rather see you dead. I wish it was *you* who had died so I wouldn't have lived to see this day.'

'What do you care? You have no idea what I do. You're too busy having a good time with your new fancy pants boyfriend. I wish I *was* dead.

I'd rather be dead than live here with you. Go to hell!' She ran into her bedroom and slammed the door.

Maria screamed after her, 'You apologize or leave this house and never come back.'

'Make me!'

Maria was about to force the door open when she caved in and went slack. 'I won't forget this,' she said, but her voice was tired and defeated.

CHAPTER 15

April 1943

A Few Days Later

E va had not apologized to her teacher or returned to school despite Maria's protests and insistence. She knew she had to get a job as she believed Maria when she told her that if she did not start paying her rent within a month, she could no longer live there. Eva found a job as a factory worker and was home after an early shift. Maria was out and Solveig had not come back from school. She was often at Ragnild's house these days and sometimes had supper there.

She paced around the house, sat on her bed, and opened a book. She flipped the pages over, moved her pillow up, and then threw the book down. She looked in the kitchen for a snack, but there was nothing apart from some potatoes and gray wartime flour. There was no bread, no butter, and what remained of the last jar of jam was so tart it made her eyes water. That would be where her mother was, queuing with all the other women, waiting in line in the hope of fresh bread and the occasional black-market egg.

Eva changed into some trousers, a loose blouse, and tied a sweater around her waist. She headed out for the town hall and docks some ten minutes' walk across Johannes Gate, leading up to Palace Park and past the notorious Theatercafeen.

Oslo Fjord was full of German and Norwegian naval ships, which had all but replaced the fishing boats. She walked to one of the few remaining fishermen and asked how much the prawns cost. When he replied, she just laughed and walked on. The fisherman returned to his chores and threw some shells into the water. A flock of seagulls squawked and fought each other, rising in a swirling white cloud above the black water. Eva breathed in the smell of fish and boat oil as she braced herself against the cool breeze. She walked along the docks and back through town. She crossed the road several times to avoid any confrontations with soldiers and stopped at a few shop windows to survey the shabby products of recycled clothes and the dull packaging of scarce goods.

She walked back through town into Frogner Park. She stopped to sit by a statue of a young woman holding her plaits in her hands and dancing with one leg raised and bent at the knee. There was avenue after avenue with statues of people of all ages in an endless variety of poses. They were all rudely healthy, sturdy, buxom, and unashamedly naked, fashioned in smooth white granite or bronze.

By now it was starting to get dark, but she carried on walking through the trees, up and down the steps, and in and out of the recesses. She stopped and looked down to the lake by a statue of a crying baby. She was sure that if it were alive, its mother would hear it from five miles away. When she had walked around the park twice, she went out the other end and walked through the Vestre Gravlund. She stopped at a plain stone grave.

Inger Magnhild Halversen

January 2nd 1926 – November 27th 1942

Beloved by God

Eva bent down and took some weeds out of the shrubs and miniature rosebush growing in front of it. She caressed the branches and patted down the soil around the remaining plants. When it was clear, she sat in front of the grave and wept. Ages later, she had no idea how long it had been, she looked up. It was getting dark. She set off for home back through the park.

The main entrance of Frogner Park was massive. It had white marble columns and black wrought-iron gates, patterned with an abstract geometrical flower-like design, topped by imposing square lights. Eva winced as she saw swastikas hung from the tops of the gates, a travesty against one of Oslo's most cherished monuments. As she approached the gates, she saw a group of soldiers smoking by the pedestrian side entrance. She looked around to see how she could avoid them, but she knew that this was the only way out and besides, they had already spotted her.

'Hey,' yelled one of the guards in German, 'what's a beautiful girl like you doing out here all alone? Come and give me a kiss!' He closed his eyes and stuck his head forward, miming a kiss. The other guards laughed. *'Kyss meg!'* shouted another.

Eva went bright red and marched past them, folding her arms around herself and staring straight ahead.

'Nice breasts,' said another, holding his cupped hands in front of his chest, weighing them. 'Big and good enough to eat,' he continued opening his mouth and letting his tongue hang out.

'A hot blonde. Does the princess have a blond pussy? I'd like to see,' jeered another.

'Shut up, you swine,' shouted Eva in German as she quickened her pace.

'Ooh, the girl is feisty! Bet she's good in bed.'

'I think we need to teach her a lesson. She should show us more respect.'

Eva had learned enough German to understand and stuck her tongue out at them.

One of the soldiers grabbed hold of her and slapped her. 'You Norwegian slut, you've got it coming.' Eva struggled and screamed, but there was no one nearby. The other two joined in and between them they dragged her back into the park and out of sight into the trees.

Soon Eva's screams were muffled as they pushed her head into the grass and pulled down her trousers. Riotous laughter and foul swear words resounded across the park. Few Norwegians understood such basic German, but the sounds of drunken soldiers yelling and laughing were all too familiar in these times.

Eva gave up fighting and kicking as it just made them hit her more. When she screamed, they gagged her. In the end, playing dead seemed to speed things up. She was not sure how many of them there were, but she thought it was five. One of them even told her to smile and stop pretending she did not like it. She just stared at the sky and tried to imagine she was one of the clouds or that she really was dead. That would have been better.

After all the cheering and laughter, the soldiers fell silent and seemed almost shamefaced, or was it that having achieved their goal they had simply lost interest? Just in case anyone might attribute any remorse to them, one of them spat in her face and swore.

'Stuck-up bitch,' said one.

'Whore,' said another as they set off.

Eva shook the dirt out of her hair, picked up the torn remnants of her underwear, and stuffed them in her bag. She heaved on her mud-stained trousers and pulled her sweater over her head. She was shivering so much she could hardly do up her bag, and her teeth chattered as she drew in her breath and sobbed as she breathed out. Her face was wet with tears, saliva, and snot. As she wiped her face on her sleeve, she wondered how much was her own and how much was the soldiers'. She shuddered in disgust then drew herself up, shook her head, and set off home.

In the park, all was now quiet. Clouds rippled in the lake, turning from pink to lilac and then deep blue. If anyone had stopped by the lake, they would have seen a full moon reflected silver in the stillness of the water and would have paused to breathe in the peacefulness of the night.

★   ★   ★   ★

Eva stumbled into the kitchen, having run all the way home. Her hair was tangled and wet, her right cheek was blue and swollen, her legs were scratched, and her blouse was torn. She hurt everywhere, but the worst feeling was the wetness in her ear as if a slug had been there.

Maria was busy in the kitchen frying some onions and minced lamb augmented with ground beef heart. She spoke to Eva without turning her head.

'Where have you been? I thought you were going to go back to school. Your teacher called here very upset with your behavior last week and I promised her you would apologize. She said she has never had a pupil be so rude to her before.'

Eva marched out of the kitchen and slammed the door.

'Eva? How dare you walk out on me when I'm trying to talk to you?'

Eva went into the bathroom and shut the door. She found a pair of scissors in the cabinet, took them, and looking in the mirror held out a handful of hair. She cut across it. She repeated this all around her head until the floor was full of wavy, golden hair. She then dug the scissors into her lower arms near her wrists, leaving deep scratches which bled onto the floor. She ran the bath, shivering as the water slowly filled the bath. It was lukewarm and she continued to shiver as she got the nail brush and soap and scrubbed herself. She scrubbed until her skin was red and raw. She washed the short, uneven hair that was left on her head with soap over and over again.

Finally, she got out of the bath, wrapped herself up in a towel, and sat on the floor. She watched her blood as it continued to ooze from her cuts and dabbed it with the towel. She felt as if she were looking down on herself from a great height, looking at an actress in a movie, or as if she had been levitated out of her body and no longer existed in this time.

Eva's reverie was interrupted by persistent banging on the door and her mother's yells. It was as if the volume had been turned down and was now reemerging. Her mother banged again.

'Eva, you've been in there for over an hour. What is going on? If you don't open the door I'll . . .' Her mother banged again then tried the door. Eva was startled when the door opened. Hadn't she even locked the door?

Maria barged in then screamed.

There was Eva sitting in the middle of the bathroom floor surrounded by tufts of hair. Down both sides of the insides of her lower arms were long crooked red lines, with some puncture wounds, a couple of which were bleeding. The blood was trickling down over her hands and onto the floor. Her face was covered in blood over her eyes where she had wiped her face, and there were patches of bloodstains over her newly cropped hair and the bath towel wrapped around her body. Her cheeks had pale streaks where tears had washed away the blood, some of which had started to congeal.

'*Oh my god!* What the hell has happened? What have you done?' shrieked Maria.

'*Go away,*' screamed Eva, 'leave me alone. I hate you. I hate all of you. I hate this bloody war and I hate myself.'

Solveig rushed out of her room

'What's happened? Is Eva ill?' she said, trying to look past Maria into the bathroom.

Maria stopped her going in and closed the door.

'She has had an accident, but it is not serious. She will be all right. Go back to your room and don't come out until I have finished in the bathroom. We'll have supper as soon as we've sorted this out.'

'But I want to help,' said Solveig. Maria pointed at her room and stared at her until she headed back.

Maria got a dustpan, mop, and bucket from the cupboard and took out a sheet from the bottom of a pile at the back of the airing cupboard. She returned to the bathroom and ran a bath. The hot tap spluttered and the cold water came out a pale, rusty brown.

'Eva, get back into the bath.' She frowned and tutted as she looked at the blood-stained towel. 'This will have to go in the bin. What a waste. Do you have any idea how hard it is to get hold of these things?

'I don't care. I just want to die,' said Eva, starting to cry.

'Stop that nonsense now. Don't you think we all feel like that sometimes? What if I let those thoughts take over? Who would look after you and your sister?'

'I don't care.'

'Eva, if you don't get into the bath right now I will slap you so hard you'll care about it all right.' Maria turned the taps off and mixed the water. Eva got in.

'Ugh, it's cold.'

'It's perfectly okay. You don't know what cold is. When I was a child, we had to wash in water from the fjord.'

Eva started washing her arms. Maria filled a large jug kept by the bath with water from the hot tap and poured it over her head, rinsing off the blood. She brushed up the hair and started cleaning the floor with a mop.

'I'll let you have the large bath towel. Here, don't put it over your arms, though. I don't want to ruin another towel.'

Eva wrapped herself up in the towel, which was warm from the airing cupboard, keeping her arms outside and sitting on the edge of the bath. Maria took a small bottle of iodine and some cotton wool out of the cabinet. She inspected the wounds and dabbed iodine on them. Eva recoiled with pain. Maria then tore some strips of sheet and wrapped then around both of her lower arms. When she had finished, she rubbed another towel over Eva's hair and straightened it with her fingers.

'What happened, Eva? You look like you've been beaten up.'

'I'm fine.'

'You're not fine. What happened?'

'Nothing, I tripped over and fell down some stairs.'

Maria narrowed her eyes. 'Something *has* happened, Eva, but why would you tell me? I'm just your mother. But I'm telling you, whatever it is, it's no excuse to kill yourself. Fight back. You have to fight back. We all have to fight back. Okay?'

Maria stopped her tidying, pulled some hair behind Eva's ear, and put her arm around her. 'Now go back to your room and get dressed. Tell Solveig that you were trying to bleach your hair but it went wrong and you spilled some bleach on your arms.'

'Yes, Mama.'

Eva, she mused, *always so angry.* She paused. 'We'll have to go to the hairdresser tomorrow.'

After Eva had gone back to her room, Maria sighed and continued to clear up. She then went into the kitchen and warmed her hands over the stove. She shuddered. What was going to become of them all?

CHAPTER 16

Oslo

Two Months Later, Tuesday

June 22ⁿᵈ, 1943

S ummer was approaching with its long light evenings and nights, which never became completely dark. Early on one of those light mornings Eva woke up feeling nauseated again. It had been like this for several mornings, but she had just put it down to fatigue and hangovers. She was working long hours at the factory and going out most nights, so it was hardly surprising really. She had gone to bed early to catch up with some sleep as she was beginning to get deep shadows under eyes and feel faint in the afternoon.

She got out of bed with an overwhelming urge to vomit. She ran to the bathroom, bent over the toilet and retched, but nothing came up apart from a small quantity of colorless fluid. She stood up and felt the room circle, staggered a few steps, and slid to the floor. Her face was shiny with perspiration, and her hands were cold and sweaty. Solveig's worried face appeared in the door.

'Are you all right. Eva?' she asked.

Eva raised her head and sat up.

'It's fine, I'm just feeling sick. It made me faint, but I'm all right now.'

'I'm going to get Mama,' said Solveig. 'You look just like Inger did when she was ill.'

Before Eva could reply, Solveig had disappeared and was knocking on Maria's door. Eva got to her feet and swayed. She felt dizzy as another wave of nausea hit her. She sat down and held her head in her hands. She was never going to be able to go to work today. She groaned and sighed, but she could not risk losing her job.

Maria came in with Solveig hurrying after her.

'What's this? Solveig says she's really scared you are going to die if you don't go to hospital right away.'

'I'm fine,' replied Eva, 'Solveig, why do you have to make such a fuss?'

'What's going on?' said Maria. Eva recounted her symptoms and Maria narrowed her eyes.

'When was your last period?'

'What? I don't know. What's that got to do with this?'

'I was exactly the same as that when I was pregnant with you.'

'Pregnant?' Eva looked horrified. 'That's impossible.'

'Are you sure? When was your last period? It must be a while, as I haven't seen any washed sanitary towels in the airing cupboard for weeks.'

'Well, I haven't had a period for ages, but they're always irregular and worse since I've been working so hard and been terrified all the time.'

'You've lost weight, but your waistline isn't as slim as it used to be.'

'I just thought that was because of all the weird food we eat.'

'I thought something was different. Now I know what it is. My god, you're pregnant. That's all we need. And who would the father be?'

Eva groaned again. 'I'll go and see the doctor. I'm sure it's just a stomach bug. Not that you would care; you're too busy having a good time with your millionaire boy-friend.'

'That's quite enough,' said Maria, 'I just hope to God I'm wrong.'

Maria left the bathroom and went back to her bedroom. Solveig saw her coming and ran back to her room before Maria could say anything to her. She had heard everything.

Eva went to leave the bathroom, but stopped and bent over the toilet again. Nothing came up, but she could not stop retching. She now started to feel scared. What if she was pregnant? Could that really have happened that night in Frogner Park? Who knew which of those drunken oafs could be the father? But no, surely it couldn't be. Her mother was just being mean. Eva managed to leave the bathroom and get dressed. She would rather die on the factory floor than risk being fired.

Two days later Eva was no better. She had not kept any food down and if she so much as took a sip of water, she started retching again. She took the morning off work to see the doctor and sat in a crowded waiting room for three hours until she was called.

The waiting room was poorly lit, crowded with people of all ages. There were pale children sniffling or sitting listlessly on their mother's laps, a mother with a baby who cried the whole time she was there despite a lot of shushing and offers of help from other women, an elderly man with a dark yellow complexion and sunken cheeks sitting so still he might have already died, and several people who coughed continuously and blew their noses into soaked handkerchiefs. If you weren't ill before you got here, Elsa mused, you certainly would be by the time you left. With no ventilation, the place must be teeming with germs.

The doctor looked weary as he came into the waiting room and surveyed the overcrowded waiting room. His suit jacket was open, his tie loose and pulled to one side, revealing his strained shirt buttons that allowed a glimpse of skin. Eva imagined him sneezing and all his buttons flying off.

'Eva Halversen,' he called.

Eva rose and followed him into his consulting room. It looked as disheveled as he did, with piles of books and magazines on one side of his desk, a stethoscope, auroscope, and ophthalmoscope, with other pieces of equipment strewn across his desk and thread-worn chairs. His sat down behind his desk while Eva sat down in front of it. The chair was a long way from the desk so she stood up and dragged it forward.

'No,' he said, 'you don't need to move it nearer. I can see and hear you perfectly well there, and I have to guard against catching infections.'

'Sorry, doctor.'

Dr. Borgen leaned back in his chair and rotated it slowly backward and forward while he looked at her notes.

'Mmm. I see. . . Yes. Perfectly healthy apart from some infected scratches on your arms in June. . . We wondered if you were depressed because you had cut your hair, but no mention of any other mental health issues. . . Yes, I see your sister died, oh, only seven months ago. My condolences. So, what can I do for you, young lady?'

Eva looked down at her hands and told the doctor about her vomiting.

'Mmm, any other symptoms like an upset tummy, sore throat, fever, food poisoning?'

'No, just the vomiting, er, and I have been feeling very tired and sometimes I feel faint.'

'Is the vomiting worse at any time of day?'

Well, I have been feeling sick for over a week now, it's only been two days that I have actually been sick, although not much comes up. Usually the nausea wears off by lunchtime and then I just feel tired. Same with the retching. I'm fine by the afternoon.

The doctor gave her a hard look. 'When was your last period?'

Eva blushed deep red and looked away from him. 'Um, not for a while, not since, er, well, just not for several months.'

'I have to ask this, young lady. Have you got a boyfriend?'

'No. Is this relevant?'

'It could be very relevant. Have you had any sexual relations?'

'No, I mean, um . . .' Eva burst into tears.

'Yes or no?'

Eva wiped her eyes and screamed out, *I was raped, okay?*'

'Did you report it to the police?'

'Of course not. They were soldiers and no one will go near them. I just wanted the whole thing to go away and pretend it hadn't happened.'

The doctor was silent for a moment then stood up.

'I am going to get a nurse.'

'I don't need a nurse.'

'No, but I do. I will need to examine you.' Eva knew what he meant and shuddered.

When the nurse came back in, the doctor told Eva to take her underpants off behind the curtain, which hid the examination table, and wait under a sheet. The nurse came in and prepared a small tray with a speculum, torch, rubber gloves, and some lubricant. Eva looked at the tray with increasing dread.

The doctor came in and proceeded to examine her. Eva gritted her teeth as he did a vaginal examination with his other hand pushing deep into her lower abdomen. She gasped at the cold of the speculum as he inserted it and gasped again as she felt it stretch inside her. The nurse was busy assisting the doctor but looked over to her and smiled.

'Nearly finished,' she said, 'you've been really good.'

Great, thought Eva, *that makes up for everything then. I may have been raped and got pregnant but everything will be all right because I was really good about the examination.*

When she had dressed and returned to the desk, the doctor looked grave.

'I'm afraid there's no doubt that you are pregnant. Your uterus is the size of a grapefruit, which makes you about ten weeks pregnant. Vomiting is a very common symptom.'

Eva sat and stared. 'I can't have a baby. I just can't. I have to get rid of it. You've got to help me.'

'I'm sure you know that it is against the law, unless the mother might die from pregnancy or unless the baby will be stillborn.'

'I'm sure my mother will kill me,' said Eva, 'or God knows I might have to do it myself.'

'It is nothing to joke about, young lady.'

'If you knew my mother, you would know it's not a joke,' said Eva as she rolled her eyes up and shook her head. 'Oh god, what am I going to do?'

'I'm sorry I can't help you. And if you'll excuse me, I have more patients to see, people who really are ill and need my help.'

'Sorry to waste your time, doctor.' Eva tossed her head and marched out of the surgery.

The doctor did not reply, but after she left he muttered to himself, 'These young women, they all say they've been raped, but I've seen them cavorting around with their German boyfriends. Then we're supposed to fix it for them, all because they can't be bothered to be careful.'

As Eva got to the door, the nurse who had helped Dr. Borgen ran after her.

'Hi,' she said, out of breath and whispering, 'I heard what the doctor was saying. He can't help you, but I know someone who can. I have to rush, but here's her address. She doesn't have a phone, I'm afraid, so you'll have to write to her. God bless you.' The nurse gave Eva a note and rushed back inside before Eva could even thank her.

Eva looked at the note. A wave of nausea came over her and she bent down over the gutter and retched. She had to sit down. She walked a few steps and sat down on a bench by a bus stop. She was shaking, perspiring, and her hands trembled. She would not be able to go to work today so would have her wages docked. She did not want to go home as her mother might be there and she could not face her. Even though her mother had suspected she was pregnant, she would still be furious. Her friends? What would they know? She could not risk news of her pregnancy getting out anyway.

The address on the note was on a familiar street near the town hall. She might as well go there now; it was not far. She walked slowly, stopping whenever she could to rest on a bench or to retch. Eventually, she got to the door of a beautician's parlor. The sign on the door directed her to go upstairs.

A bell rang as she opened the door leading to a small reception area. The desk was empty and the two adjoining doors were shut.

'Hello?' called Eva. In a moment, a young woman wearing a tightly fitting white jacket, skirt, and high heels came out of the door marked TREATMENT ROOM I.

'Hello. Are you the eleven o'clock?'

'No. I have come to see'—Eva looked at her note—'um, Birgit Westphal. Is she here?'

'Oh, sorry. She's not here at the moment. Can I take a message?'

'When will she back?'

'Oh, I'm not sure. She'll be back soon, I think. Sorry, it's just me today and I need to get back to my client.'

'I'll wait, if that's all right.'

'Suit yourself.' The beautician returned to her client.

Eva looked around her. The posters on the wall were faded and showed covers from magazines such as *Vogue* and *Harper's Bazaar.* There were shelves on one wall with various face creams, mascara, lipstick, nail varnish, and perfumes. As she turned to the opposite wall, she caught her breath. There was a large picture of the Fuhrer with HEIL HITLER written below. Beside it was another poster of a young woman with long blond plaits, curls around her head, a golden tan, and a smiling face, holding a red flag with a black swastika in a white square. She was wearing a white shirt, navy blue skirt, and necktie. At the bottom, it read RUND DEUTSCHER MADEL IN DER HITLERJUGEND. Eva knew enough German to translate it, at least the bit about a German maid in the Hitler Youth. Could this be the right place? She examined the note again. She might as well wait. What did she have to lose anyway, apart from her pregnancy?

Eva stirred as an older woman asked her if she had an appointment.

'No, I, er, are you Birgit Westphal?'

'Yes. And you are?'

'Eva Halversen. A nurse at Dr. Borgen's surgery gave me your address.'

'Ah, I see, you better come in here then. I have someone due at twelve o'clock, so we can't be long.'

They went into TREATMENT ROOM 2 and sat down in a cramped space with barely enough room for a reclining chair.

'Well then, Eva, I can guess what you have come for. But you better tell me more.'

Eva hesitated. 'How do I know that you won't report me to the authorities?'

'Why would you think that?'

'I saw the posters.'

'Oh, those. Look I promise you, I'm not a Nazi; in fact, I hate the whole lot of them, but I have to make a living. A lot of the women who come here are wives of German officials or, more often, girlfriends of high-ranking soldiers. I even had the wife of one of the chief Gestapo agents last week. They come here to have their nails and faces done for all these parties they seem to go to and, believe you me, I see a lot of them who have got caught.'

'Got caught?'

Birgit laughed. 'You know, got in the family way. Everything I do is in the strictest confidence, in exchange you must tell no one about me. So tell me what you need.'

Eva told her about her visit to the doctor but did not mention the rape. Birgit nodded.

'The only questions I ask are medical ones. I have no need to know anything about you.' Birgit asked her a few things about her general health, recent infections, vaginal discharge, previous pregnancies, and living conditions.

'Why do you want to know about where I live?' said Eva.

'I prefer to work in my clients' homes as there is less risk of getting caught.'

'But my mother is there and, well, I don't want her to know.'

'I can do it here, but I charge more.'

'How much will it be?'

'Five hundred kroners.'

'What? I can't afford that.'

'Maybe your mother or boyfriend will help you pay.'

'She hasn't got any money, and, oh never mind,' said Eva.

'It's up to you.' The bell on the door clanged. 'That's my next client. I'll have to go. Let me know what you decide.'

Eva left without saying goodbye. When she got out, she realized she had forgotten to ask how Birgit did it. She had heard terrible stories about girls and women who had died after chemicals such as bleach or diesel oil were injected inside the womb, rubber catheter tubes being inserted and left inside only to lead to death from overwhelming sepsis, or women who bled to death after knitting needles were inserted. But she was more scared of having a baby. She could not imagine facing the disgrace, losing her job, and looking after the poor mite who would come into this world fatherless and at risk of being discovered as German. And even if the abortion was safe, it was too expensive.

Eva fretted back and forth as she walked home. She had heard that hot baths and brandy could set off a miscarriage. Was that just an old wives' tale or was it worth a try?

CHAPTER 17

Later That Day

E va got home early and was relieved to find no one at home yet. It was early afternoon and Solveig would still be at school. She was always going back to her friend's house anyway, so she was often not home until after supper. And Mother? God only knows, but she seemed to be out all the time at the moment.

Eva took off her coat and shivered. It was cold despite the time of year. She went into the lounge and opened the drinks cabinet. Not many bottles there—only a small amount of Remi Martin brandy left. At the back was an unopened bottle of Aquavit. Mother only drank brandy or whisky, everything else being kept for a rare guest. Maybe the Aquavit would be just as good as brandy, maybe better. She took it into the kitchen and set the first of several kettles on. It would take a while, but she would have a deep boiling hot bath and drink the Aquavit.

* * * *

A couple of hours later, there was a loud banging on the door and Maria shouting.

'Eva, open the door. What are you doing in there?'

Eva woke up and for a moment couldn't work out where she was. She was lying in a bath of cool water, shivering. There was condensation everywhere and her mouth felt dry. She tried to answer her mother but just slurred. She squinted as the light hit her eyes and saw the blurry outline of a half-empty bottle of Aquavit at the end of the bath. With a shock, she remembered everything.

'Shurrrite. I'm awrrite.'

'Open the door at once.'

Eva slipped several times as she got out of the bath, splashing water onto the floor as she slipped back. She managed to climb out and fell onto the floor. She clambered up and staggered to the door, fumbling with the bolt. As soon as the door was unlocked, Maria pushed it open. Eva had fallen on the floor again. In a moment, Maria wrapped her in a towel. She put her arms around her and swept her hair back from her face. 'What's wrong?'

Eva opened her mouth to speak, then her face crumpled and she sobbed loudly. 'I'm pregnant. I don't know what to do. It wasn't my fault. It was the soldiers in Frogner Park. They forced me. I didn't want to do it. It wasn't my fault,' she slurred in between sobs.

Maria rocked her backward and forward, shushing her every time she let out a new burst of sobs. 'I had a friend many years ago who tried to get rid of a baby with whisky and a hot bath, but it just gave her a terrible hangover.'

'Arnge you angry?'

'I've been angry all my life, Eva, but where has it got me? That's why your father left me. All the rows, all the anger, but for what?'

'You won't throw me out of the house?' said Eva, giving an occasional silent sob.

'I've already lost one daughter. I don't want to lose another one. We'll have to work it out. But for now, I'm going to help you get your pajamas on and get you to bed.'

Eva smiled. She felt as if she was a tiny child again with a mother she had not seen since before Solveig was born. She felt miles away from herself, her problems so far away they were almost invisible, and she was floating in mist, with just the warmth of her bed and her mother's voice.

* ★ ★ ★

The next morning Eva opened her eyes and for a moment felt good. Then memories of the day before cut through the haze, and pain seared through her head. She felt as if she had been flattened by a German tank but had refused to die. It would be so much easier to die. She groaned as she thought of going to work. She could barely remember the night before and had no idea how she had got into bed. Her last memory was of a steaming bath and Aquavit. She remembered an angel stroking her hair and speaking to her as if she were an infant. The angel looked just like her mother, or was it her? Her mind closed over and all she could think about was the throbbing pain in her head and how exhausted she felt. She pulled the duvet over her and went back to sleep.

'Eva,' shouted her mother, 'Eva, time to get up.'

'I'm too tired.'

'Having too much to drink the night before is not a good enough excuse to miss work. Do you want to lose your job?'

The thought of getting the sack put a shot of adrenaline into her. She could not remember ever feeling so ill and yet she had to go to work. After brushing her teeth and a quick wash, she pulled on yesterday's clothes. She managed to brush her hair and apply some makeup. Her eyes were puffy and she had dark circles under them, contrasting starkly with the pallor of her face. Her lips were bloodless and when she applied her red lipstick, she looked more like a voodoo doll than the beautiful young woman she was. Her hands trembled and she nearly fainted a couple of times.

When she came into the kitchen, Maria was getting breakfast for Solveig who had not emerged yet. Eva's work started earlier than Solveig's school, so they usually ended up having breakfast separately.

'And how are you this morning?' asked her mother.

'I've never felt worse in my life. I can hardly stand up and I feel really sick.'

'Well, that's the consequence of drinking all the Aquavit.'

'I didn't drink all of it.'

'Well, you might as well have. You must have had at least half of it anyway. Look at the state of you.'

'I wasn't doing it for fun, you know.'

'I know, but that doesn't change the fact that there's hardly any of my Aquavit left.'

'I thought you said you would help me.' Eva wondered if the angel who had comforted her last night was just a vision.

'Go to work and we'll talk about it tonight.

*   *   *   *

Eva struggled her way to the tram stop and waited in the queue. She stared blankly ahead as the tram headed for Nordstrand, where the factory was. Quite a few of the other passengers, mainly women, were workers at the same factory. After Eva got out, one of the women ran after her.

'Eva, what are you doing here? You looked really ill yesterday and you look terrible today. Shouldn't you see a doctor?'

'I have,' replied Eva. 'There's nothing wrong with me, just fatigue.'

'Come and work next to me today and I can cover for you if you are sick or faint again.'

'Thank you, that's really sweet of you.'

Eva took her place beside her friend on the factory floor. They were sewing clothes, mostly utilitarian jackets, and trousers this week. There were different batches all the time. Last week they had been sewing women's blouses and the week before that, children's clothes. The jackets they were working on at the moment were difficult because the fabric was coarse and areas where machine stitching could not reach had to be sewn by hand. It was hard to drive the needle through, and even though they had thimbles, it was common to end up with pricked fingers. Woe betide anyone who got spots of blood on the clothes.

Eva could hardly sit up straight, and her head kept falling forward as she fell asleep. Her friend kept waking her up but had to concentrate so hard on a particularly complicated bit of sewing around the buttonhole of a jacket that she did not notice their supervisor coming through.

'Miss Halversen,' a voice boomed out, 'we don't pay workers to come here and sleep. You weren't here yesterday, and today you have hardly done anything in the last hour. We're not a charity, you know. Come to my office now.' The supervisor beckoned her to follow him as he walked across to the opposite end of the factory floor to his office.

'Explain yourself, Miss Halversen,' he said as they sat down on either side of his desk.

'I've been ill with a stomach bug,' said Eva, 'but I didn't want to have any more time off sick.'

'You will have to get a doctor's note. Are you sure that's it? Some girls are out all night at jazz clubs and the like with their boyfriends. I'd hate to think that you were one of those. But I have heard rumors.'

'Rumors? What rumors?' replied Eva.

'Yes, rumors, you know, boyfriends and carryings on.'

'That's ridiculous. I've been ill.'

'You better get a doctor's certificate then, madam. You can go home now, but if I don't have that certificate on my desk tomorrow morning you'll be fired.'

'Is that all, sir?'

'Yes, go home.'

★   ★   ★   ★

Eva was relieved to be going home but annoyed at the prospect of going back to see the doctor again so soon. Perhaps she would see that helpful nurse who could just ask the doctor for her. But what were these rumors? She couldn't imagine why anyone would spread rumors about her. She took the tram back to the city center and went to the surgery. She looked for the helpful nurse but could not see her. Instead there was a waspish receptionist who told her the doctor could not give her a sick certificate unless she saw him.

She went into the dingy waiting room, squeezed herself into one of the few remaining seats, and closed her eyes. She could still hear the snuffling, crying, and coughing that seemed to be obligatory in a doctor's surgery, but had no wish to see any of it.

A familiar wave of nausea came over her, but she had learned to suppress the urge to retch as it made things worse. She was almost asleep when she heard her name called. How long had she been waiting there? The room was quieter, and there were more spaces with several new people settled in. She followed the doctor into his waiting room.

'Hello again, Miss Halversen,' said the doctor. 'What can I do for you so soon after the last appointment?'

'I have to have a certificate for work. I missed time yesterday and I have been sent home because the vomiting has been so bad.' She was not going to tell him about the Aquavit.

'Well, lots of women have a bit of vomiting when they are pregnant and still manage to get to work. It's not an illness; it's a natural healthy part of being pregnant.'

'Yes, but this has been really bad.'

'It will settle and, meanwhile, you have to learn to manage it better. Eat less rich food, drink small amounts of water frequently, and just a glass of milk for breakfast.'

'Do you have any pills to stop it?'

'No, not for something that is not an illness.'

He took a pad of sick certificates from the side of his desk, wrote one out for her, and handed it over the desk. 'Here, I have signed you off for a week, but I don't expect to see you again until you start feeling the baby moving. Then we can check how your pregnancy is going and make arrangements for the delivery.'

Eva thanked the doctor and took the note. On her way out, she had one more look for the helpful nurse but had no luck. She noticed a young woman about her age had come into the waiting room. It was obvious that she was due to have a baby any day now. Eva shuddered. That could be her in seven months' time. But no, it could not be. She could not let this happen.

On her way home, Eva took out the doctor's certificate. The doctor had written, *Vomiting and dehydration due to pregnancy*. How could he do that? How could he think that she would want anyone to see that? He could have just put *Vomiting and dehydration* on it. But no. Why not put *Vomiting and dehydration due to pregnancy after being raped by German soldiers and seven months after her sister died from undiagnosed appendicitis?*

Or maybe that would not be enough of her personal information to give out. Eva was so angry that she had forgotten her nausea and fatigue and was tramping home at a fast pace.

When a group of soldiers outside the gates of Palace Park waved to her, she yelled out *'Go to hell you bastards'* so fiercely that instead of the usual taunts and laughter, they looked almost scared until one of them yelled out, 'Not getting enough, eh?' And then they all laughed.

Eva was so furious she felt like going back and laying into them. But even in her anger she knew this would be dangerous, and so she just carried on home.

That evening her mother seemed to have forgotten that they were going to have a talk and carried on as if nothing had happened. She created a supper that was almost edible and, considering the few ingredients she had to work with, was a triumph.

Solveig was in high spirits and would not stop going on about every single detail of her day at school. Ragnild had a huge smudge on her homework and had got told off by the teacher. Mrs. Ostby told Solveig that her story about a dog which had lost his mother was the best story she had read all week and that Solveig was a great storyteller. But her writing needed to be neater—and how did she get the pages so grubby and crumpled? Solveig went on and on. There was not going to be a single thing that Solveig did that day that they were not going to be told about.

Despite the fact that Maria was clearly not listening, and just said a vacant 'hmmm' every now and again, and despite the fact that Eva was sitting like a statue, not eating, or talking, and hardly breathing, Solveig's high spirits were not in the least dampened. If everyone talked as much as Solveig, Eva thought, no one would ever listen to anyone, and if we all ended up deaf it would make no difference.

CHAPTER 18

Oslo

Wednesday

June 23rd, 1943

The next morning Eva decided to go to work and pretend that she had not been able to get a certificate. With a bit of luck, the foreman would forget. He knew she was a hard worker normally, and he had so many other things to deal with. If she had the sack, they would have to find a replacement for her. So maybe he might overlook her bit of time off sick.

When she got to work, she waved at her friend but her friend looked the other way. Eva sat down in front of her sewing machine and picked up the jacket she had been working on. When she looked up, she could see the other women giving her dirty looks and whispering to each other. Then she saw the foreman coming toward her with an expression she had never seen on his face before. His face was twisted with disgust and hatred. Eva felt adrenaline shoot through her like a cold shower.

'You are not welcome here. Pack your things. You are leaving.'

'But what about my sick certificate?' Eva had been going to make an excuse to stall for time.

'You don't need one now because you are sacked.'

'But I don't understand . . . what?' Eva went red and burst into tears.

'*Nazi whore!*' yelled out one of the workers from the other side of the factory floor.

'*Nazi whore!*' yelled some more.

'That's not true,' cried Eva.

'Oh yes?' said the foreman. 'I've heard the rumors. Do you think people wouldn't notice that you are pregnant?'

'I'm not. *It's not true,*' shouted Eva.

The woman on the sewing machine next to her stood up and turned towards her.

'We knew it. You're such a stuck-up madam. Think you are better than us, do you? We saw you flaunting yourself in your tight sweaters and skirts. Think we didn't notice how rounded you've become and that glow on your face. We knew when you started being sick in the mornings. Oh, we might be below you, but we are not stupid.'

'I'm *not* pregnant and even if I were, what makes you think I've been with a Nazi anyway?'

One of the other women replied. 'I know your neighbor at Kristian IV flats. The only person she's seen coming to your flat is a Nazi officer, and since he left you've been going out a lot. You've been seen talking to soldiers at Theatercafeen, and we know that that same Nazi officer goes there all the time. It doesn't take much to put two and two together.'

'I've only been there once and it was a mistake. That's ridiculous. How could you think I'd have anything to do with that old man?'

'Money makes the world go round, they say,' said another worker.

All the women started yelling '*Nazi whore, Nazi whore*' until the place was in uproar.

'Ladies, *ladies,*' bellowed the foreman. 'That's enough. Get back to work, all of you. We've got to get these jackets finished by the end of the week.'

Gradually the din died down and Eva put on her coat and rushed to the door. She did not look behind her and knew there was no point saying anything. She had a pretty good idea who the neighbor who spread the rumor was, but what could she do? She had been found guilty in the court of vicious gossip, based on fear and hatred of the Nazis and anyone seen to collaborate with them.

After she had walked a few yards, she heard footsteps running behind her. She wondered whether to run away, she felt so scared. When she turned around, she saw her friend.

'Eva, I'm so sorry. I was scared they would label me too and I didn't want to lose my job. But now I don't care. I don't want to work with those women anymore.'

'It's okay. But don't lose your job on my account. The women are just as scared as we are. They have to take it out on someone. I just wish it didn't have to be me.'

'I didn't know you were so wise.'

'Nor did I,' said Eva as she smiled and gave her friend a hug. 'Go back and forget about all this. There's no point in you losing your job as well.'

'I don't know. I feel bad.'

'Go on, we're in a war. We all have to survive as best we can. Go back before they notice you have gone.'

'Yes. You're a good person, Eva. I'll miss you.'

Her friend kissed her and waved goodbye as she ran back to the factory.

Eva stood and watched her go. She wondered if she really was a good person or if all her mean acts had caught up with her and this was a terrible punishment. But she didn't believe in God. Maybe the trolls were real after all. Eva told herself off for her ridiculous thoughts and started back for home. What was she going to tell her mother?

When Eva arrived home, she wrapped herself up in the comfort of her duvet and tried to sleep her troubles away. But it was hot and light seeped in everywhere, bringing visions of all those angry faces. A toxic wave of shame spread through her, bringing nausea in its wake. In an attempt to drum out the thoughts, she got up and busied herself in the kitchen. Solveig was due home from school soon, and she thought she would surprise her mother and make supper. She checked the cupboards. They were well stocked with potatoes from her mother's shopping trip yesterday, with onions, a cabbage and several scrag ends of lamb. She rummaged the cupboards and found a packet of pepper corns. Perfect. She could make *farikal* with added potatoes.

She was well into this when her mother returned home.

'What are you doing home so early?'

Eva could never predict how her mother would react to anything, and the last thing she needed now was another row. She could not bring herself to tell her mother what had happened. She could imagine her mother telling her it was her fault or, worse, she might storm down to the factory the next day and demand that they stop telling lies and give Eva her job back. Her mother was harsh with her children but would defend them from outsiders to the death. Eva muttered something about her doctor signing her off for a week and that it was fine with her boss. Maria was too busy checking the stew bubbling on the hob to be suspicious.

'Mmm, *farikal,* just what I was planning. But you've put potatoes in with it.'

'I thought it would make it more filling, and the potatoes absorb the juices. The Irish put loads of potatoes in their stews and that's the whole point.'

'How come you're such an expert on Ireland now?'

'I did go to school, you know. We learned about that in cookery.'

'Eva, I've been worrying about you all day. It's making me ill.'

Eva wondered if that was true. She looked as though she had been having a good time with her rich boyfriend. Not so much a boyfriend as a fat bald old man-friend. He was so much older that her. Whatever did she see in him? In her mind, she heard the taunt she had heard at work, *Money makes the world go round, they say*, then she thought, *That's what they think about me and it's not true, so if I think that about my mother, I am just as bad as them. I have been found guilty of a crime I did not commit. Do I want to do the same to someone else, even if it is my mother? And maybe she has been worried about me.* Eva thought all this in an instant.

She tried to smile at her mother but instead she burst into tears. She hadn't planned to do that. 'I don't know what to do. I can't have a baby, not now, not after what happened.'

Maria sat down and beckoned her to do the same. 'I've heard terrible things about what happens to babies born to girls who are not married,' she said. 'The Nazi doctors make the hospital notify them and then they send their doctors to inspect them and look at the records of the mother. If the mother and the baby have blond hair and blue eyes, they take the baby away and send them to Germany to be adopted.'

'I can't believe anyone would do that. Not even the Nazis.'

'Yes, and they tell the mothers that their baby has died and the girls tell their friends and family that they were shocked as their babies seemed really healthy. If the babies are born with any abnormalities or birth problems, they take them away as well, but not for adoption. They tell the mothers the same thing, but this time it is true. Their babies are dead, but not from natural causes.'

'That's monstrous. Where did you hear about this anyway? It just can't be true.'

'I have a friend whose daughter is a nurse in one of the Lebensborn nursing homes and she hears a lot. Her daughter also has friend who is a nurse in the maternity hospital, and they see and hear things as well. They are sworn to secrecy, but you know how secrets can leak out.'

'I wouldn't want to have a child and have it taken from me.'

'You could go to stay with your grandfather and grandmother and have the baby there. When the war is over, you can come back and I'll help you look after your child.'

'I don't know. I'm scared to have a baby and I'm scared of an abortion.'

Just as Maria was about to reply, Solveig came in. She ran into the kitchen looking upset.

'Why are there horrible things written on the door and all over the wall? And why are there lots of people outside?'

'What? I didn't see anything when I came home,' said Maria.

'I'm scared,' said Solveig, putting her thumb in her mouth.

'I'm sure it's nothing. I'm going down to check,' said Maria.

Eva had gone so pale she looked a sickly shade of yellow. 'Mother, I think I know. I can't believe they would. I . . . er,' Eva couldn't go on. She shivered and buried her head in her hands.

'For God's sake, *tell* me. What?' said Maria. Eva brought her knees up to her chest and turned away. Maria shook her. 'You have to tell me. If you don't, I'm going to slap your face.'

'At the factory today, um, at the factory today, all the women there were calling me a Nazi whore.'

'How dare they? Let's hope this has nothing to do with that or they'll be sorry.'

Maria marched out and onto the street. The door was daubed with wet paint spelling the words NAZI WHORE, and on the wall were the words SHAME ON YOU. There was a small crowd of people, mostly young men and a few women on the other side of the street chanting, 'Norway for the Norwegians! No Nazis and no Nazi whores!'

Maria shouted at them, 'My daughter has never been with a Nazi. She's a good Norwegian just like you.'

'You're the mother, aren't you?' shouted one of them.

'She's the wife of a police collaborator,' shouted another. Maria recognized her as one of the neighbors from the ground floor.

'Wife of a traitor, mother of a traitor,' said a few more voices, and then they all joined into this chant.

'That's not true,' shouted Maria above the din. Eva had been watching this from the window. She had told Solveig to go into her bedroom. When they started threatening her mother, Eva went downstairs. She came out, squeezed past her mother, and stood in front of her.

'My mother hasn't done anything wrong. My father is not a traitor and someone is spreading lies about me. I have never been with a Nazi. I swear to God. But if you want a fight, have it with me, not with her.'

'Eva,' gasped Maria, 'for heaven's sake, get back. They wouldn't dare do anything to me.'

Before Eva could reply, the mob had crossed the road and two men grabbed her arms. Then another grabbed her middle as she kicked and screamed. Maria tried to fight them off, but they flung her to one side and another man punched her in the stomach, making her fall to the ground. When some more men had hold of Eva's legs so that she could no longer kick or move, two women came and grabbed her hair. They both had scissors and started cutting handfuls off.

'You better keep your head still or you'll get poked in the eye. You don't want that, hey, bitch.'

Eva gave up struggling and slumped. When the women had finished, the men let Eva go. Maria was sitting on the pavement, crying and screaming *'Bastards'* at them.

'You got what you deserved,' said one of the women. 'That should teach you a lesson.'

With that last retort, the mob left. After they left, several neighbors came down to help them up. Eva was dazed and Maria was crying.

When Maria and Eva came back into the flat, Solveig ran out. When she saw them, she ran up and hugged them. Maria asked Solveig to help her get Eva into bed.

Eva just murmured 'I'm so sorry' and 'Thank you' and 'I'll be all right.'

Maria poured some of her Remi Martin into a mug, mixed it with a small amount of hot water and a teaspoon of their scarce supply of sugar, stirred it up, and told Eva to drink it.

'What after all the Aquavit last night?'

'Forget about that. This is medicine. It will help with the pain and get you to sleep.'

Eva sat on the bed and rubbed her hands over the bruises on her arms. The pain gave some reality to the assault on her. It reminded her of the pain she had felt after that night in Frogner Park.

Behind her tears she could feel a cold burn of anger rising from her chest. The anger had been latent for so long: her father's abandonment of them, her mother's self-absorption, Inger dying needlessly because there were too many children with upset stomachs, no petrol for the ambulances, and no hospital beds. Inger, who died just because of the war. The war, the interminable, dreary, miserable war, with all its restrictions, people disappearing never to be heard of again, people who died in bombings, people who died of malnutrition in war camps, and resistance heroes who were shot in the streets.

And now she was pregnant. Who were they to judge her and reduce her to this state of fear and dread? She had spent too many days imagining the ways she could have an abortion, the horror stories of abortions gone wrong, and too many days thinking of the humiliation of being pregnant and without a husband. She had wondered if any of the men she knew would marry her and accept the child as their own, but there was no one. And now, the neighbors and everyone she knew believed she was pregnant with a Nazi. She *was* pregnant with a Nazi, but it wasn't her fault.

Her anger ebbed away like a wave recedes, dragging pebbles after it, and she gave in to silent sobs. Like all waves, this one would recede for a while but would come back with as much force as ever. She reached for her mug and took a deep draught of warm brandy, frowned, then took the rest in one go.

She lay herself on the bed and felt the warmth of the drink spread into her limbs and into her mind. She put her hands on her abdomen and felt the small bump. Inside her was a tiny being that was innocent and had not been hurt by anything in the world. She felt herself floating out of the swirl of tormenting thoughts and, rising above it, she felt love. Was it the medicine or was it the new life inside her? It was a new feeling, a sparkle of light in a sea of black. She drew her duvet over her and fell into a blissful sleep.

*   *   *   *

After saying good night to Eva, Maria went back into the kitchen and saw that Solveig was crying. It made her feel sad and so inadequate that she had been unable to protect her from all this, from all the horror of this war. Brisk routines, harsh discipline, and the forbidding of self-pity were not enough for what had just happened.

'Come here, Solveig,' she said.

Solveig went over to her and Maria gave her a hug. 'Those people have gone now. Somebody has been telling lies about Eva and they thought she was a collaborator, but we know she is not and never would be. Eva will be all right. She is a very strong girl.'

'What about you Mama? I heard you shouting and screaming.'

'They tried to hurt me too, but they had no idea how hard I can fight. I'm all right.'

'I want to be good at fighting too. I'm scared they'll come back,' said Solveig, nestling into her mother's side.

'They won't ever come back. The war is very scary for all of us, Solveig. But we have to be brave and strong. You think you can do that?'

'Yes, Mama,' said Solveig, but she did not look too sure.

Maria lifted the lid to the *farikal* and a delicious smell of lamb steamed out. 'One good thing, the *farikal* is perfect. Now, we have to eat to keep our strength up. Want some?'

Solveig smiled and got some knives and forks and plates.

'That's better,' said Maria as she ladled out two large portions. 'Now, I want to know what you did at school today.'

★   ★   ★   ★

After Solveig had gone to bed Maria finished her chores and checked to see if Eva was all right. It was a relief now that they were both asleep. She took her shoes off, lit a cigarette, and sat down with her feet up on the table. The sky was pale gray with a uniform layer of cloud, and she could hear people on the streets below. It was after ten, but with the light nights it felt much earlier.

She thought about her new boyfriend, Edvard Gregersen, who liked to take her out for meals, dances, and ply her with whisky from his vast cellar when they returned in his Chevrolet to his extensive house in Parkveien. He had managed to keep his vast ship-building business going somehow, but she decided not to ask too much about that. It made a change to have someone admire and flatter her, but she knew the relationship was doomed. The novelty was wearing off and beneath the charisma of his wealth and powerful bearing, he was dull. Their conversation was awkward and she kept running out of things to say. He would talk at length about the shipping business and his adult children who had settled in America and had never contacted him since his wife died. She would find herself stifling her yawns and pinching her leg under the table to prevent herself from falling asleep.

She knew he was expecting her to make love to him soon and so far, she had managed to make her excuses. But he was becoming pushy despite his charm, and even though she tried, she could feel no desire for him. Herr Wolff was more attractive, and she had seen how he used to look at her, but he was a Nazi and seeing him in his uniform killed any spark of forbidden desire and made her recoil in dread.

She missed Johannes, damn him. She was still furious at him, but thought about him every night. She yearned for him to love her and be with her, and she fantasized about revenge. She wanted him to yearn for her as much as she did for him, and then see her go off with a younger, more handsome, more brilliant man as she laughed in his face. She wanted him to beg her to come back to him and for her to refuse. She wanted him to hurt as much as she did.

But where did all her anger and hatred get her? She thought about how grief had turned her mother into such an invalid; always complaining about her health, and always saying such mean and spiteful things about everyone. Occasionally, her mother might forget how injured she was by life, and a smile would bring back a hint of the person she used to be and whom her father still tried to revive even after all these years.

Maria could hear her mother in her own spiteful comments and in her own enduring sense of misfortune and rage. And who could argue that she or her mother were not entitled to feel hard done by? But did she want to end up like her? Maria leaned back and stared into the pale haze of the late evening sky. It was too late for her mother, but it was not too late for her.

She missed Inger every day, even though she had felt burdened and drained by her and the other two. She must have loved Inger to feel so much pain. She thought about Eva and Solveig. Neither of them deserved the grief and misery of this war. They deserved something better. Maria felt lighter in her chest as she swore to make it up to them. She wondered what would happen to Eva and the baby. She had some money to help with an abortion, or money to look after a baby depending on what Eva wanted.

She saw some dark clouds move over the pale gray and turn the sky dark blue. Heaven knows how they would all cope, but at least things were steady with Solveig. Or so she thought.

CHAPTER 19

Oslo

Monday

June 28th, 1943

I t was a sunny morning toward the end of June. Maria no longer joined Eva and Solveig for breakfast, preferring to stay in bed and drink the freshly brewed coffee she bought on the black market with every bit of money she saved from the housekeeping.

Johannes sent her a monthly allowance, although he often needed a reminder. A sharp phone call usually sufficed. This was topped up with checks her father sneaked out of the house when her mother was not looking. Solveig still cycled up to Else and Torhild's house at Blommenholm every week to bring food waste for their pig and collect any eggs or fresh vegetables they could spare. Else was still away and Aunt Torhild had to manage on her own. Maria and the girls went up there for Sunday lunch and their parents came down every few months.

A week after she was sacked from the clothes factory, Eva managed to get a job in a shop with a friend of Maria's. Solveig still went to school held at different locations, as the main local school was still occupied. Lessons were held in a church hall regularly, and now that they had most of their teachers back they could go to school almost full time.

The sun streamed in the open window as Eva made porridge. There was a scraping of honey left and Eva instructed Solveig to rinse out the jar with a couple of spoons of warm water until it was all melted. In a moment, they were sitting in front of large plates of porridge with the reconstituted milk and honey shared equally.

'I miss Papa,' said Solveig.

'It's no good missing him,' said Eva, 'he's living with his girlfriend now.'

'I don't believe that.'

'And what do you believe then?'

'I think he still loves us all and wants to come home.'

'One of your fairy tales?'

'Why is everyone so horrible about Papa? You and Mama don't care. I hate you both!' cried Solveig.

'Grow up and stop being so stupid,' said Eva.

The girls finished their breakfast and Solveig went to the hall to get her schoolbag. Maria came out in her dressing gown.

'You off then? Eva, get some cheese if you can, and some fish on the way home from work. Here's some ration cards.'

'Do I have to? Last time I had to wait for two hours and when I got there, the only thing that was left was some disgusting heads of herring and tiny crabs. The shopkeeper said I should have gone much earlier. Why can't you go this morning?'

'I have to hem my black skirt and put some new buttons on my jacket.'

'Ooh, have you finished putting the collar on?' said Solveig

'Yes, it's nearly finished. Then I am having my hair done. I won't be here for supper tonight. I am meeting Edvard.'

'Why do *I* have to do everything?' said Eva. 'It's bad enough having to do this boring job.'

'It was you who walked out of school, Eva. You could have studied and tried to make something of yourself, but no, you were "too bored" at school. Well, I've got news for you, madam. Some things in life *are* boring, but you have to stick to them. That's called being a grown-up. What if *I* gave up every time I felt "bored," huh? Do you think I enjoy slaving away every single day to keep you two clean and fed?'

'You didn't do much when we were little, did you? Maybe it was you who was too bored and tired to be bothered to look after us. How many times did you send us away to Granny's? And she didn't love us either.'

'I was ill. And it was hard to do anything. It wasn't my fault. I missed you and Inger a lot when you went to Bronnoysund. I wish I had been able to be there more.'

'It was always about you and your illness. It's never your fault. Papa was too busy and you were too "ill" to care. Well, I've got news for *you*, mother. You are not the only person in the world to suffer. In case you haven't noticed, it was hard for me and Inger too.' Eva paused and looked upward. 'At least Inger doesn't have to suffer any more of this crap, which is called our life.'

Maria stepped toward Eva and raised her hand to slap her face.

Eva grabbed her hand. 'No, Mother, you won't ever slap me again. I am as big as you are and I'm big enough to win a fight.'

Maria struggled for a moment then sat down, and put her hands over her forehead.

'I'm sorry. I miss Inger so much, but it's not your fault. Let's not fight, I'm too tired.'

Eva sat down beside her and put her arm on her shoulder. 'I'm sorry too,' she said.

'And I miss Inger every day too,' said Solveig, 'and Papa, I miss him all the time.'

'Come on both of you, you'll be late,' said Maria, waving them off.

*　*　*　*

Later that morning the pupils at school were having a break. Solveig was sitting in the garden outside the church hall, chatting to Ragnhild and giggling as usual when one of the boys in her class swaggered up to her.

'Your father's a Nazi!'

'No, he's not! He's a policeman.'

'All the police are Nazis.'

'No, they're not, because my father isn't and never will be a Nazi. *Your* father's a Nazi.'

'Solveig's father is a traitor, a Nazi, a collaborator, a Jew-killing Nazi,' sang the boy. His friends repeated the taunts in the same singsong voices. Solveig marched up to the boy and punched him in the face. He fell over and yelled. When he sat up, there was blood streaming down from his nose. His friends ran off to get the teacher, and in a moment, Mrs. Ostby came back and bent over the boy. She helped him up, took a hanky out, and showed him how to put pressure on it. She told the boys to take him into her makeshift office inside the church building.

'Solveig, come with me at once!' When they were in the classroom, she sat down at her desk and made Solveig stand in front of it. 'This isn't like you. What has got into you?'

'He called my father a Nazi!'

'I don't care what he said. You shouldn't have hit him. There's no excuse. What do you think we are fighting for in this war? You can't go around attacking people just because you don't like what they say. That's what the Nazis do.'

'I'm sorry. I didn't mean it. I'm not like them. Honestly, I'm not.' Solveig burst into tears and wiped her nose on her sleeve.

'Here, take this,' said Mrs. Ostby, handing her a hanky. 'I know you are a good girl, but I am very disappointed with your behavior today.' She wrote a short note, put it in an envelope, and handed it to her. She then escorted Solveig to the boy and instructed her to apologize. Solveig was very crestfallen and puffy-eyed when she did so. The boy just gloated back. Solveig set off, sent home in disgrace.

When Solveig got home, Maria was in the living room sewing the last button on her jacket. She had already done her hair and makeup, and the scent of her Arpêge hung heavily in the air.

'What are you doing home?'

'Teacher told me to give you this,' mumbled Solveig, handing her the envelope. Maria tutted impatiently and took it over to her desk. Solveig slunk out to her room.

'I have to go in a minute,' said Maria as she took out the letter.

Dear Mrs. Halversen,

I am sorry to have to write to you, but Solveig
was very naughty today. She punched Petter
Stavig in the nose and made it bleed.

   She is late at least once a week, never
has her homework in on time, and does not pay
attention in class. I have been going easy on
her because of your family bereavement, but
that was months ago now and she cannot go on
like this. Hitting Petter today was the last
straw. And now she has started to tell lies.
She says he called her father a Nazi, but
Petter is a nice little boy and would never
say a thing like that.

                    God bless you.
                 Yours Sincerely,
                   Glenda Ostby

Maria frowned. 'Solveig!'

'Yes?' said Solveig, looking terrified as she ran back in.

'What happened?' said Maria. Solveig told her the story. 'Did Petter really say that?'

'Yes, he did. I know Papa is not a Nazi. He's a really brave policeman, isn't he?'

'Of course he is, and he would never be a Nazi. Don't let that stupid boy upset you.'

'Where is Papa? We haven't seen him for ages now.'

'I expect he's just working hard. Sometimes they can't tell us what they are doing and we just have to wait.'

'But he's been away for longer than ever this time.'

'I don't know. Maybe he's gone to Sweden, maybe he's gone with his girlfriend,' said Maria more to herself than to Solveig.

'What if he hasn't gone to Sweden?'

'How should I know?' Maria dismissed her and picked up her pen.

June 26th

Dear Mrs. Ostby,

My daughter does not tell lies. She is perfectly well-behaved at home and does everything I ask her too. I can only assume that you do not know how to keep order in your own class. I have enough problems of my own here without having to do your work for you.

Yours Sincerely,
Maria Halversen

She put it in an envelope and wrote the teacher's name across the envelope, underlining it with a flourish.

'Take this back to your teacher now.'

'But she sent me home today. Can't I take it tomorrow?'

'No, take it to the school now and tell the teacher I told you to go back because I am going out and there will be no one to look after you. Have you got the key?'

Solveig checked the key on a long band around her neck and nodded.

'Make sure you get your homework done before I get back,' added Maria.

Solveig headed back to school and, despite Mrs. Ostby's, surprise walked in and handed her the letter. The teacher put it on her desk as she was still teaching class and did not stop Solveig from going back to her chair. When class was dismissed, the teacher read the letter. 'No wonder Solveig is the way she is,' she said, shaking her head.

On the way home, Solveig was still smarting from the unfairness of it all. She barely noticed the German soldiers roaring past on motorbikes or the new graffiti on the wall leading up to the palace, with FREEDOM and NORWAY written on it in large red letters. These sights were commonplace.

On the high wall, someone had stuck a cartoon of a fat man eating a Norway-shaped pie with QUISLING, 'SAVIOR OF NORWAY' written under it.

She walked past a queue of women outside a shop which had an open door and boarded-up windows. Outside the door were several stalls with vegetables and signs saying SOLD OUT or SPECIAL OFFER. There were some small children who had joined together to play in the road. One had screwed up a poster to make a ball to play catch with. Solveig picked it up as it came in front of her and threw it back at them, only for it to land in the same place as she had picked it up from. They laughed and ran to collect it.

It was late afternoon when she let herself in the flat. Eva would not be back for some hours yet, and her mother was out for the rest of the day with that horrible fat man, Mr. Gregersen. She went to her mother's desk and looked through the drawers. One was locked. She spent some time searching in the unlocked drawers, in her mother's wardrobe, and finally in her jewelry box. There in the bottom layer, next to a silver watch and several strands of tangled beads, was a tiny key on a silver chain. She took it out and tried it. The lock clicked open.

Inside the secret drawer were several piles of envelopes tied with red velvet ribbon. Solveig recognized her father's handwriting on some loose envelopes on top. She flicked through them and read the most recent. It was dated some five weeks before.

Dearest Maria,

I hope that you and the girls are well. I can come and collect them this Sunday at four o'clock. Tell them to wear their best dresses because we are going to the theater. I was given free tickets by my police chief.

I have tried to phone you so many times but the receiver just clicks off. I know it is you. I need to speak to you. Can you let me up to the flat this time? It will only take a moment.

Give my love to the girls. Eva looks just as beautiful as

*you were at that age. You still are. And Solveig, well, she is
so funny. She makes us all laugh.*

Ever Yours,

Johannes

On the top of the letter was an address. Solveig repeated it to herself ten
times and continued to repeat it as she replaced the letters and the key to
their exact places. She went into her room, took a notebook from her desk
and wrote the address down in tiny letters on the back page, then hid it
under her pillow. She thought about the date on the letter. That was over
a month ago.

She had been so excited as she and Eva had dressed up in their best
party clothes, but their father had never come to collect them. As the
evening went on, they changed into their pajamas and she had cried all
night. Eva had pretended she did not care, but even Solveig could see it
was an act. Mama had said that he was always doing things like that and
we should just get used to it.

Solveig knew her father wanted to see her really. Something very bad
must have happened. Even if he did not want to see Eva, who was always
so rude to him, she knew he would want to see her. He still called her his
little princess. She knew he would never ever be a Nazi or any of the awful
things everyone said about him. She wished it was Mama and Eva who
had disappeared and that she could go and live with him.

She stopped her daydreaming and frowned at the letter. Something
bad had happened and no one was taking any notice. Then it dawned on
her: If no one else was bothering to find him, it would have to be her. She,
Solveig Halversen, third daughter of Johannes and Maria, would have to be
the one. She drew herself up to her full height and smiled. She was going
to go and find him.

CHAPTER 20

Tuesday

June 29th, 1943

The next morning Solveig started off to school as usual. Maria had seemed in an unusually good mood and was up and dressed, cooking them waffles for breakfast. The jam was sour and there was no butter, but it was still a treat.

When Eva set off to her work, Solveig carried on as if she were heading to Mrs. Ostby's class in the church hall, but after walking two hundred yards she turned back on herself. She went past some school friends who waved and asked where she was going. Solveig told them she had forgotten something and would be there soon. Her friends just laughed as she was always doing that.

As soon as she was past her fellow pupils and heading in the direction of the palace, she took out her notebook. She went to the tram stop and checked out the sign. With the help of some fellow passengers, she managed to get to Smedstad and, having been given further directions, found the street where her father now lived. It was wide and tree-lined with several large houses on one side and on the other two large blocks of modern flats.

She went to the ground floor flat of the address and rang the doorbell. She repeated this several times, getting longer with each press. She walked over to the window and knocked for several minutes, then sat dejectedly on the porch. She was just about to ring again when a lady called out of the window from the flat above. When Solveig asked about a policeman called Johannes Halversen, she told her to come up.

'Come in, my dear,' the lady spoke gently. 'Have you come far? You sit there and I'll get you some water.' Solveig sat down on a sofa with the most cushions she had ever seen. They were embroidered in bright colors with birds, wild animals, and flowers. On the table was a tapestry the lady was working on with lengths of wool in rich colors. The lady had left some thick spectacles nearby. When she came back into the living room, the lady saw her looking at the tapestry.

'It keeps me busy. My two boys are off fighting. One of them is in England and the other, well, I don't know where he is.' She pointed to a photo on the mantelpiece. 'Who could imagine those little boys growing up so strong? My husband, God rest his soul, would have been so proud. It's just me here now. So tell me who Johannes Halversen is.' Solveig explained. 'Yes, I see. So he's your father, is he?' She went back into the kitchen and brought out some homemade biscuits.

'Thank you,' said Solveig, trying not to look too hungry.

'I don't know if I can tell you much, and I'm afraid it might not be very helpful,' she said as Solveig nodded, 'but I have seen a policeman coming here often, and I think he was living here. Klara, the lady who lives downstairs used to talk to me sometimes and said she hoped she would marry him one day.' Solveig looked puzzled and upset. 'Sorry, my dear, I'm only telling you what I know.'

'It's okay.'

'Sometimes his car would be parked here every night for a week or more, then it wouldn't turn up for several days or sometimes longer.'

'We haven't heard from him for over a month now,' said Solveig.

'Yes, that sounds about right. I haven't seen either of them since a black car came in the early hours of the morning and four men in black uniform came. They banged on the door and I could hear Klara talking to them after they went in. She sounded upset, but I couldn't hear what she was saying. It was starting to get light and I couldn't get back to sleep. As soon as it was morning, I went to the flat, knocked, and rang but there was no answer. The door was unlocked so I went in. Their coats were still there and your father's police car was still outside. Later that day another police car drew up and one of the policemen got into your father's car and drove off. But it definitely wasn't your father. I was scared for days that someone would arrest me, but we had no more visits.' Solveig was listening with wide eyes.

'Who were the men?'

'I don't know. They just had black uniforms. I was scared to look out again in case they saw me.'

'What do you think happened?'

'My dear child, there's so much we don't understand. We have to trust that God is with us. I pray that he will give us all courage and that one day this war will end.'

Solveig got up, thanked the lady, and walked back out into the street. It was hot and sunny. There were a few wisps of clouds in the clear blue sky, and birds singing in the tall trees lining the street. The gardens were vibrant with flowers, and the smell of freshly mown grass suffused the air. All this was lost on Solveig, who stared down at the dusty gray slabs of pavement with occasional patches of tar melting in the heat.

A gust of wind unfurled a red flag in one of the gardens. It contained a black swastika encircled in white, and on the garden wall in broad brushstrokes, which had trickled down to the pavement were the words DEATH TO ALL COLLABORATORS.

* * * *

Solveig took the tram back to Karl Johans Gate then set off to the police headquarters at Mollergata, but when she came to the entrance she nearly ran away. The doors were open, but there were two policemen on either side. She was not sure from their black uniforms if they were police or Gestapo, but when she overheard them speaking in Norwegian and saw that they did not have red swastika armbands, she decided to continue. She hunched her shoulders as if that would make her less visible and walked in the ample space between them.

'Stop. No entry,' shouted the younger of the two.

Solveig knew she would be stopped but still jumped. When she turned around, her face had gone red and her legs shook.

'I, er, I need to find my father,' she mumbled.

'Go home. Children aren't allowed here.'

'But he works here.'

'Then he'll be busy.'

'Please help me,' she said as her face crumpled and tears streamed down her cheeks.

'Hey, Per,' said the other policeman, who looked as if he should have been retired long ago. 'You've upset her now. She's only a kid.' He bent down and smiled.

'Hey, don't cry,' he said as he produced a hanky and handed it to her. 'Why have you come to the police, and where's your mother?'

'My father works here, but he hasn't come to see us for over a month. My mother doesn't care; no one cares except me, and I know he wouldn't just leave us.'

'What's his name?'

'Johannes Marius Halversen,' said Solveig proudly.

'Oh, Johannes,' said the older man to himself. 'He's your dad, is he?'

'Do you know him?'

'Know him? He's one of the best police inspectors I've had the honor to know.'

Solveig beamed. 'My father.' She nodded.

'No, we haven't seen him for a while now. We never know what assignments they have been on. He might have been sent somewhere, but we wouldn't know.'

The younger policeman, who had been pacing up and down the hallway just inside the door, vigilant to people passing outside and inside, joined in their conversation.

'I heard someone say they thought Johannes was working for the resistance. But there have also been rumors that he was a Nazi spy.'

'Shush, someone might hear,' said the older man. 'No one knows whose side anyone is on. I try to keep out of it all and just do my duty.'

'It's too dangerous to do anything else,' said the younger man. He bent down to Solveig and spoke softly. 'Your father is a good man. No one thinks he was a spy. But if anyone in the resistance is caught and not killed by the Gestapo, they would be arrested and taken to Falstad Prison, up north.'

'I know he's not a Nazi spy and I know he's not dead,' said Solveig as she struggled to keep more tears at bay. She wiped her eyes fiercely. 'Falstad Prison? Where's that?'

'Way up north somewhere, who knows?' replied the young man, shrugging his shoulders.

'How do you know about Falstad?' said the older policeman.

'It's surprising how much you can learn when you have to accompany prisoners to and from Grini.'

'Grini?' said Solveig. Like everyone else in Oslo, she had heard of the horrors of nearby Grini Prison, where political prisoners were tortured, starved, and held in solitary confinement.

'They don't send policemen to Grini. If he was arrested, he'd go to Falstad Prison all right. But it's hard to know anything. You should just go home and see what your mother says,' said the older policeman.

Solveig wiped her nose on the hanky and handed it back to the older policeman.

'Thank you,' she said. 'I know my father is safe and I'm going to find him.' She held herself upright and walked out of the police station, screwing her eyes as she came out into the sunlight.

Inside the two policemen resumed their posts on either side of the entrance.

'She'll be lucky,' said the older one. 'I hope her mother sorts her out for her own sake.'

'She's just a kid. She probably boasts like that all the time,' said the younger one as his attention moved to the cleavage of a young woman in a tight summer blouse passing by on the other side of the street.

CHAPTER 21

Later the Same Day

Solveig came home much later than her normal time, and her mother and sister had already started supper. Solveig's food was congealing on her plate, laid out on the table.

'And where have you been?'

'Sorry I'm late. I, er, I—'

'I have been worried sick,' said Maria.

'I went home with Ragnhild,' said Solveig. It could easily have been true.

'Really? Well, I phoned their house and her mother said you had not been there at all today.'

Solveig went bright red and sat transfixed, staring at her mother as if dumbstruck.

'I am waiting for an explanation. It better be good!'

'I . . . I, er, just went for a walk.'

'I don't believe you. If you don't tell me the truth, there will be no supper tonight or breakfast tomorrow.'

'But I haven't had anything to eat today.'

'Well, then . . .' After another long silence, Solveig stammered as she started to tell her story.

'How did you know where your father is staying?'

'Papa told me,' she lied.

'He had no business telling you where his girlfriend lives.'

'There was a really nice lady in the flat above, and she told me that they might have been arrested,' said Solveig before recounting the rest of the story.

'It could have been anything. It could have been some of his police colleagues collecting him to go out on a call and his girlfriend might have just been shouting at him because she was annoyed,' said Eva.

'Yes, but she has disappeared as well,' said Solveig.

'We don't know that, do we?' said Eva. 'She might have gone away on holiday, or gone to stay with relatives somewhere. Lots of people are doing that these days.'

'Maybe they met up afterward and have gone over to Sweden together. That's what I think. What does he care about us?' said Maria.

'No, I know he's gone. He's gone to Falstad Prison.'

'What makes you say that?'

'Um . . .' said Solveig, starting to stammer again, 'I don't know. Someone at school said they knew someone who was arrested and sent there.' Solveig looked down at the floor as she said this, and Maria peered at her suspiciously.

'What nonsense. Someone is filling your head with rubbish.'

'No, Papa has been arrested and no one cares!' Solveig burst into tears and ran to her room.

'I don't know what she's been doing, but she's been up to something. She's such a hopeless liar,' said Eva.

'She's so childish for her age. She's probably making it all up to get more attention, and now she hasn't eaten her food.' Maria got up wearily and walked down to Solveig's room. She knocked on the door and after a few more moments of crying, Solveig emerged.

'Come on. Come and eat supper. I queued all day today and managed to get some lamb and extra potato,' said Maria. 'You have to eat. Come on.' Solveig followed her mother back to the kitchen and sniffed as she sat back up and started to eat her food.

'Poor little Solveig,' said Maria in a softer voice than normal. Solveig ate every morsel of food on her plate, even though it had gone cold. The lamb was fatty but tasted delicious after a week of fried, salted, or pickled herrings. Solveig chewed on it for a long time and, when her mother had her back turned, wiped up the last of the gravy with her fingers.

⋆ ⋆ ⋆ ⋆

The next morning Solveig walked to school as usual. In class Mrs. Ostby got them to open their schoolbooks to the page they had studied the previous day. When she asked them to produce their homework, Solveig did not even bother to look for hers. Usually the teacher would tell her off, but after the exchange of correspondence two days before, she had decided to ease up. She did not want any more of Mrs. Halversen's unpleasant letters.

Usually Solveig was lively in class and asked too many questions, but she spent the lesson just staring out of the window. The teacher assumed that she was still upset about the fight she had had with Petter Stavig. He was back to his usual boisterous self despite some residual swelling and bruising around his nose. The class was busy and she had no more time to reflect on Solveig or Petter as the lesson went on.

At the end of the morning session, Solveig went up to her teacher and asked her if she knew where Falstad Prison was. When she asked her why she wanted to know, Solveig said that a neighbor had said that her son had gone there. Mrs. Ostby told Solveig she had never heard of it, did not know if it existed, and advised her to ask in the library.

As soon as school was over, Solveig heaved her rucksack over her shoulders and went straight to the library. When she got there, she went over to the librarian and asked her about Falstad Prison. The librarian frowned and went to look for her colleague upstairs. They whispered together for a while and the other one came down.

'Why do you want to know where Falstad Prison is?'

'My father has been sent there.'

'Who told you that? You could get arrested for spreading false information, or your mother could anyway.'

Solveig looked so disappointed that the second librarian beckoned her to come with her into the office. 'I *have* heard of it. There is a prison by that name near Levanger, which is up near Trondheim, and you're right, political prisoners are sent there. But you must not tell anyone I told you that.'

'Why not?' replied Solveig

'Don't ask. There are people working everywhere who know a lot more than anyone realizes. Shush.' The librarian raised her finger to her lips.

'Thank you.' Solveig repeated the names of the places to herself as she went to the maps section and took out an atlas that was so large she could hardly carry it. She went through the towns at the back and after some time found the page. She spent about an hour looking at different pages and writing down the names of the places and some other names in her school notebook. She worked out that Levanger was some way north of Trondheim, which was some five hundred kilometers north of Oslo.

That evening Maria was meeting her friend Mr. Edvard Gregersen. Maria left a note asking Eva to heat up the little bit of lamb and potato she had saved up from the previous day, mix it with some thinly sliced swede, and fry it up in some lamb dripping. Eva told Solveig that she had no intention of cooking up the swede and that Solveig could have her food as she was not hungry. Solveig had wondered if Eva was on a diet because she was starting to look a bit fat around her tummy, and Solveig knew how much Eva liked to be slim.

Eva and Solveig carried on like that for another week, with Maria out every night and leaving notes next to bits of food in the fridge. She came in long after both the girls had gone to bed and was still asleep when they got up in the morning. She would then go straight out again to join queues, look for bargains in dress shops, and meet her boyfriend.

Eva cooked potatoes and fish or meat scraps but omitted the vegetables. In the wooden rack in the corner, the cabbage wilted, gnarled roots of parsnip turned brown, and the turnip developed soggy black spots. Half a packet of war mince went dark brown and mottled with furry blue areas. Whenever the fridge was opened, the kitchen would fill with its pungent odor. Maria left increasingly angry notes which Eva screwed up and threw down the rubbish shoot and finally a note telling Solveig to take the whole lot to her aunts' pig in Blommenholm and that if they wanted any more food, they would have to get it themselves.

During that week Solveig would make a detour past the railway station on her way home from school. She would stop and check the lay of the land as far as guards and ticket collectors were concerned. She had no money and no pass, so she had to get past the ticket collector without being seen. She checked out the times the train to Trondheim set off and noticed that there was usually a queue and often women traveling with small children. Sometimes there were men and women with large amounts of luggage.

She went to the library several more times and took out atlases and made notes in tiny writing at the back of a school exercise book. She abbreviated names of places along the way and wrote the numbers of miles between places, calculated using a piece of thread she had taken from her mother's sewing box and measuring it between places and against the scale just as she had been taught at school. The librarians assumed she was doing a project and helped willingly.

She had pretended to be unwell and developed a false cough so that when she was away from school for a couple of days, her teacher would not suspect. When the teacher asked her for a note from her mother, she pretended she had forgotten it at home. Mrs. Ostby was happy to leave things as they were. Solveig had walked around the station several times looking for different approaches. After several days, she felt ready to go. She would travel on a school day as her mother would not suspect anything until after she was due home, by which time she would be well on her way.

The night before she set off she took all her schoolbooks out of her rucksack and hid them under her bed. She replaced the books with two extra cardigans, a shirt, a spare pair of trousers, some socks and underwear, and some pieces of bread she had wrapped in a dishcloth and hidden under her bed. She packed her smallest doll, Topsy, at the bottom, and at the top were her exercise book and a couple of pencils. She took the photo of her parents and sisters, which was taken when she was a baby, out of its frame, hid the frame under her bed, and after tearing out a page, put the photo in her exercise book. She wrote a note, folded it and put 'To Mama' on top.

She got ready for bed as usual and lay under her duvet looking out at the sky. It was summer and the sky was gray, the light barely fading after the sun reluctantly tipped below the horizon. She did not sleep at all that night. The train to Trondheim was due to set off at eleven fourteen.

CHAPTER 22

Monday

July 5th, 1943

The 11:14 to Trondheim

Early the next morning, after rushing out of the house before even Eva was up, Solveig arrived at the station. She walked up and down the street outside the station, repeatedly checking the clock and making a note of the people and guards. At ten o'clock she walked in and spent some time looking at the magazines in a small wooden kiosk just inside the station, then she sat on a chair and pretended to read her book.

Over the next hour several people came to the terminal for the eleven-fourteen to Trondheim. There was an elderly man with a large suitcase and some cages with chickens on a trolley, together with a wooden crate of vegetables. There was a young woman kissing her boyfriend and crying. About half an hour before the train was due to leave, a woman came in with two children, one baby in an oversized pram and a boy no more than about three. The woman looked harassed and had difficulty keeping hold of the boy. A station guard helped her carry her two bags. She sat down, took her baby out of the pram, and shouted to her boy as he ran off across the station. When he returned, she slapped him and grabbed hold of his hand so tightly he cried again.

At eleven o'clock another guard went to the entrance to the platform and indicated to them to come on to the platform. Solveig waited until they had formed a queue and chose a moment when the ticket collector was talking to the elderly man about his baggage and the other guard was hoisting the woman's two suitcases. She slipped in between the trolley with the chickens and the woman and went on the other side of a couple of people who were queuing. The young man was waving goodbye to the young woman who was keeping her hand outstretched, trying to hold on to him for as long as possible. The little boy, who had managed to wrench his hand free, ran up to the chickens making clucking noises, then fell over and grazed his knees. His mother put the baby in the pram, pushing aside some clothes and shopping bags and ran over to him. He cried loudly as she picked him up.

'*My car!*' he shouted.

'There it is,' said the old man, pointing under his cart. He bent over stiffly then knelt down to retrieve it. 'Here,' then to the little boy's mother, 'he's a fine young lad, reminds me of my grandson.'

'Thank you,' she replied, then said to her son, 'Say thank you.' The little boy just buried his face into his mother's skirt. 'Sorry, he's shy.'

'Ha, no one wants to talk to strangers these days. He's quite right!'

'You can't take that cart on the train!' bellowed the guard.

'But how else can I take all my things?' replied the old man. The ticket collector explained that they could store the cart for him. The old man groaned and heaved his cargo onto the platform. As he started loading it, the young man who had just waved one last kiss to his girlfriend came to help him.

The woman was now pushing the heavily laden pram with one hand and gripping her son's with the other. The other guard followed behind with their suitcases. In all of this melee, Solveig managed to hide behind the old man's things and creep onto the platform unnoticed. She crouched down near the cart as it was being unpacked.

Very soon more people were milling about on the platform. The train drew up and as the young man was helping the old man load the last of the wooden crates onto the guard's van at the end, she jumped on. The old man saw her but showed no reaction. The guards were busy with the luggage and collecting the last tickets as two young women ran onto the platform out of breath. They had barely managed to get on when a loud whistle went off.

Once the train was up to full speed, Solveig walked down the corridor. The first carriage was full. In it the old man was clutching his chest and breathing fast. He took a silver tablet case out of his pocket and, without looking down, took a white tablet out. He placed it under his tongue and stared right at Solveig. The young man next to him tried to help, but he just laid his head back and indicated for him to sit down again before closing his eyes.

Solveig carried on down until she found a carriage that had a couple of free seats. She got in and sat on the edge of her seat, keeping her bag on her lap, and turned to look out of the window. Tall ornate buildings gave way to wooden houses with larger gardens, which soon gave way to open countryside. There were endless rows of fir trees and silver birch with delicate branches and slender trunks so close together that only a fox would be able to squeeze through. Gradually the flat expanses came less often and low black hills rose gently in the distance. The train passed long thin islands in lakes and fjords, occasional clusters of red farm houses, gently rising fields, and more stretches of spindly silver birch and thick pine forest.

As the journey continued, there were fewer fields, more patches of forest, which were getting thicker and darker, while the hills were getting steeper and closer. Every now and again there would be a grass embankment covered in tall pink and blue lupines. The train droned on for hours. Solveig left the carriage several times to put her head out of the open window across the corridor. Her face became sooty and her hair tangled and flecked with tiny bits of white ash. She had been offered some food by the young women in her carriage but having been brought up to be proud and not accept charity, she had declined even though she was ravenous. She ate half of her own sandwich as soon as she could without appearing to be desperate. That would have to do for lunch.

Every now and again the train stopped but not many people got on or off. There were flags with swastikas over the railway buildings, but apart from that everything looked peaceful and normal. The scenery blurred into one never ending scene for Solveig as she dosed and day dreamed through the long hours of the journey.

Shortly before they were due to arrive in Trondheim, she awoke with a start as the train stopped at a tiny station. Solveig looked at the sign: HEIMDAL. She had no idea where this was. She heard shouting and a couple of Norwegian policemen came onto the train. Solveig's two carriage companions brought out their tickets and travel passes. She sat up, pulled her bag off the floor, ran down to the toilet, and locked the door. Outside it was quiet for a moment, then the commands and footsteps of the policemen got louder. She held her breath and put her fingers in her ears.

There was a loud knocking on the door. She stood up on the toilet and tried the window. It was barely big enough to put her bag through, let alone her whole body. The knocking got louder.

'If you don't come out, we'll break down the door.' Solveig crouched against the wall and covered her head with her arms. 'Stand back or you will get hurt!' There was a huge crashing noise as one of the policemen shouldered the door then kicked it. After a moment, the door cracked open. Solveig was crouched between the wall and the toilet, with her arms covering her head. She raised her head just enough to peer over at the intruders.

'What are you doing in there?' shouted one of the policemen.

Solveig was mute.

'Where are your travel documents?' said the other.

Then as there was still no answer: 'You better come with us.'

One of the policemen dragged her out of the train while the other one took her bag and emptied the contents out onto the dusty concrete of the platform. Solveig's notebook and pencils dropped out.

'What's this?' said the first policeman, looking at the last page of the notebook with its initials and numbers. 'It looks like a code,'

'Shameful. The resistance are even using children as messengers these days,' said the other policeman as he scrutinized the notes. 'Who gave you this notebook? Who are you meeting?'

'It's my own notebook from school,' said Solveig, 'and I am going to see my grandparents.'

'What does TT11.14 mean, and why has it got *Falstad Prison* here?'

'Our teacher told us about it.'

'You expect us to believe that?'

Behind the policemen she saw the young man who had helped with the cages and crates being held by the guard of the train. His hands were handcuffed behind his back.

'Are you with him?' said the policeman.

'No,' said Solveig

'Is she helping you?' he said to the young man.

'No, I don't know her at all.'

'I'll believe that when I see it,' said the guard.

The old man came out of the train and walked down to the guard van. He ignored the small gathering of policemen and their detainees and started to unload his crates and cages, stopping to catch his breath as he did so. He kept looking toward the entrance of the station. As he was unloading the last crate, a woman dressed in baggy trousers, muddy brogues, and a head scarf came running toward him with two teenage boys. They embraced and the boys started to carry the luggage. The old man picked up one of his suitcases, then staggered for a few steps, clutching his chest and collapsed.

The woman ran toward him with a cry and the two boys dropped their loads and ran over. The old man was pale with perspiration pouring down his face. He managed to sit up with the lady's help. He was crouching forward with both his arms folded in front of his chest. The woman loosened his collar and looked in his coat pockets. The old man fumbled in his inner coat pocket and brought out his pillbox. He was just about to open it when he had another spasm of pain and dropped it. He went limp and the woman struggling to hold him and retrieve the tablets shouted for help. The guard left Solveig and ran off to the station office. The policemen left their prisoner and ran over to the old man.

As soon as their backs were turned, the young man made a dash for the railway tracks. He jumped down and ran between the tracks, bending forwards as his hands were still handcuffed behind his back.

'*Come back!*' shouted one of the policemen.

The other one got up and as they chased after him, one of them fired his gun. They disappeared farther along the track and two more shots were heard. There was more shouting and a final shot, followed by a yell from the young man who collapsed over the rails. The passengers looking out of the windows of the train were motionless, as were the family of the old man who was starting to regain color.

Solveig, who had gone into a trance when she was arrested, now came to. She scooped her clothes and notebook back into her bag and ran across the platform through the station buildings and out onto the road. She ran up the main street, which had only a couple of shops and a few white painted houses, and keeping close to the fence she turned off the into a narrow track with fields on either side.

As soon as she came to some trees, she climbed over the fence and hid. The trees were close together and it was dark inside, so no one could have seen her from the road. She wrapped her arms around her knees and caught her breath. She listened for engine sounds, footsteps, or shouts. After a few minutes, she heard a car engine grow louder then recede. She held her breath and drew herself into a tighter ball around her bag. The car drove past slowly, and she could see the policemen looking out. They carried on driving until they came to the nearby farm, then returned to their car after speaking to a woman there. As they drove past her hiding place again, Solveig held her breath and closed her eyes. The engine receded and this time she heard no more. She waited for ages to be sure, then shivered. It was late afternoon and still light and sunny, but she was sitting in dense shade on damp moss with pine needles. She was hungry, freezing cold, and scared.

She took her doll out of the bag and sat her down on her lap.

'We have to be really strong. We have to find Papa.' She nodded her head then put Topsy back in her bag. She brushed the pine needles off her trousers and cardigan and climbed out of the copse. She walked back to the center of the village and onto the main road. It was quiet now. She looked up at a clock over the village hall—a large wooden house painted dark yellow—and noted that it was getting on for six o' clock. It was still bright and sunny and would stay like this for hours yet.

She walked on the road leading away from the station and found a signpost. It was twelve kilometers to Trondheim. She checked her scribbled notes which said it was another forty-eight kilometers from Trondheim to Levanger and nearby Ekne, where Falstad prison was. She kept her eyes on the road, not noticing the soft curves of the fields or the dark hills reflected in streaks of purple with pale blue and white over the inlets of the fjord.

CHAPTER 23

Later the Same Day

Trondheim

Solveig kept walking as the road meandered through steep hills giving way to flat, wide fields with misty gray hills in the distance. The farms were larger now with white houses and huge dark red barns nearby. Occasionally cows grazed and she even saw a moose running toward the woods at the top of a long golden field. Sometimes the road would go right next to a lake and she could go across long grass and drink some water. She stopped for a picnic in a cluster of trees and ate a squashed piece of bread with a smear of margarine and scrape of red currant jam. She was able to check the signs to Trondheim when she went through the many tiny villages dotted around there. No one thought anything of a girl of her age walking along the road that late in the evening. Children often had to run errands for their parents, many of whom were farmers or tradesmen and had extra work to do.

Eventually she came to the outskirts of Trondheim. The sky was turning faintly mauve on the horizon with a couple of golden-edged clouds, and her shadow was long. There were wooden houses up and down hills with views across the huge expanse of fjord around which the city nestled. Although it was nearing midnight, people still walked up and down the street, older children cycled past, couples walked slowly arm in arm. People had scuffed shoes, bare feet, wooden sandals with thick bands of newspaper nailed so they were secure, frayed sleeves, patched knees of trousers, children with clothes that were too tight or much too large, many worn at the cuffs with mismatched buttons and holes in the elbows. Solveig in her baggy sweater, grimy trousers, and dusty socks blended in perfectly. No one noticed such an ordinary sight as a little girl trudging slowly, late at night, carrying a heavy bag and looking scared.

She needed to go through the center so she could find her directions toward Levanger. She carried on down the cobbled streets toward the docks where she hoped to find a shed or somewhere she could sleep for a few hours. She walked past bars, restaurants, many of which were full of German soldiers drinking and talking loudly, their arms around local girls. The shops were closed and boarded up for the night. On a few she saw old graffiti, on others yellow paint with remnants of stars and No Jews signs. Some had broken windows and others had flags with swastikas outside. All these were familiar sights to a girl from Oslo.

She walked into the dock area. Across the wide fjord, there were small boats moored to a wooden jetty, larger ships anchored off shore, and further out were a couple of grey battle ships with German flags and soldiers on guard on deck. The water looked dark, opaque, with glints of pink and purple reflecting the heavy sky in the distance. Solveig walked farther in and eventually saw some rowing boats set ashore with tarpaulins over them. They were in a deserted area and, looking both ways, she lifted the corner of one of the covers. It peeled back easily and there was plenty of space. She could smell the tar on the thick ropes coiled inside and a musty seaweed smell, but it was clean. She climbed inside and put back the cover. In her bag, she had saved a small piece of bread, and although it was hard and dry, she bit into it hungrily. She finished it all and, after putting on a spare sweater and extra socks, went to sleep curled around her bag with Topsy tucked into her sweater.

* * * *

The next morning she was woken by two fishermen. She blinked as they tore back the cover of the boat.

'What? What's going on here?' said one roughly.

'Looks like a runaway,' said the other. Solveig clutched her bag closer to her, got hold of her red rag doll, and looked for an escape route.

'What are you doing here?'

'Please don't tell the police I'm here.'

'The police? Are you in trouble?'

'No, it's just that I have run away from home and the police nearly caught me at Heimdal Station.'

'Why have you run away from home?'

'My father is lost and I want to find him. He's at Falstad Prison and my mother and sister don't care and they both *hate* me,' she said, her face crumpling as she was no longer able to hold back her tears.

'I don't think a little girl like you should be going to a prison. Once people are lost, they are lost. No one ever finds them. Nothing good ever happens in this blasted war.'

'Everyone says that. I don't care what anyone says; I am going to find him.'

'Hey, Olaf,' said the other fisherman, 'now look what you've done. You've made her cry.'

'Don't cry. Shush, shush,' said Olaf. 'Don't . . . er, look, who knows what anyone should do?'

Solveig wiped her nose on her sleeve and listened.

'We just mind our own business,' continued Olaf, 'so what you do is up to you. I suppose if you can make it this far, you're grown up enough to carry on.'

Olaf helped Solveig out of their boat. 'I guess a traveler like you could do with some breakfast. Want some?' Solveig nodded cautiously. Olaf took two massive pieces of bread with cheese out of his backpack and handed one to her.

'Thank you,' said Solveig as she sat down beside the two men. She ate ravenously and both men laughed.

'She's got an appetite almost as good as yours,' said Olaf. When Solveig and the fishermen had finished eating, she asked them the way to Levanger. They pondered this for a while, arguing between themselves before they managed to agree on a route. Basically, she wanted to go over a couple of bridges, follow the docks until she got to the main road, which should then be signposted. Solveig repeated the directions back to them a couple of times and after she waved them goodbye kept repeating the directions to herself until she had learned them off by heart. She checked her book. It was forty-eight kilometers to Levanger.

She set off more cheerily than the day before and found the main road. The streets were quite busy now as people went to work. It was a sunny day and, concentrating hard on her directions and wary of police cars, Solveig had not paused for a moment to reflect on what she had left behind at Kristian IV Gate.

CHAPTER 24

Oslo

Monday

July 5th, 1943

While Solveig was walking to Trondheim, Eva was having a humdrum day at work, and Maria was out with Edvard Gregersen.

She had instructed Eva to make sure Solveig had supper and to look after her until she got back. Maria had spent most of the day getting ready for her date: putting tucks in her jacket so it showed off her slim waist, using oil to hide scuff marks on her black high heels, and making an invisible mend in a seam in her ivory blouse. She had sold her amber beads months ago, but she had Eva's red silk scarf which she folded as a neck tie. She spent ages adjusting her clothes and applying mascara eked out with charcoal from old matches and using some cochineal food dye she had found at the back of the cupboard to color her lips. As she clicked down the main street, she held her head and shoulders high with the haughty stare of a woman who knows she looks stunning. She braced herself knowing that today she would have to end it with Edvard. The night before she had allowed him to kiss her, hoping that she would warm into his embrace, but she had been left cold. She had pulled herself away and pretended she was ill.

Eva came home from work at the normal time and because Solveig was often out late playing with her school friends, she had not been concerned when Solveig was not there for supper. She took the last of the bread and cut a thick slice of salami. Maria cut slices so thin they were almost translucent, but Eva relished something more substantial. Maria had been softer on her than usual, maybe because of their row, or maybe because she was pregnant. With that thought, she cut herself another generous slice and ate it without anything else.

Her feet ached from standing in the shop all day, and she was sure that if she smiled one more time at a customer her cheeks would get stuck forever. Her arms were tired from unrolling meters of fabric only to roll them up again, and occasionally, when a customer finally found something they wanted, measuring and cutting the required length. The most exhausting thing was having to say how lovely the material was, what a good choice, and how well they suited the lady. She could feel how they looked down on her; they with their parties to dress for and their rich husbands or boyfriends. Many of her customers were German women, wives of officers and administrators, who could afford the opulent materials. They took no interest in her; after all, in their eyes she was only a shop girl.

Eva had never felt invisible before. The experience of people looking straight through her as if she did not exist was strange. She had never imagined how other shop girls had felt, as she had never looked at them or thought about them herself. She was no different from the ladies who came into the shop, she thought.

Occasionally, when one of her customers was accompanied by a man, husband, boyfriend, lover, or who knew what, she was aware of becoming visible again. Despite the pink overall jacket she had to wear, the men would inevitably peer at her intently, averting their eyes when their lady friends turned toward them. Eva knew that she was nothing but a shop girl to them as well—but with the potential to gratify certain desires before being quickly discarded. Eva had become wary of men and on the rare occasion one of them ignored her and was totally attentive to his lady friend, she felt glad to know there were exceptions.

Her boss was one of those. She was grateful for his kindness and easygoing humor. He treated her like a daughter and took an interest in what she had to say. They often commiserated about life in Oslo under the swastika. He was an efficient businessman, insisting that he had to "sell to everyone" to earn his living and have enough to pay his staff, all two of them. He also insisted that he did not exclude Jewish women, although some of his shopkeeper friends had started to do that. Signs saying No Jews were almost universal. The shopkeepers did this in order to allay the risk of their windows being smashed and to avoid visits from officious German soldiers questioning their backgrounds, or worse. But he had his limits, and would rather go to prison and sell up his business than collaborate this way with the Nazi regime. There would be no Nazi signs on his shop window. But the German women, they had not done him any harm, and he needed their patronage.

Eva mused on her day, ruminated about her mother and all the rows they kept having despite her mother seeming more able to acknowledge her problems. As soon as those thoughts cleared, the ever-present worry of the life growing inside her returned. Soon it would be obvious and she would have to tell her boss. She still wondered if she should have an abortion. It was not too late, and she had managed to save half the money she would need. But it scared her. She could not imagine having a baby. How on earth would she look after it? But she could not bear the thought of giving her baby away to someone else, although they might be able to give her baby a better life. Maybe she should give her baby to someone—but what if the Nazis heard about it and took it to Germany? Would her baby have to become one of them? She shuddered at the thought.

She never thought about the father. This baby had nothing to do with those soldiers. Her baby was beautiful and it belonged to no one but her. She was surprised how she already felt attached to this little being inside her. She knew that even though there was no way she could look after a baby, she could not kill it either. She would just have to find a way.

Exhausted after a hard day's work and absorbed in her own problems, she curled up on her bed and fell asleep.

*   *   *   *

Shortly after midnight Maria returned. She was drained. It had taken her all evening to tell Edvard that there was no future in their relationship, and then it had taken a long time for her to manage, as his initial pleadings turned to anger.

She came into the silent flat, turned on the hall light, and went in to check on Solveig. No Solveig. Maria pulled back the covers on the bed and checked under it. She ran into the lounge and checked the settees and under the table. No Solveig. She checked the kitchen, but still, no Solveig. She must be in with Eva. Maria flung open Eva's door and put on the light, but all she could see was Eva curled up in bed asleep.

'Eva, wake up. Where is Solveig?'

Eva roused herself and sat up. 'What do you mean where is Solveig?'

'You were looking after her today.'

'What? Well, I haven't seen her. I thought that she would be with Ragnhild as usual and would let herself in.'

'Oh my god, I've been out with Edvard and just got back.' She stopped to think. 'Do you know where her friend lives?'

'No.'

'Her surname?'

'Yes, it's Blom.' Maria ran to the phone and asked the operator to put her through. The phone rang for several minutes.

'Hello?'

'It's Mrs. Halversen. I am sorry to phone you so late. I am Solveig's mother and I wondered if Solveig was staying the night.'

'No, no, she's not.'

'Are you Ragnhild's mother?'

'Yes, and I know Solveig very well. She's a lovely girl. Ragnhild hasn't seen her for a few days now. I thought she'd been ill.'

'Oh, I see.'

'Is everything alright?'

'I'm sure we'll find her. Maybe she's gone to her aunt's. So sorry, I hope I haven't woken you.'

'I hope everything is all right. Good night.'

'Thank you. Good night.'

Maria went into Solveig's room and looked for her bag. It was gone. She looked in the wardrobe and noted that both her sweaters were missing. At the back of the wardrobe she saw the hidden dolls and noted that the smallest of the three was missing. 'Topsy,' she said to herself. She saw Solveig's letter where it had fallen onto the floor. She recognized the envelope as one from her locked writing desk. On the front, it said *To Mother*. She opened it up and read the pencil-written note.

Dear Mama,

I have gone to look for Papa. Everybody says he is a Nazi but I know he is not. A policeman who knows Papa told me they think he is in Falstad Prison. I want to live with Papa when he gets out of prison and I am never coming home again.

I am sorry.
Solveig

Maria came out with the letter and stormed down to the sitting room. 'Eva!'

Eva came out of her bedroom.

'Do you know anything about this?' said Maria, shoving the letter into Eva's hand. Eva read it and shook her head.

'No, I had no idea, honestly.'

'Do you think she's making this up?'

'Who on earth would know? She's always imagining things, so nothing would surprise me.'

Maria walked backward and forward and backward and forward to the window, opening the blackout curtains each time and peering down at the street below.

'She can hardly organize herself to get to school, let alone to some prison. Maybe she is sulking again and is hiding out somewhere. I'm sure she'll come back soon,' said Eva.

Maria phoned Else but Torhild answered and said she had not seen Solveig and Else was still away. Maria tried to phone Johannes at his girlfriend's, but the phone gave a disconnected signal. She took the phone and asked the operator for police HQ. When she got through, she demanded that they contact Police Inspector Halversen immediately, asked them what on earth they meant when they said that he did not work there anymore, accused them of deliberately concealing his whereabouts from his wife, and then screamed at the duty sergeant until he put the phone down on her.

She phoned the German headquarters and demanded to speak to Officer Wolff, but the duty telephonist said he would not be there until the morning; that, no, she could not send someone to his house; and, no, she could not tell a civilian his home address. The phone went dead as Maria swore and shouted down the receiver. How come no one was ever there when she needed them? Where could Solveig be at this time of night?

She threw on a cardigan and went for the door. Eva went to follow her but Maria said she should stay there in case Solveig came back. Maria ran off and knocked on every single door in the block of flats even though it was one in the morning. Some neighbors said they were sorry to hear that and would look out for her, some were annoyed at being woken with such loud knocks on their door that they were scared it was the Gestapo, and some just slammed the door in her face. Maria searched the courtyard and cellar and then went down the street calling for Solveig. She went all the way to Palace Park and back, to City Hall and the docks, and down all the nearby streets. Finally, she came home exhausted, her high heels and sheer stockings caked in mud, and her cheeks streaked with black mascara.

Eva came rushing out but Maria shook her head.

'I don't know what to do, she could be anywhere.'

Eva put her arm around her and led her into the kitchen.

'I'm sorry, Mama. I just thought she was at Ragnild's house as she is always over there these days.'

'It's not your fault, Eva. It's my fault for not knowing what was going on. I haven't really seen her for a whole week.

'I thought she was fine and that everything had settled after she gave that boy a nosebleed,' said Eva.

'Ha!' said Maria. 'He deserved everything he got. Calling Johannes a Nazi. The brat.'

'Good for her.' Eva smiled, then shivered. 'What are we going to do?'

'I don't know. I'll make some more phone calls in the morning and report her missing to the police if she hasn't got back. What else can we do?'

Maria went into the lounge and poured herself a large glass of home-brewed vodka which she had traded for an old coat of Eva's. She paced up and down the room, smoked, and poured herself several more glasses. She stood by the window, looking down one end of the street then the other. Where could she have gone? Where on earth was Falstad? There was no way Solveig could travel anywhere without any money. She could have drowned in Oslo Harbor, been run over, been taken by soldiers. Maria shuddered. Her mind was a riot of fear.

Outside there was the eerie light of midnight under a sheet of gray clouds. Footsteps came and went but none of them were Solveig's.

CHAPTER 25

Morning of Tuesday

July 6ᵗʰ, 1943

In the morning Maria stirred on the living room sofa. She shivered with cold and as she sat up, she groaned and clutched her head. She got a shawl from her bedroom and went into the kitchen for a glass of water. She had gone up and down to the window all night and checked Solveig's room so many times she knew every wrinkle of her duvet off by heart. She pulled some old boots on, went downstairs, checked the cellar and courtyard again, and peered down the street.

It was too early to phone anyone, so she brewed her coffee—or rather, the burnt dried peas—strained it into a small cup, and grimaced as she took a sip. She boiled a large kettle of water and took it into the bathroom. After several minutes of clanking and thumping from the pipes, she poured the contents of the kettle into the bath. Steam rose and filled the bathroom. She lay back in the pale brown water which barely covered her legs and closed her eyes. Where was Solveig? Where was Johannes? What was she going to do? And Eva, what was to become of Eva?

Maria dressed quickly, still shivering on this cold summer morning, and went back into Solveig's room. This time she was thinking more clearly and started an inch-by-inch search of Solveig's room. She discovered a library book under the bed. It was an atlas. She turned the pages over and saw some towns marked in pencil. *Trondheim. Levanger.* But they were miles away. She checked the wardrobe and noted that as well as her two cardigans, she had taken her old slacks and several pairs of socks and underwear. Solveig had packed for a journey all right.

Maria went to the phone and asked the operator to put her through to police HQ. The receptionist recognized her voice but was unable to get her off the phone until she promised to put Solveig on their missing persons list. Maria knew perfectly well that they had no intention of doing anything.

She dreaded the thought of discussing anything with her mother but phoned Bronnoysund anyway. After several long rings, she got through.

'Maria here, yes, I'm sorry, I know it is only six in the morning. It's an emergency. Just get Father, please. All right, all right, Solveig has disappeared, okay? For God's sake, *please*, just get Father. Yes, well, I am talking to you like this and I will keep ringing until I speak to him.'

When her father came to the phone, she burst into tears but managed to tell him what had happened between sobs. Her father repeated the names of the towns.

'She said in her letter she was going to Falstein or Falsborg Prison, or whatever the hell it is called. Oh, here it is,' she said, peering at Solveig's note which she had left by the phone. 'It's Falstad Prison.'

'I think she's clever enough to get there. I'll phone you back when I've found out more.'

Maria paced backward and forward, looking down to the street every few seconds, going into Solveig's room and checking the cupboards and under the bed, then rushing back into the sitting room thinking she had missed the phone.

After a few minutes, which had seemed like hours, Maria's father phoned her back.

'I have found out where Falstad Prison is.'

The phone whirred.

'Hello?' said Maria, then after the whirring was over: 'Where is it?'

'North of Trondheim,' he shouted as the phone crackled again.

'What?'

'Never mind. We'll sail down the coast.'

'Won't that be dangerous?'

'No, it's just another fishing trip.'

'What if she's not there? What if you can't find her?'

'She will be there and we will find her. We have to have faith.'

The line crackled again and Maria did not hear the last bit.

'Be careful. Thank you,' she shouted down the line.

'Bye,' shouted her father.

*　　*　　*　　*

Jorgen placed the receiver and sat in the chair, waiting for Ruth to come in. As if on cue, she appeared.

'So, what's going on? What does your favorite daughter expect you to do about Solveig?' she said in her kindest voice, as was her way when she was at her most annoyed.

'She thinks Solveig has run away to find her father.'

'Good god. How could Maria let her do that? I always said she was too lenient. And now she has a child that disobeys her and runs off. And as for that good-for-nothing husband of hers, well, so he's disappeared, has he? Good riddance.'

'Whatever Maria has done or not done, Ruth, Solveig is missing and we have to find her.'

'You mean Maria wants *you* to find her.'

'Yes, I am going to get two of my men and sail there. Apparently, the prison is very near a small harbor in Ekne village near Levanger, so if we set off after lunch we should get there tomorrow afternoon.'

'What? Are you crazy? You are letting your daughter make you risk your life? I can't believe how selfish she is.'

'That's enough, Ruth, I am going and nothing you can say will change my mind.'

'As if anything I say ever could,' said Ruth as she raised her head and glided out of the room.

Jorgen sighed. He usually gave way to Ruth's wishes, but his granddaughter was in danger and if there was any hope that he could find her, he would. He hastened himself to get prepared for the journey ahead.

★   ★   ★   ★

After Maria had finished her call to her father, she sat and imagined the ensuing conversation between her parents. It was bad enough having to tell her that Solveig was missing, but what about Eva's news? Maria shuddered at how her mother would react to Eva being pregnant. She felt her body caving in with exhaustion at the thought of the recriminations, the blame, the shouting, and the crying that would ensue; then all the guilt she would feel as her mother would retire to bed with terrible pains and breathlessness.

Sometimes Maria wished a heart attack would really kill her mother. But then she felt even guiltier and was overwhelmed with a sense of paralysis, the same feeling that she had had ever since she was a child. And, for all her mother's protestations of poor health, Maria did not really believe her. Her mother just wallowed in the attention it gave her. But then with another pang of guilt, Maria had to remind herself that the illness may be real, or at least partly real. Perhaps she was more critical of her mother than she should be, but that thought did not make her feel any less angry or any less weary. Maria felt as if all her energy had disappeared down a plughole and she was being sucked down into the void.

She shook her head. She steeled herself as she thought of the only other person she could think of who could help her. Herr Wolff. Why could she never free herself from this accursed man?

She phoned the German headquarters and despite the early hour managed to get through to him.

'Hello. Herr Wolff?'

'Hello, Mrs. Halversen, how can I help you?'

'Solveig has gone missing,' replied Maria and proceeded to tell him the story, finishing with 'Falbourg or Fastin Prison or something like that.'

'Ah, Falstad Prison, I know it.'

'Is my husband there?'

'I can't say, and even if I knew, I couldn't tell you.'

'You don't have to say anything Herr Wolff, but I know that you know where he is. I just know. If you don't answer my next question, I will take it that that is exactly where he is.' She paused and inhaled deeply. 'Is my husband in Falstad Prison?'

There was no answer. After a long pause, Maria said, 'I will draw my conclusions from that as I said.'

'Yes,' said Herr Wolff, 'you may draw your conclusions, but I have not told you anything.' He paused, drew a breath, and spoke more softly. 'It's been a while. How are you?'

'Just fine, thank you, Herr Wolff,' retorted Maria. 'One daughter is dead, one is pregnant, and the other has gone missing. How could I be happier?'

'I am very sorry, and sorry for my question. Eva is pregnant?'

'Thank you for your help, Herr Wolff. I have a daughter to find, so if you'll excuse me not wanting to chat about my private life, I need to get back to my search.'

'Of course. I hope you find her soon, Mrs. Halversen.'

* * * *

After they concluded their conversation, Herr Wolff called his secretary and told her to cancel all his meetings for that morning. He picked up the phone and asked the operator to put him through to Falstad Prison. The phone rang for several minutes.

'Hello, this is Officer Wolff; I need to speak to Governor Schmidt.'

The guard at the other end of the phone asked for his credentials and Herr Wolff gave them impatiently and demanded to speak to the governor again.

'He has given orders that he is not to be disturbed unless there is an emergency in the prison.'

'I can assure you this is very urgent and I must speak to him immediately.'

'He is still in his quarters, sir. It is seven and we don't expect him here until nine. Then he has meetings all morning.'

'Get him on the phone. That is an order.' The guard put Herr Wolff's call on hold and rang the governor's quarters. The governor had a house just outside the prison and was sitting at his desk with a large glass of whisky. Eventually he answered the phone.

'Yes, what?' he said angrily, slurring his words. The guard explained. 'Okay, put him through.' The governor waited a moment, then said, 'Good morning, sir.'

'I am looking for a girl who has run away from home. She might have tried to visit her father who is at Falstad prison. She is only ten years old, but we think she is traveling up there.'

'What is the name of the prisoner?'

'Police Inspector Johannes Halversen,' said Herr Wolff.

'I have not had any reports of a young girl looking for anyone. How would she know that he is here? If I do see her, I will have to arrest her.'

'She is only a child so you will not arrest her. You have to keep her safe.'

'We can't babysit for local Norwegian children. This is a prison.'

'Just keep her safe. Tell one of the nurses to look after her until I have her collected. I will deal with her then.'

'The nurses are too busy. I can't expect them to neglect their duties.'

'I expect you to keep me informed.'

'I don't take orders from you.'

'Who is your superior? I shall contact him right away. And, governor, it is obvious that you have been drinking.'

'I have not had a drink since last night when I was off duty.'

'It is obvious that you are drunk. You are in charge of a prison. You are never off duty. I shall have to report this. Now tell me where Inspector Halversen is.'

'With respect, Officer Wolff, what concern is that of the Wehrmacht? I take my orders from the SS.'

'You do not need to know, Governor Schmidt. It is classified and I am under orders from my superiors to have him taken back to Oslo for further questioning.'

'I will have to check this, sir.'

'Yes, of course,' said Herr Wolff, 'but I will have to report your behavior to your superiors.'

'Oh really?'

'I can assure you, friends tell me things, and there are friends who know how to make life uncomfortable for people who obstruct the activities of the Wehrmacht. I am sure you understand my meaning?'

Herr Wolff was bluffing, but he knew how things worked in the SS and in his own ranks, and he was confident that Governor Schmidt would be well warned.

'Mmm, let's see. It's not a name I remember.'

Governor Schmidt pulled some cabinet drawers in and out and opened a book of records. He pretended to be looking through them. If the prisoner had any information to give, it would come to him first. Good results helped him gain favor as far as promotion was concerned. He ran the prison his way and no one questioned him. That was the way he wanted to keep it.

If he said Johannes Halversen was there, the Wehrmacht might come sniffing around, interfering in things that were no concern of theirs. He knew that his superiors in the SS were not concerned about the high mortality rates or methods used to extract information. They were pleased with the results of his interrogations and the intelligence it produced. Yes, he was doing his bit for the Third Reich and did not need any outside interference.

'No, sorry, there's no record of him being here.'

'That's wrong,' said Herr Wolff. 'I know he was sent there. I have seen the records at headquarters.'

'They must be wrong, because he has never been here. Or maybe he tried to escape on his way here and had to be shot. It happens quite often.'

'There would be records of that then.'

'Well, not here. I'm sorry I can't help you.' Governor Schmidt could always blame his secretary for misfiling or misreading records if he needed to.

'If I find you are hiding something, I will make sure you pay. Heil Hitler,' said Herr Wolff.

'I'm sure you will. But if you don't mind, I have to get back to work. Oh, and I will have to tell the overmaster as this is highly irregular. Heil Hitler.'

Herr Wolff knew Governor Schmidt was lying about Johannes Halversen, but it was beyond his authority to do any more. He knew that the SS intelligence would be interested to know his connection to the prisoner. Johannes had been arrested for spying, obstructing the deportment of Jews from Oslo, and helping them escape. As such, Johannes was guilty of one of the worst crimes against the Third Reich, aiding and abetting Jews. Herr Wolff knew that if he was suspected of trying to help Maria's husband and was suspected of collaborating, he could be arrested for crimes against the Fuhrer, an offence which was punishable by death.

He swore and walked over to the window. *This accursed war.* Here he was exiled in this godforsaken country, fighting to make Germany conquer all. He had started to believe that the Third Reich was a fantasy in the mind of a man capable of unthinkable atrocities. He had heard rumors of executions on a scale never dreamt of. He had always thought that this was anti-German propaganda, but he had heard stories whispered behind closed doors which were harder and harder to dismiss. But he was a soldier and had to fulfill his duty to his country. It was not his place to question the judgment of his superiors.

Herr Wolff walked back to his chair and picked up the phone. He knew that Governor Schmidt would be only too pleased to report him and that the Gestapo would soon be on to him looking for any irregularities. And they would find them. Why stop now? After a couple of rings, the phone was answered by Maria.

'Mrs. Halversen? I am really sorry, but I am told there is no record of him having arrived at Falstad Prison.'

'What? What do you mean he's not there?'

'To tell you the truth, I know he was sent there and that the governor is lying to me. But I don't know if your husband is still there or even if he is still alive.'

'I have a good mind to go to the prison myself and demand to see him,' said Maria.

'You must not go there. They will immediately have you arrested as a fellow resistance fighter. And many resistance fighters are executed without a trial.

'God damn it, I hate this war. How am I going to find my husband?'

'I am very sorry, Maria, er, I mean, Mrs. Halversen. I think he must be dead. It is beyond my jurisdiction and there is nothing I can do.'

'Yes, I see.' Maria paused, then calming herself continued, 'Officer Wolff, I never thought I would have to be grateful to a Nazi, and no matter how much I hate that, I have to say that I know you have put yourself out for us and I have to thank you for that.'

'I have been honored to help you, Mrs. Halversen. I am sorry I have not been more successful.'

'Goodbye, Officer Wolff.'

'I wish we had met at another time and place. Goodbye, Maria. Good Luck.'

★　★　★　★

After the call Herr Wolff looked through the papers on his desk. There were reports on Norwegian resistance fighters, sightings by collaborators, and collected evidence. There were edicts from the Fuhrer giving orders as to how German soldiers should conduct themselves and instructions on positioning of troops and training. Herr Wolff was one of the few officers who read every word of every article which came his way. He ordered the notes and had his secretary file them so that he could easily find any information he needed. He would work out who he needed to meet and where, and what strategic plans would be made. His secretary helped him organize his diary and things ran smoothly. Occasionally, he was called to interrogate prisoners but usually he left this to the German police and other less senior officials, who would then report back. His main mission was to organize, deploy, and discipline the troops under his command, and he pursued this with total dedication and efficiency.

But today was different. He found himself yearning to see Maria again despite her eternally cool attitude to him. Even if Solveig had made it as far as Falstad and not had any kind of accident or mishap on the way, she might be discovered by guards and they would assume she was working for the resistance, and it would not be long until the SS would be on the trail of her mother.

He turned back to his paperwork but found himself looking past the papers to images of his wife and children, fading as they always did to that of Maria. He got up, paced toward the window, and went around his desk several times.

His secretary, who worked in an adjoining office, looked in through the open door and raised her eyebrows at him. He smiled at her.

'Yes, I know. I have to finish the report today, but'—he shook his head—'I can't even see the pages. I've got a migraine. No, I have to leave. Tell the general that it will be on his desk tomorrow.'

Herr Wolff gathered the papers he had been working on and put them in his briefcase. He also took the photo of his wife and children and, unlocking his drawer, took out a gun. He turned his back to the door and checked the gun for bullets, although he already knew it was loaded. He looked around the office where he had spent so many hours for so many months dedicated to the German army and to the machinations of the Third Reich.

When he was a young soldier, he had risked his life willingly and felt proud to do his duty. But now, in this brutal regime, with so many arrests, executions, and street killings, he had started to feel cheated of honor and defiled. If punishment was deserved that was one thing, but some of the people looked to him like ordinary folk. He used to believe the teachings against the Jewish people and had suppressed his own knowledge. But now he was haunted by images of families he had seen dragged out of their homes. Fathers, mothers, children, terrified into silence, or crying, begging to be freed. Seeing young men fleeing only to be shot, followed by increased wailing from the women and shouts of anguish from the men. He found he could no longer believe that Jewish people were any different. He had betrayed them by keeping silent and continuing to do his duty. He was an army man and his duty was to serve, but he could no longer separate himself from the actions demanded of him and of his soldiers. He felt he was imprisoned in a nightmare from which he would never wake, unless he was dead. He had had enough. He needed honor, even if it meant death.

He called his two loyal men and told them that they were to drive him up north on a secret mission, and that they would have to set off right away.

*   *   *   *

After her conversation with Herr Wolff, Maria phoned the railway station, noting how little time was left to pack. It was eight o' clock and she and Eva would have to catch the eleven-fourteen train to Trondheim. She looked in her purse. She had been saving for some black-market coffee for weeks but would have to spend it on a taxi, if she was lucky enough to get one. She looked for her and Eva's passports and set about waking Eva and packing. They would have to travel light.

She went to her bedroom and dressed in her smartest suit, her favorite silk blouse, the red scarf, and her highest heels. She applied her makeup with an extra smudge of cochineal food dye for lipstick. She pulled herself up to her full height in front of the mirror and tossed her head. There may be a war going on but she, Maria, had standards to keep.

She went in to check on Eva, expecting her to be dressed; instead she was writhing in her bed.

'Eva?'

Eva turned to answer, then caught her breath as a wave of pain came over her. She winced, curled up in a ball, and after a couple of moments released her grip and took a deep breath. Perspiration was running down the sides of her face and her hair was damp.

'Oh,' Maria said with a gasp as she worked out what was happening. She pulled the duvet back and, as expected, saw that the sheets were soaked in blood. This time she was not going to wait around for an ambulance. She went straight to the phone and called a taxi. There was no way anyone could stop her from taking Eva to hospital.

Eva went into another spasm and let out a shriek of pain. Maria rubbed her back and held her until it subsided.

'Eva, a taxi is on the way. We're going to Rikshospitalet. Put your dressing gown on.'

Eva did not reply as she contracted into a ball again. Maria rushed to the airing cupboard and took out several sheets and towels, then went downstairs to wait for the taxi. Very soon the driver had come up to help and they were on their way to Rikshospitalet, just ten minutes away on Pilestredet.

Maria told Eva to lie on the seat and bend her knees. She knelt between the seat and the back of the driver's area, gripping Eva's hand each time a spasm of pain came over her. She kept telling the driver to go faster and cursed every time they had to stop at a traffic light or were held up at a junction. The taxi driver shouted, hooted, and barged his way through, ignoring the blaring horns that greeted him in response. The only person who was quiet was Eva as she gritted her teeth and held her stomach. Finally, the taxi screeched to a halt in front of the emergency entrance and the driver rushed in to get help.

Maria helped Eva sit up and helped her out of the taxi as a couple of nurses came with a wheelchair. As they wheeled her off, Maria instinctively checked the back of the taxi and saw that there were no stains left on the seat. She paid the driver and ran after her daughter.

CHAPTER 26

Toward Levanger

Tuesday

July 6th, 1943

Solveig had already walked five kilometers by the time Eva and Maria had reached the hospital. She was well on her way toward the coastal road. It was another hot sunny day and she was in her blouse and summer skirt, all wrinkled from being in her bag. She watched for traffic and as soon as she heard an engine she hid in trees, or behind fences, or sometimes lay down in a dent in the ground or in long grass. Not many cars went past. There were a few tractors, and on one occasion several motor bikes. They sounded just like the German motorbikes she was always hearing in Oslo, but she did not dare look to check. She had eaten all her rations and had no water and no water bottle. She took a few detours down to the edge of some of the fjords to drink, had a few rests hidden in trees or grass, and would constantly check her notebook.

By mid-afternoon she was dragging herself along and had started to limp. She went off the road across a narrow strip of long grass into a wood. The trees were close together and it was dark inside despite the strong sunshine. She had just enough space to walk between the narrow tree trunks and find a mossy area where she took off her shoes and socks. A few blisters had broken and the congealed blood made her socks stick, so it hurt when she took them off. She squinted at her feet and rubbed them. There were large blisters on her heels and several of her toes were now bleeding. She pushed her toes and the soles of her feet into the cool, damp moss and, despite her hunger and fatigue, sighed with relief. She curled herself up into a little ball and fell asleep.

She was soon startled out of her drowsiness by the sound of motorbikes. She put on her spare socks and her shoes, tying the laces more loosely as her feet were now very swollen. Her stomach was gnawing with hunger and she felt dry. By the time she reached the next village, she could hardly walk and had stopped making any effort to hide if a car went past.

Walking out of a grocery store was a stout woman dressed in baggy trousers, sturdy boots, and a loose shirt. She shook the hand of the shopkeeper vigorously after he had counted some notes into her hand. A couple of young lads unloaded the last two metal urns of milk and a large sack of potatoes off the back of a wooden cart. She got up into the front of the cart and pulled the reins of a white and tan horse. Solveig limped toward the old lady and asked if she had some spare milk.

'That was my last delivery for today. Hey, are you all right?' she called as Solveig started to limp past. Solveig did not look up or answer but gripped her bag and kept walking.

The old lady shook the reigns and caught up with her in a few steps. 'Hey, where are you going? You look like you need a lift.'

'I'm looking for my father. He's in Falstad Prison,' she replied.

'Falstad Prison? That's no place for a young lady to be going.' Upon seeing Solveig's face, she added, 'Well, missy, you're in luck. I know all the farmers around here. My farm is near Levanger, but I can take you to a farm right next to Falstad. They have prisoners working with them. We all help out when we can. Here'—she took out a metal bottle and unscrewed the lid—'have some water.' Solveig turned the bottle up and glugged and glugged until it was empty.

'Sorry, I didn't mean to take it all,' said Solveig, looking scared.

The old lady laughed. 'Bless me. Don't worry. Blossom here is a strong old horse. She'll get us to Gustav's farm in a couple of hours. I think we'll survive.'

The old lady asked where she had come from and listened gravely while Solveig talked.

'There's nothing up at the prison, just a lot of barbed wire and German soldiers posted outside.'

'My father is there.'

'No one is allowed inside. Where are you from? You should get back home.'

'I'm not going back. My mother is horrible all the time. So is my sister. I hate them both.'

'I bet your mother loves you really. Did you have a row?'

'I'm just trying to find my father.'

'Lord bless you.' She crossed herself.

As soon as they were on their way, the old lady took some bread out of her bag. 'You look like you need some of this.' Solveig tore off several pieces and ate so fast that her cheeks bulged. As they continued, she became drowsy with the pleasant breeze, the distant cries of seagulls, the buzzing of flies, and the steady drum of hooves on hard mud, clattering more loudly on stretches of road.

The horse and cart ambled its way on dirt track roads, passing inlets from the fjords and various farms with their white wooden houses and dark red barns. Some of the fields were golden, and some pale green, flickering as wind swept over long grass with feathery tufts at the end. Some fields were stripes of bare earth and dark purple with seagulls dotting the lines. Every now and again crows flew overhead, their deep caws contrasting with the shrill cries of the gulls. There were banks pink with wild lupines and woods heavy with the fragrance of pine and damp earth.

At last they came to a white farmhouse gleaming in the sun: Gustav's Farm. The old lady climbed down from the cart, fastened the horse to a wooden fence leading to one of the barns, and called out. A young lad came out. She had a quick word and he went to the second barn to get his father. They shook hands and as the old lady spoke to him, he frowned and nodded. He looked sternly toward Solveig who was ready to run away if necessary. The old lady came back.

'He says you can stay here, but you will have to sleep in the barn. They already have his brother's family staying, and there are two other people staying in one of the barns. He says you are not to ask them any questions and not to talk to anyone. There are spies everywhere and no one can be trusted.

Solveig nodded. 'Can't I stay with you?'

'I wish you could, but I live too far away.' On seeing Solveig's stricken face, she added, 'Old Gustav isn't as bad as he looks. You'll be safe, I promise.'

Solveig nodded mutely as the old lady set off. She was just picking up her bag when the farmer's wife came out. She was wearing a large red apron, waterproof boots despite the heat, and a scarf tied around her hair. She was drying her hands on her apron.

'Hello, I am Gerda, and you are Solveig?' Solveig nodded, still mute. 'Come and give me a hand. You can tell me everything in there.' Solveig limped in after her and the farmer's wife peered back at her against the sun. 'You better let me have a proper look at you.'

They entered a long kitchen with a massive pinewood table and fourteen heavy wooden chairs. She told Solveig to take her shoes and socks off and climb up onto the table. Solveig obliged, pulling her socks off with great care as she gritted her teeth. Gerda bent down to inspect them.

'Mmm, they look bad.' She filled a basin with cold water and put it on the chair nearest Solveig and moved it over. 'You better let them soak in here.' She took a tea towel and rinsed it out. 'Here. Clean your face and hands on this and you'll be right as rain in a moment.' Solveig did as she was asked and handed a grimy cloth back to the farmer's wife, who laughed and threw it to one side.

'So, tell me why you are here,' she said as she pushed her elbows deep in hot, soapy water and wiped a seemingly endless number of plates with a worn-out sponge. Solveig continued her story as the farmer's wife started making pastries in a gigantic wooden bowl. Solveig had never seen so much flour.

'Dry your feet off, and let me get you some sandals. You need to let those feet heal in the open air.'

She wiped the dough off her hands and returned a moment later with some worn brown leather sandals. 'They're a bit big but they'll do.' She heaved up a basket, moving the handle up her arm and lifting it to rest on her hip. 'Let's get your message to one of the prisoners. They are waiting for the guard to escort them back to the prison, so we better be quick.'

Solveig did her buckles up very tight and found she could walk all right in them if she curled her toes hard down. She put her own shoes and remnants of socks back in her bag and put it over her shoulder.

As they went behind the house, Solveig saw eleven prisoners sitting on a pile of logs which they had been working on that afternoon. There were a couple of shovels leaned up next to them. They were all quite young and they were wearing identical uniforms with shirts and trousers made from a thick, crude material only a little finer than sackcloth and about the same color. Their dull metal buttons were done up tightly at the top, and each of them had marks crudely painted in bright yellow on the upper part of their left sleeves. Most of them were large Vs and one of them had a thick T and a couple of thinner stripes above it. They all wore flat caps in the same material which perched on top of their heads, some like pillbox hats and others pressed flat like berets. They looked strong and quite cheerful in their dusty uniforms and thick lace-up boots.

Solveig paused a little way in front of them as they waved to the farmer's wife, who gave them pieces of bread and butter out of her basket. She gave one of them an envelope which contained three letters and some pills. He took off one of his boots, folded the envelope, and put it inside. Solveig took out her notebook and searched for her pencil. She took all the contents of her bag out until she found it. The lead was blunt, but she could just make her words legible. She wrote a letter to her father and paused upon seeing Topsy out on the grass next to her worn socks and spare clothes. She tore out the page and folded it five times into a small solid square. She then pushed it up inside her doll's sweater, took out one of her frayed socks, and tied it around the waist. She went toward the prisoners and with a nod of encouragement from the farmer's wife went up to the one on the end nearest her and extended the little red doll.

'Can you give this to my father, Johannes Halversen, please?' He looked puzzled, then said something to her in a foreign language.

'My father, Vater, Papa, Johannes Halversen,' she shouted.

'Ah, your Papa,' said the prisoner sitting next to him.

'Johannes. Halversen. Here. In. Prison?' said Solveig in English.

'I ask. We come back here tomorrow, yes?' Solveig gave him the doll and he hid it inside his sleeve under his arm. 'Johan Havverrhs . . . I ask,' he said, rolling the *r*. Solveig repeated the name and he repeated it more correctly.

The farmer's wife ran over to Solveig, grabbed her arm, and pulled her into the door of the barn next to them. 'Shhh, hide under the straw. The guards are coming to collect the prisoners.'

Solveig crawled behind the door and covered herself in the scratchy straw which smelled of horse manure. Dust filled her nostrils and she flinched as a mouse darted over her feet to the other side. She felt fleas hopping on her legs. She was too terrified to sneeze or scratch or scream. She closed her eyes, curled into a tight, little ball, and stayed motionless, hardly breathing, until the shouts and orders from the guards subsided and the footsteps of the prisoners faded.

After the prisoners had gone, the farmer's wife dashed into the barn and shook her little guest gently. Solveig emerged with dust all over her face and strands of straw and muddy grass attached to her hair and clothes.

'It's okay, they've all gone,' said the farmer's wife laughing as she scraped some of the straw off her. 'I'll show you where the bathroom is so you can have a wash. Then you can help me finish getting supper ready.'

Solveig lay places for fourteen people. After they had been called in, she sat down and was silent throughout the bustle of their late supper. She was happy to mingle with the farmer's family. In addition to Gustav and his wife, there were three grown-up sons, the farmer's brother, his wife, and their four children, all younger than Solveig, and two young men who were guests.

She had not seen as much fresh milk, fresh fish, or fried pork for years. Even the cabbage was special with bacon bits and butter on it. She sat saucer-eyed, and tried not to stuff her food down too quickly. After a great deal more chatting, and some time after the smaller children had gone to bed, the farmer's wife popped out and came in with couple of blankets.

'I'll take you to the barn next to the house. There's some clean hay on the ledge up the ladder. Our two guests will be down on the ground. They're very quiet and won't trouble you.'

Solveig climbed up to the hayloft and spread one of the blankets out. There were dogs barking, cows clinking their bells, cats meowing, and scurrying noises of mice nearby. She could hear the voices of the family through the open window of the kitchen. But despite the noise and unfamiliarity of the place, she felt safer than she had for a long time. There was no threat of air raids, no distant gunshots, no motorbikes or cars slowing down in the street below, no heavy boots coming upstairs, no shouting and crying, no doors slamming, no banging and pleading outside locked rooms. Despite the absence of her red rag doll, she was soon deeply asleep.

CHAPTER 27

Falstad Prison

Late afternoon, Tuesday

July 6th, 1943

T hat same evening, while Solveig was setting the table for supper at the farm, the troop of prisoners carried on their walk back to the prison accompanied by guards. The mud track came down a gentle slope toward a wide expanse of fields. Across a straight single-track road between Falstad Woods and the small harbor in the village of Ekne was Falstad Prison.

In the center of a vast expanse of flat ground surrounded by barbed wire was a square, single-story white structure with four joined corridors surrounding a central square courtyard. Along the four inner walls was a wide corridor with a series of high archways so that all the rooms had access to the courtyard. Around this central building was a wide yard of mud, cracked and dried in the summer's heat, and around the perimeter of the compound were numerous long wooden huts where the prisoners slept, crowded into narrow bunk beds jutting out of the walls. Surrounding the whole complex were double fences formed in a lattice of barbed wire with extra rolls of barbed wire at the top of each.

In one of the corners of the double fence was an elevated platform with steps leading up to a high wooden tower where two armed guards stood looking over the whole site. At the entrance was a high wooden gate painted white with a triangle stretching over it. At the bottom of the triangle, between two parallel horizontal beams stretching across the whole gate, were tall capital letters saying:

SS STRAFGEFANGENENLAGER FALSTAD

There were two guards in front and three just inside. They had peaked caps with silver badges, and jackets with shiny silver buttons and four pockets. A couple of them held rifles in their right hands, arms bent on the ready. Their uniforms were a similar color but darker and finer than the baggy clothes of the prisoners.

A few prisoners in their regulation jackets and trousers were walking around the yard when the farmhand prisoners returned. Others were returning from a day building roads, some by jeep, all accompanied by heavily armed guards. There were several guards walking up and down, each one with a rifle slung across their shoulders.

All the returning prisoners were lined up, and some prisoners who worked within the camp joined them. Ten guards came out and started shouting orders in German. The guards inspected them and went up to some of the prisoners and checked their pockets and felt over their jackets and trousers. One of them confiscated a small parcel from a returning road worker, unwrapped it and, upon seeing some bread, threw it on the ground and trampled over it. He then took his rifle and rammed the handle into the prisoner's back, pushing him onto the ground where he kicked him. The other prisoners stood in silence with their heads bowed as the prisoner's screams resounded over the compound. One more kick and he was silent. Two of the guards dragged him by the feet, his face scraping over the hard mud and stones, into the main building.

The Russian prisoner, who had spoken to Solveig earlier, still had the doll safely under his sleeve when he entered his hut. He took it out and hid it under the layer of straw and newspaper that did for a mattress on the lower bunk. He took his boots off, unwrapped the rags which served as socks around his feet, put them under his pillow, and sat on the floor next to his bed. The others came in and when one of the Norwegian prisoners entered, he asked him if he knew a 'Johan Havvesen'.

'You know him? Little girl come for him,' he said in English.

'I ask,' replied the Norwegian prisoner.

'She bring doll,' said the Russian as he took it out from the mattress.

The Norwegian took the doll and hid it as the first prisoner had done. He waited until the guards shouted out *'Essen,'* and went out into the yard with the other prisoners to form a long queue in front of a wooden table with several huge metal urns of thin soup. Each prisoner carried their own metal bowls which were used alike for tea, water, and so-called food. If they were lucky, they would get a lump of bread to go with it. A couple of guards splashed out their portions.

Although guards patrolled the queue, the prisoners could talk and it was easy to trade objects. Some had found cigarettes or food in parcels left for them on the roads nearby by the villagers and farmers. There were sometimes medical supplies and sometimes socks or even leather for shoes. The Norwegian prisoner asked a few prisoners if any of them knew a Johannes Halversen. One of them nodded. He did know him. Johannes had been working on the fences in the compound and stayed in a hut on the other side. He had been in the sick bay for the last week. He would give the doll to Torfinn, who was older than most of them and had a much sought-after job as a cleaner. The Norwegian prisoner soon reached him in the queue. He tried to approach him a couple of times but the guard saw him move out of line and shouted at him to get back to his place.

The cleaner saw that he wanted to make contact and after mealtime took a mop and bucket and went over the hut. The guards took no notice of him as he was often instructed to clean out places and he was supposed to act as a spy for them. Prisoners often fell ill with dysentery and, having inadequate facilities, would end up spending a whole night covered in vomit and soiled with liquid feces. Torfinn was the clean-up man, often carrying feverish and dehydrated men singlehandedly to the sick bay. The guards were only too happy to give him a wide berth.

As soon as he was inside the hut, the Norwegian prisoner gave him the doll which was still tied up with the sock. To avoid suspicion, the cleaner went up to the guard and told him that one of the prisoners had severe stomachache and needed some medicine. He asked if he could go to the sick bay to get some from the nurse. As the guard looked over to him, the Norwegian prisoner came out of the hut and bent over as if in pain and appeared to vomit. The guard nodded. The cleaner walked over to the main building and asked to be let in to see the nurse.

He walked down a white corridor with large windows and into a wing which acted as a sick bay. If a prisoner was very ill, he would be transported to Innherred Hospital in Levanger, the nearest town, usually as a one-way trip. Prisoners with episodes of dysentery or abdominal pains would be given some medication and bed rest, and those who survived would be returned to work as soon as they could walk.

They had usually lost a huge amount of weight and were barely able to pick up a spade, let alone spend twelve hours of strenuous hard labor in the summer heat. The other prisoners would help but the guards would yell orders and hit them. It was quite common for them to collapse and be beaten until they had to be carried back to the prison.

The patients in the sick bay would be given extra food rations if they could keep it down and were expected to stay in bed and sleep. It was a good place to be and sometimes a prisoner would pretend to have colic or would inflict an injury on himself in order to stay there. It was risky because twice a week on any random day the camp doctor would come and if a prisoner was believed to be feigning an illness, the punishment would be severe. A malingerer might have to crawl along the entire width of the courtyard backward and forward many times on his stomach assisted by the boot of a guard, or be showered, naked, in freezing water, or just simply be beaten up in front of the other prisoners. The prison needed its workers, though, so the younger, stronger ones would not be so severely punished.

There were two prisoners, both political prisoners, who were doctors. They were allowed to help in the sick bay but were subject to the same rules and regulations as the other prisoners. During their shifts, they did everything they could to delay prisoners returning to work and would often overplay the symptoms. They had to be subtle, though, to avoid the guard nurses discovering them.

The cleaner walked into the sick bay and smiled at the nurse, a female guard in a uniform identical to the other guards except that she had a skirt. She was sitting in a small office area next to a bare room with four beds. Each bed had a table and light beside it and was well covered with blankets over crisp white sheets. Only two of the beds were occupied. One man was asleep and the other was coughing continuously and spitting bloodstained phlegm into a metal cup by his bed.

In the office was a medicine cabinet, a desk with a typewriter and telephone, and shelves with files. The guard was playing solitaire with two packs of cards and smoking.

'Hello,' said the cleaner in German.

'Hello, I suppose you want something,' said the guard wearily.

'I need some medicine for prisoner number thirty-nine, hut four. He has really bad colic and has been sick.' After discussing the symptoms, the nurse gave him a bottle of Kaolin and Morph.

'Fancy a game?' said the nurse. The cleaner dealt some cards and they were soon engrossed. The nurse offered the cleaner a cigarette and a swig from a metal flask she produced from the drawer. The cleaner took a large swig, coughed, and then smiled.

'What is this? Turpentine?'

'Homemade vodka from Afdalen farm. Got a good kick, yes?' She laughed.

'Nurse,' called the patient who was coughing all the time. 'I need a drink of water.'

'Not again. Go back to sleep.'

'Please, I'm so thirsty.'

'Wait, I'll be there in a moment.' She went back to her cards.

'Miss,' said the cleaner, 'I'll get him some water. You can finish your cigarette.' The guard leaned back and nodded. The cleaner walked over to the patient and got his metal cup, pulling a face as he looked at the contents. He took it to a kitchen next door, rinsed it, and filled it to the top with water. When he got back, he turned his back to the office window so that the guard could not see the patient. He lifted him up to sitting position and helped him drink. The patient's face was drawn and his lips were swollen and chapped.

'Johannes Havveson?'

'Halversen, yes, why?'

'I've got this for you. A little girl gave it to one of the Russians and said she is looking for you.'

'That's not possible,' said Johannes, leaning back against the pillow. 'No one knows I'm here.'

'She asked for her father and gave this doll.' The cleaner produced the doll. Johannes sat up and took it.

'Topsy.' He looked pleased for a moment then frowned.

'But how did she get here? Where's her mother?'

'The little girl wants to see you.'

'But I can't even stand up, and the guards would never let her in.' He had a coughing fit and clutched his chest in pain. He looked for somewhere to spit. The cleaner produced a grimy handkerchief.

'Here, you can keep it,' he said as Johannes spat out some more pink-stained phlegm. His eyes were bright and his face and pajama top were wet with perspiration.

'I'll come back to see you in the morning if I can. I think the Russian said he would see the girl tomorrow at Gustav's farm, but it wasn't easy to understand him.'

'Thanks,' said Johannes, coughing again. He looked at the doll then dropped it on the floor as another coughing fit started up. The cleaner went back into the office and saw the nurse guard taking another swig from her hip flask.

'What took you so long?'

'That patient has a really bad fever. Is Doctor Hartmann coming tomorrow?'

'We never know when he will come.'

'Maybe that patient should go to hospital.'

'Are you telling me how to do my job?'

'No, of course not, miss. Want another game?'

'I'll win this time, you'll see.' She smiled and settled back into her chair. After another half hour the cleaner went back to his hut and the nurse leaned forward on her desk and went to sleep.

*   *   *   *

Johannes slept for several hours despite his cough and woke in the early hours of the morning. It was quiet, apart from birds singing and the breathing of the other patient who had been up several times in the night to use the toilet next door. Johannes leaned over to have a drink and saw the doll on the floor. So it wasn't a dream after all.

Seeing no sign of the nurse, he moved himself so that he was on his stomach and could lean his arm down. After some wriggling and stretching, he managed to reach the doll and bring it up. The effort brought on a coughing fit which he tried to suppress for fear of annoying the night nurse and bringing her out of the office. He felt a wave of heat and perspiration break out across his forehead and upper lip. He wiped his face and noted the stubble of several days there to remind him how long he had been in the sick bay.

He took the doll and, noticing a small piece of paper sticking out from under its jumper, untied the dirty rag wrapped around it and pulled it out. He saw it was a note, smoothed it out very carefully, and with frequent glances at the window and door, he read it.

Dear Papa,

I want to see you and get you out. I miss you very, very much.

Lots of love
Solveig xxx

He smiled, then tears came to his eyes. He folded the note, put it back under the doll's sweater, retied the rag which he noted was the remnant of a dirt-ingrained sock, and put it under his pillow. He started to sweat and shiver as his coughing started up again. He was finding it hard to catch his breath.

At six in the morning the nurse came to him and took his temperature. She recorded it and asked him to sit on the chair next to his bed as she changed the sheets. He struggled onto the chair and shivered again. The nurse pulled the pillow out and as she did so the doll dropped out.

'What's this?'

'Just a doll, I made it for my daughter,' he said between coughs.

The nurse examined it. 'It's filthy, just a dusty old bit of rag,' she said in German. The note was poking out. 'What's this?'

'Nothing.'

'I'll have to report this. We can't have any coded messages here.' She marched off, leaving him on the chair. As soon as she had gone, the cleaner came in with his bucket and mop, his get-in-free ticket to anywhere in the prison. Johannes was starting to fall off the chair and the cleaner ran over to him and helped him back onto the bed.

'Thank you,' said Johannes, stopping to catch his breath between each word. 'I need to write a note.' The cleaner slipped into the office and once he confirmed that the coast was clear, he took an old envelope out of the wastepaper basket and a pencil from the desk.

The cleaner helped Johannes sit up and lean over to write it. He wrote laboriously, trying to stifle his coughing as he did so. When he had finished, he asked the cleaner to go to hut two and fetch a cigarette case from under the floorboard next to the third bed on the left. It was made from tin from a soup bowl retained after one of the meals.

The guards were wise to this practice and now counted the bowls after each meal but sometimes miscounted or did not bother checking if there was a discrepancy. If the guards did notice one missing, rather than go through a lineup and probable beating, the prisoner concerned would pretend that they had just noticed a dropped bowl and return it. The Russians were always aiming for an opportunity. One of them had taught Johannes how to use a stone to hammer the metal flat and carve it with sharp-edged stones or tools which occasionally went 'missing' from the prison supplies. Johannes had managed to make a thin oblong of metal and some of the other prisoners who were good with their hands helped him fold it over so it was large enough to hold ten cigarettes and small enough to hide in the palm of the hand or under a belt if needed. They helped him seal the side and fasten a lid so it could open. This was delicate work which needed time and patience.

The cleaner went across the yard to hut two and found the cigarette case. He passed his finger over the smooth surface and admired the simple design. Johannes's cigarette case had his initials, JH, in large letters in a square in the middle with *Falstad 1943* underneath in smaller letters. On the curved top was his full name and on the back in another simple square was *Maria*, and under her name in smaller letters were *Eva, Inger,* then on the next line *Olav, Solveig,* so it made a square. All the letters were in ornate capitals so the reader had to look closely to discern them. The cleaner swept the wooden floorboards and then washed them with the mop and bucket he had brought over.

He went to the utilities area to get some clean water and carried it to the sick house. He stopped in the doorway and overheard the conversation between the camp governor and the nurse guard. She was still there from the previous night.

'Nurse?'

'Yes sir?'

'Don't waste my time with any more of the prisoner's toys and children's nonsense.' He handed her the rag doll which had been torn open at the front and the letter which was crumpled into a tight ball. He had looked at it but could not understand a word:

Kjaere Papa

Jeg vil se deg og komme deg ut. Jeg savner deg veldig veldig mye.

Mye kjaelighet
Solveig xxx

'I thought it might be a coded message, sir.'

'It's just the scribbling of a man with delirium.'

The nurse stared sullenly after him and dropped the doll and note into the wastepaper bin. She then started handing over duties to a younger nurse guard who had just arrived to take over the shift. Without a glance at the cleaner, the night nurse went back to her quarters.

The new nurse went over to Johannes with a mug of water and sat him up. She dipped in a hanky and dabbed it over his face. Johannes looked up at her and smiled.

'Ah, it's the pretty one.'

The nurse smiled and went to the other patient who was stirring and asking for a hand to go to the toilet. She helped him up and escorted him out. When she had left the room, the cleaner crept over to Johannes and handed him the cigarette case. Johannes took the note he had written, put it in the case, and handed it back, indicating for him to get it back to the girl. He had a resurgence of his coughing and held his arms tightly over his chest, grimacing with pain every time he coughed. He then sank back onto the pillow and closed his eyes.

The cleaner left with his bucket and mop and walked as quickly as he could without raising suspicion, to join the prisoners who were lining up to go out to work. He crept into the line and, finding his Russian, gave him the cigarette case.

Later that day, when he returned to the nurse's office, the cleaner saw some frayed red material half covered with discarded reports. He extracted the remnants of the doll and gave it to one of the Russian prisoners. A week later the doll was sewn back together again and on her skirt was a name and date in Russian. By the time the prisoner had been sent back to Gustav's farm, Solveig was long gone, so he gave it to Gustav's youngest niece. Topsy was given a new name and from then on was carried everywhere by the little girl.

CHAPTER 28

Falstad Prison

Early Hours of Wednesday

July 7ᵗʰ, 1943

O vernight Herr Wolff's two men took turns driving and Herr Wolff sat in the back, staring out of the window with unseeing eyes. The car went as fast as possible along the narrow roads, winding by fjords and up and down low mountains.

In the early hours of Wednesday morning, their car drove to the front gate of Falstad Prison. One of the men got out and spoke to a guard who had climbed down from his lookout post as the car approached.

Herr Wolff's man explained their mission to the guard, who peered into the back of the car and saluted the official passenger. Herr Wolff saluted back and showed him a wallet inside which was a silver badge appropriate for his rank. The guard nodded and the men drove into the courtyard. They were shown into the governor's office and informed that as it was only four in the morning, they would have to wake him.

The guard who went to fetch the governor had to knock long and hard on his door. The upstairs window opened and Governor Schmidt shouted down at the unfortunate bearer of the news. When he heard that Officer Wolff was demanding to see him, he cursed and slammed the window shut. He pulled on yesterday's shirt and crumpled trousers still on the floor where he had tumbled into bed after his usual nightcap. A woman stirred in his bed, looked at the time, and groaned. She put the sheet over her head and went back to sleep.

When the governor was dressed, he left his house, still buckling his belt, and walked to the main building with the guard. He entered the office and saw a senior Wehrmacht officer in full uniform standing in the middle of the room with his two men on either side.

'Good morning, Governor Schmidt,' said Herr Wolff, saluting him.

'Good morning, Officer Wolff, and to what do I owe the pleasure of your visit?'

'You know perfectly well. I am looking for Police Inspector Johannes Halversen. I know he is here and I demand to see him now.'

'Why would you be interested in a Norwegian resistance traitor? It's not normal procedure.'

'He is needed for questioning in Oslo and I intend to bring him back with me.'

'I have not been informed of this. I should be notified properly if any prisoner is to be transferred.'

'As I said, governor, this is a secret mission and not for you to know.'

'I can only act if I have a written order from my overseer.'

'Take me to him now,' said Herr Wolff.

'He is *not* here and you have no right to be here either. You must leave or I shall call Hauptsturmfuhrer Ehmer.'

Herr Wolff drew out his gun. 'Show me the admissions diary.'

Herr Wolff's men went on either side of the governor and got hold of his arms.

'If you take your thugs off me, I'll get the book.'

Herr Wolff nodded to the men and followed the governor, pointing his gun into his back. The governor produced the book and after Herr Wolff had indicated for his men to restrain him again, he looked through the admissions. He remembered the date that he had been informed of the arrest. Anything pertaining to Maria was of note to him.

He looked for the date when he would have expected an entry with Johannes's name, and checked a few days after and above. At that precise date was a name which had been crossed out with a solid black line across each of the columns so that it was impossible to know who had been written there. He pointed to it and looked at the governor.

'No record of Police Inspector Halversen, but what is this?' he said, pointing to the black line. 'You are hiding his admission.'

The governor laughed. 'That could be anything, you have no proof that your Norwegian spy friend was here.'

Herr Wolff raised his gun. 'Take me to him now.'

The governor shook his head. 'He's not here, and even if he was, how do you think you would find him?

'Take me to the prisoner's huts.'

'Or what? Are you going to kill me? What would your bosses say then? And if you did find this Inspector Halversen, how far do you think you would get?'

Herr Wolff put his gun back in his holster. 'I will make sure you are punished for this. The hiding of prisoners is against the law.'

'I can assure we have orders to insure the safety of our staff and other prisoners, and if any prisoner violates that we are entitled to do whatever is necessary to restore peace. And I can also assure you that there is no one called Inspector Halversen here.'

Herr Wolff knew he had been defeated.

'I shall report this,' he said as he indicated to his men that they would leave.

'And so shall I, officer.' The governor sneered. 'Drawing a gun, threatening a prison governor, and helping a Norwegian spy escape are crimes.'

'We shall see.'

Herr Wolff summoned his men and started to walk back to the car.

'Heil Hitler,' he said as he saluted the governor. The governor smiled.

'Heil Hitler.'

Herr Wolff walked with his head held up high and allowed his men to open the door for him and resume driving. It would be a long journey back to Oslo and he had little comfort as he thought about his life, his destiny, and his misguided feelings.

*   *   *   *

It was evening by the time Herr Wolff returned to his town flat. He felt the humiliation of failure. He had failed as an officer, failed as a husband and father, and now he had failed Maria. He had been unable to save Inger, unable to protect Eva, and now was unable to rescue her husband and unable to find Solveig. It was because of his obsession with Maria and his desire to gain favor with her that he had ended up like this. He wondered if he would have fulfilled his desire with Maria if she had ever let him anywhere near her. His behavior had been impeccable but his lust was a betrayal of the sanctity of his marriage to Katherina. The thought of that made him feel even more ashamed but did nothing to quell his yearning for Maria.

His wife lived in another world to him, and she believed in the dream of the Third Reich. She would never understand his doubts. She was strong and independent, the children were growing up, and he knew that they would survive perfectly well without him. He was sorry that they would have to be told he was a traitor to the Fatherland, but in serving this regime he had become a traitor to himself.

* * * *

Herr Wolff was ready when they came to his office the next morning. He knew it would not take long, but he was surprised at how quickly the officers from the SS came. They would have phone records, the reluctant report of his secretary, and the record of where his former lodgings were. They would have all the evidence they needed.

Herr Wolff put on his cap and his jacket with all his medals. He was in full uniform as he stood up and saluted the SS officers when they came in.

'There's no need for handcuffs,' he said after they had gone through the formalities of the arrest. 'I will not try to escape.'

'You are accused of crimes against the Fuhrer. You will be handcuffed as an example of what happens to officers who betray the Fatherland.'

Herr Wolff stretched out his wrists and smiled ironically.

All those years of service and sacrifice to protect his country, only to end up like this. But he knew who he was. He had served with honor and remained a faithful soldier. He held his head up high and looked every inch the true soldier that he was.

A few days later, he was marched out of his cell in Grini Prison. He walked to his position in front of the firing squad and, after refusing to wear a blindfold, saluted before he fell to the ground.

CHAPTER 29

Falstad Prison

Wednesday

July 7ᵗʰ, 1943

A few hours after Herr Wolff's humiliating encounter with Governor Schmidt, it was still early morning and the prisoners for Gustav's farm were lined up for inspection. The guards asked them to raise their hands and empty their pockets, the usual routine where the guards checked them for anything which could be used as a weapon. The prisoners were used to this and allowed the guards to do their search. The guards were usually slack at this, but there had been an alert last night as a planned escape had been apprehended. The Russian prisoner showed his empty pockets and raised his arms but not as high as usual as his shirt was tucked in. The guard examining him pulled his arms up higher, pulling the rest of his shirt up and causing a small package wrapped in rags to fall onto the ground.

'Eet ees my lunch,' said the prisoner bending down to pick it up.

'Not so fast,' said the guard, pushing him out of the way and grabbing the parcel. He unwound the material and brought out a metal case. 'And what is this?'

'Eet vos wrong parcel, should be my lunch,' replied the prisoner.

'Do you think I'm an idiot?' said the guard, pushing the rifle butt into his chest with enough force to push him to the ground. The prisoner tried to get up but the guard kicked him in his sides and legs until he gave up struggling. The accompanying guard called for help and soon several guards ran toward the fray and pulled the prisoner, now semi-conscious, across the yard. One of them took the cigarette case and hurried toward the governor's office.

The other prisoners destined for Gustav's farm stood by in silence. They knew only too well what would happen if they tried to defend a fellow captive. When the guards returned, they walked quietly after them toward Gustav's farm. They were each burning with rage, unable to act and unable to say a word.

The governor was called and met the guards and prisoner in a holding cell near the sick bay. He took the case and studied it. He was familiar with the techniques used for these handmade objects and recognized the initials, JH, as the same as those of the prisoner that the interfering Wehrmacht officer had asked about. It was too much to be a coincidence. He looked at the enclosed note. It was hard to decipher as the writing was so shaky, but he had an idea of what it meant, even though it was in Norwegian:

Dearest Solveig

I am so happy to get your letter. But you must go home to Mama and wait for me. I will be home soon.

All my love

Papa xxx

Governor Schmidt did not understand Norwegian, but he could understand: 'I will be home soon.' The prisoner obviously had an escape plan, was writing in code and using his own daughter as a messenger. If this Johannes Halversen was a spy and escaped from prison, he, as governor, would be in deep trouble. He was not going to take any risks.

* * * *

Back in the sick bay, Johannes heard the young nurse arguing with two guards.

'He has pneumonia. He is really sick and has to stay here.'

'He is a spy and the governor must talk to him right away.'

'I shall report you to Doctor Lohr. He is more senior than you.'

'Governor's orders overrule your Herr Doctor's. Get him up at once.'

She came toward Johannes, looking agitated. 'I'm so sorry, they won't listen to me,' she said as she wrapped him in a gray blanket. Johannes stood and swayed while the nurse pulled his arm around her and supported him toward the door.

'Are we going out on a date?' said Johannes, suppressing a cough in order to smile.

'When you are well, I promise we will,' she said and kissed his cheek.

The guards grabbed hold of him and prodded him with the end of the rifle down the main corridor until he came to the door of a cell. When he fell over, the guards pulled him up, threw him in, and locked the door. Johannes sat on a bench and waited.

About an hour later he was shoved from the cell and dragged to the interrogation room. Inside was a large desk with three chairs on one side and one chair on the other side. The window was boarded up and there was a dim light from a bare light bulb overhead and an additional lamp on the desk by which the prison governor was reading Johannes's file. The guards dumped the prisoner on the opposite chair and stood on either side of him.

'Prisoner fifty-six, Johannes Halversen,' read the governor, no longer slurring his words, 'I am authorized by the German Fuhrer to bring justice against all traitors against the Third Reich. I have reason to believe you have given information to our enemies.' He pronounced this all in German and one of the guards, a Norwegian, translated. 'Are you Johannes Halversen, police inspector of the Oslo division?'

'Yes,'

'Yes sir!' shouted one of the guards. Johannes stared at him without saying anything.

'Yes sir,' repeated the guard, hitting him across the face with the back of his hand and sending him flying off his chair.

Johannes heaved himself back on the chair and mumbled, 'Yes sir.'

'Johannes Halversen,' continued the governor, 'I have evidence that you have betrayed the Oslo police and the Nasjonal Samling by spying for the enemy. On November 24th and 25th, 1942, you were seen going to the houses of six different Jewish families and preventing their arrests. Our informer tells me that you gave names of twenty other Jewish families to two young men who have now been arrested and executed as traitors. You were living with Klara Ramsen who had a radio in her house. We have reason to believe you were helping her to distribute lies and propaganda from enemies of the Fuhrer. Do you deny this?'

Johannes just stared back at him. One of the guards punched him in the back with his gun while the governor repeated, 'Do you deny this?' The translator continued after each man spoke.

'What happened to Klara? She had nothing to do with any of this.'

'You expect us to believe that?'

'Where is she?'

'Women traitors are taken to Germany to await trial for their crimes.'

'She is not a criminal.'

'We believe you were working with other police men and civilian criminals. If you give me their names, you will go free.'

'I know nothing.'

'You better give me their names.'

'Or what?'

'I think you know.'

'I am not afraid to die.'

'Yes, but you won't like what we do to traitors who refuse to obey our orders.'

The junior guard pulled Johannes's chair down to the other end of the room and pulled him onto another chair which had leather straps on the arms and around the back. The guard attached them and the governor got up from the desk and walked over. The second guard took a large cloth and stuffed it into Johannes's mouth. On the shelf nearby were a variety of metal gadgets, some of which were dented and some of which were bloodstained.

Down in the sick bay the young nurse who had kissed Johannes lifted her head after a muffled noise came from down the corridor. She frowned and listened intently, but no more sounds came. One of the patients called her and, forgetting the strange noise, she busied herself attending to her charges.

* * * *

Johannes had no names to confess as all the resistance fighters used code names. He understood now why some of them carried capsules of arsenic with them, because nothing would have stopped him screaming out their names if he had known them.

After what seemed like hours, he was returned to the cell where there were now two other prisoners. This secret cell was down a flight of stairs in an old cellar which had once stored food for the boarding school that Falstad Prison was originally.

Johannes was coughing and breathing in shallow gasps, his swollen face barely recognizable. All three prisoners sat on the wet concrete floor, shivering. One of them, a younger man, rocked himself backward and forward, praying constantly. Johannes and the other one stared straight ahead with blank eyes.

Johannes put his hands up to his swollen face and groaned. His lips were thick and covered with congealed blood which split as he spoke. His hands were swollen, he had red lines where wire had dug into his throat, his legs were mottled with cigarette burns, and blood trickled from puncture wounds on his legs.

'Hey, do you believe in heaven?' said the other prisoner.

'Mmm,' replied Johannes.

'I believe I will go to heaven and my wife will join me. My mother is already there. I can see her as she was when she was young and I was just a schoolboy.'

'Dunno,' muttered Johannes, struggling to get his words out, 'wish I was dead anyway.'

'Our young lad here doesn't. He's petrified. He was just a student, that's all. All he had done was paint "Freedom and Liberty: Long Live King Haakon" across a wall. I was a teacher, but they found my radio and leaflets.' The student carried on praying with his eyes closed, frequently crossing himself and crying.

CHAPTER 30

Gustav's Farm

Friday

July 6ᵗʰ, 1943

Earlier the same day, Solveig was woken by the farmer's wife. The two young men who had slept below her in the barn had disappeared over the fields hours ago, carrying heavy rucksacks and wearing boots the farmer's boys had grown out of.

'Good morning, sleepyhead,' she said. 'The prisoners are here.'

'What time is it?'

'It's really late, way after seven,' said Gerda, laughing.

'Oh, sorry,' said Solveig as she shook the straw out of her hair. She climbed down the ladder and followed the farmer's wife into the yard. The prisoners were further in the field digging a ditch alongside the neighboring meadow where several cows were grazing. They had taken their hats and heavy jackets off knowing the guards would not return for hours yet. Some of their shirts had large holes with frayed edges, revealing shoulders or areas of chest, and where buttons were missing there were safety pins with gaping holes on either side. Their shirts might have been white once but were now the color of cement and pale rust. Two of their heads were newly shaven with multiple fresh cuts on a layer of shadow against blue-white skin. The rest had no more than an inch of hair and were either deeply tanned or had old, sunburn peeling on freckled arms and noses revealing shiny pale pink beneath. Solveig and the farmer's wife walked over.

The Russian prisoner who had taken the doll the previous day was not there. Solveig looked across the field and back down, but he was nowhere to be seen. After Gerda had given the prisoners the bread stacked in her basket, she saw Solveig's head and shoulders drooped down. She too looked for the prisoner from yesterday. She walked toward one of the Norwegian prisoners.

'Where is the man who took this girl's note yesterday?'

'He could not come this morning,' replied the prisoner.

'Do you know why? What happened to the note she sent?'

'He was carrying a cigarette case and the guard discovered it. He was taken back to his hut. We are not allowed to take anything out of the prison.'

'Do you know if her father got her note?'

'Sorry, but I'm not in the same hut as him so I don't know anything about it.'

'What was in the case, do you know?'

'Probably just cigarettes. It's really hard to get hold of them. Sometimes it is good to smoke or sometimes exchange them for food.'

Solveig heard this and walked toward them.

'Have any of you seen my father, Johannes Halversen?' she shouted. But none of the prisoners there had seen him or knew his name. Or if they did, they could not put themselves at risk.

Solveig ran back to the farmhouse and Gerda chased after her. When they were in the kitchen, Solveig sat at the table, put her arms over her head, and sobbed. Gerda tried to comfort her but Solveig seemed to have stored up months of crying and now was in full flood. Gerda put her arm around her and rocked her slowly her until her sobs started to die down.

'There, there, shush,' repeated Gerda. 'You've been such a brave girl and come so far. Dear girl, come now. We'll have to get you home to your mother.'

Solveig started crying again. 'I don't want to go back. I don't want to see Mama ever again. Can I stay here with you?'

'Lord bless you, my child. Shush now. I'm sure your mother misses you very much and wants you to come home. She doesn't know where you are, she must be so scared for you, dear child.'

Solveig sniffed and nodded. 'Mmm, don't know,' she said and put her thumb into her mouth.

'You can stay here as long as you need to. Now, come on, we have work to do. Hard work is the best medicine for a sad heart.' Solveig sat quietly and, noticing that her thumb was still in her mouth, took it out and wrapped it in the edge of her sweater. She and Gerda were just getting up when Gerda looked out across the courtyard and started up. Marching up the dirt track from the road near the prison were two guards in full uniform carrying rifles over their shoulders.

'Solveig, you have to be very brave, *right now*. There are two guards coming. Maybe they have discovered something.' Solveig's grief was instantly replaced with terror. She clasped her arms around herself and started shaking.

'Follow me,' said Gerda, grabbing her hand. They ran upstairs and into the main bedroom. The farmer's wife pulled out a suitcase and some shoes from under the bed and pointed for Solveig to go under. Solveig crawled in and the farmer's wife replaced the suitcase and shoes, pulled up the sheets, and shook the blanket so it looked unmade, unpinned her hair, and ran downstairs.

The guards, both Norwegians, reached the kitchen and knocked even though it was open.

'Hello?'

'Oh, you startled me,' she said, wiping her forehead and sighing heavily, 'what can I do for you?'

'We have orders to search for a girl, about ten years old. She's needed for questioning in Oslo.'

'Oh goodness, are children being arrested now?'

'No, she's just needed for questioning, that's all. She is the daughter of a spy. Well?'

'No, we haven't seen a girl here.'

'We have orders to search your farm.'

'Go ahead.' Just as she said that, she bent double and grimaced. She stumbled, still doubled up, to the nearest chair and gasped for breath, clasping her abdomen. 'Sorry, I have been sick all morning.' She leaned forward, ran her hands over her face, and then with a groan ran down the corridor. The guards sat down and listened to loud retching coming from the toilet. In a moment, she reemerged with damp hair and shirt, looking as if she had been sweating profusely.

'I'm so sorry. Do you want to look around the barns first? I can come with you.'

'It's all right,' said one of them, leading the way.

'I have to go back to bed, I'm so sorry, but you can search any room in the house, I am here to help.'

She walked slowly to the bottom of the stairs, groaning quietly as she did so, and continued like this until she got to her room. She walked over to the bed and whispered, 'Are you okay, Solveig?'

'Yes,' came a little voice, 'but my foot is going to sleep.'

'You can move around and get comfortable. The guards have gone to the barns. If they come up here, then I'm going to pretend to be very unwell and you will have to stay as still as a statue and don't come out until I say so.'

'What if they ask the men on the farm?'

'Ha! If we told them half of what goes on here, we would all be long dead. Now, excuse me while I make some loud groaning noises.'

The soldiers spent some time searching through cattle stalls, henhouses, stables, barns, and the hayloft in the main barn, talking to the farmworkers as they went. Gustav had gone into Levanger with the milk urns, leaving his eldest son in charge. He had nodded slowly when they asked about his mother.

'Yes, one of the prisoners was also very sick yesterday,' he had said. 'I hope it is not contagious.'

'You must report if you see the girl.'

'Of course,' he said as he continued scraping the hoof of one of the carthorses.

The guards, satisfied that none of them knew anything, headed back to the farmhouse. Their uniforms were now dusty and bits of hay and mud were sticking to their boots.

'Hello?' they called on, coming into the kitchen.

There was no answer, so they went upstairs and called again. The farmer's wife got up and hobbled to the door.

'You can search every room up here, we have nothing to hide.' Then she clutched her stomach again and leaned against the wall unsteadily. They glanced inside the door, then at each other. One of them shook his head, and the other one replied putting a handkerchief over his nose.

'We can see there's no one here. Sorry to disturb you and hope you will feel well soon. But you must report if you see anything suspicious, anything at all.'

'I will do. Let me get you some eggs while you are here.'

'No thank you. We have some more farms to visit,' he said, backing off hastily. 'Thank you for your help. Good morning.'

Gerda stood motionless in the kitchen until the soldiers reached the road and watched them walk on toward the next farm. Then she ran upstairs and pulled out the shoes and suitcase. Solveig crawled out and limped over to the door.

'What's wrong with your leg?'

'It's gone all numb. I can't feel the floor.'

'If you stamp it on the ground, the circulation will come back, then you'll have pins and needles. Come on, you look like you need one of my special drinks.'

When they got to the kitchen, the farmer's wife put the kettle on and reached to the back of the cupboard for her bottle of cooking brandy. She put a tablespoon into one cup and a large glug into another. When the kettle boiled, she added a little to hers, half a cup to Solveig's, and added sugar to both.

'Here, special medicine. Sip it and you'll soon feel better.' Her hand shook as she took her own cup and drank it down in one go.

CHAPTER 31

Falstad Prison

Later That Evening, Friday

July 6th, 1943

A fter some hours, during which Johannes had passed out intermittently and the student had not once stopped rocking, the door opened. Five guards came in, bound their hands behind their backs, and put sacks over their heads. The three prisoners were shoved up the stairs out into the main corridor and with frequent pushes and prods out onto the courtyard where they were bundled into a van. Every time Johannes collapsed on the ground he was kicked until he heaved himself up. When he was seated, Johannes fiddled with the rope around his hands. It was coming loose.

'Where are we going?' asked the younger prisoner in German.

'Shut up,' replied the guard. The young man crossed himself and carried on with his rocking and praying while the other two prisoners bent their heads. The driver was accompanied by one guard at the front and the other three guards each watched a prisoner. The youngest prisoner stopped moaning for a moment, leaned forward, and vomited from under his sack all over the floor. The guard swore and rammed his elbow into the prisoner's side, whereupon the prisoner resumed his delirious chanting and crying.

'*Shut up!*' cried the guard before hitting him with the handle of his gun. The prisoner slumped forward and the noise stopped.

'I don't care if I die, but I'll be damned if I'm going to let these bastards get away with it,' said Johannes, gritting his teeth.

'I'd rather die trying than give up,' said the other prisoner.

There was a stirring and the youngest prisoner sat up and started humming tunelessly, still rocking and crossing himself.

The guard swore at them again and one of them stood up to punch him but fell over as the van skidded to a halt. They were in Falstad Woods, only a mile from the prison. There was a fierce wind blowing and it was now pouring with rain.

The guards took the sacks off the prisoners' heads and manhandled them out of the van. The two guards at the front came out with torches and pointed the way, walking on ahead. Their boots sank in mud and they made slow progress as they stepped over knots of wood and roots on the uneven ground. The three other guards had a prisoner each and drove them ahead of them, steering them between the closely packed trees. They shouted to each other, and the guards at the front waved their torches so they could be seen in the mist.

After several minutes one of the guards at the front slipped and fell into a shallow hole that had been dug some days before. The other one stopped to help him, and their torches were no longer visible to the guards following. They yelled and stumbled vaguely in their direction.

Johannes was in the front and, summoning a desperate burst of strength against his fever, yelled out, '*Now!*' He turned around on the guard just behind him, bent over, and lunged into his middle. The guard fell down and Johannes stood beside him and kicked him in the head. The guard behind him shouted and pointed his gun at Johannes, but before he could shoot, the second prisoner who was close in front of him threw himself in front of his guard's feet and tripped him up. The third guard ran toward them, shooting into the void. Johannes kicked his guard again and ran behind him to assist the other prisoner. By this time the second guard had struggled free and was hitting the prisoner over the head with his gun. The guards at the front hearing the shouts and gunfire ran toward the fray with their torches on and guns at the ready.

The first guard went back to the older prisoner and shot him five times in the head and chest. Johannes stumbled out into the forest and tripped over the tree roots as two guards chased after him. There were more shots and Johannes slumped, facedown into the mud.

The two guards with torches issued instructions and helped drag the two prisoners through the trees to a shallow hole. Both prisoners were light and slipped easily over the mud and pine needles.

'Where is the other one?' shouted the first guard. The guard who had been with the student ran back and searched for him. The others followed and shone their torches on the path they had followed, then widened their search out.

'Have you found him yet?'

'No, there's no sign.'

'Look for footprints.'

'Are you joking? I can't see a thing.'

They carried on searching for another twenty minutes until the first guard told them to stop.

'He's probably dead already. We will bury these bodies and come back tomorrow to find the other one.'

'How will we get permission from the governor? What reason shall we give for going out tomorrow?'

'We can't tell him that one of them went missing. Look what he did to Hans when he let a prisoner escape.'

'We'll tell the governor that we buried three prisoners. Anyone want to go against that?'

'Who says one of ours escaped?'

'If he's not already dead, he won't get far. What's one more prisoner anyway?'

'The governor is not going to come into these woods. Anyway, even if he did, anything could happen to a body after it has been buried. A wolf could dig one up for all I know.'

The guards covered the two bodies over with mud that had been piled up beside the hole from the previous day. They walked back to the van and drove off.

Much Later That Night

Long after the sound of the engine was lost in the rustling of the trees and the drumming of the rain, the student climbed out of a hollow only twenty yards from the track where the soldiers had been. His hands were still tied behind his back, but he managed to move slowly, frequently falling, crawling around trees, and stepping over gnarled roots until he reached a field. He dragged himself, sliding through long, wet grass until exhaustion and cold caught up with him and he lost consciousness.

Back in the gloom of the woods, the freshly dug earth was wet from the deluge of last night. In the center of a shallow grave, a bruised hand poked through and moved to clear a thin layer of leaves and mud off his face. It was Johannes.

CHAPTER 32

Gustav's Farm

Next Day, Thursday

July 8th

I t was early morning as an unfamiliar fishing boat came to the wooden pier on the fjord by the cluster of houses on the hill that constituted Ekne village. The boat had set off from Bronnoysund the previous day and been sailing all night without arousing any suspicion. The local farmers all had boats and went fishing at night.

This morning one of the farmers was checking his nets as two men moored the boat next to his. The farmer stood up with his arms folded and stared sullenly at them and their passenger, a tall, gray-haired man wearing a suit.

'Good morning,' said the man in the suit. The farmer nodded without smiling and continued staring at them. 'Have you seen or heard anything about a little girl, only ten years old, looking for her father?'

'No,' said the farmer, turning back to his work.

'Please, mister, do you know anyone who could help?'

'Where are you from?'

'I am from Bronnoysund and am looking for my granddaughter.' The farmer paused then nodded, seeming satisfied.

'You could try Gustav's farm,' he said, pointing toward the dirt track leading from the pier toward the road and pointing up to the right. 'If there's anything going on, they'll know about it there. If you don't mind me saying, there are guards and informers everywhere. They'll be onto you in no time at all, believe me. We don't see many city folk round here.'

Jorgen spoke to his men and after a few words he went back inside the boat and they set off for the farm.

The farm was soon visible across a wide expanse of fields going gently uphill on their right. In the distance to the left of a long straight road surrounded by more flat fields sat a low building surrounded by a barbed wire fence. As they neared the farm, a woman wearing boots, loose trousers, and a shirt under a brightly colored apron came out toward them.

'Hello?'

The men waved and walked up to her.

'Good morning, madam. We are sorry to disturb you but we wondered if you could help us. We are looking for a little girl.'

'Why?'

'She is our boss's granddaughter.' The farmer's wife put her head on one side and scowled at them.

'Really? Who is your boss?'

'Jorgen Jorgensen from Bronnoysund. He is looking for Solveig.'

'I don't know. Wait here and I will see if anyone has heard anything.'

She walked back to the kitchen and told Solveig who sprang out of her chair and before the farmer's wife could stop her, she ran out to the men. She knew them from the times she had visited her grandparents, and hugged them and jumped up and down for joy. The farmer's wife ran after her.

'Get back in the house immediately. There are guards everywhere.' She tried to hide Solveig between her and the men.

When they were in the house, the men explained and the farmer's wife checked if Solveig really wanted to see her grandfather. She had no need to ask as one look at Solveig's face told her that she could not have been happier at that moment. Gerda asked the men to go back to the boat and bring him back. She paused and asked them to wait a moment.

She went outside, calling her eldest son, and crossed the yard toward him when he emerged from a barn. Jorgen Jorgensen's men could hear them in urgent conversation but could only make out that the son was annoyed and the farmer's wife was insistent. Soon they appeared with a horse and cart and a farmhand.

'Okay,' she said to the men, 'You must pretend that you have come here from Levanger to exchange some fish for milk and bacon. I will give you some and you must go back to your boat and pretend you have to fix the engine in case anyone asks why you are there. Trust no one. We have to hide Solveig here. There are guards out looking for her.'

She got some brown paper, wrapped up a parcel of bacon, and put it with two bottles of milk in a string bag. There were several bales of hay and some farm equipment in the back. Soon the cart set off, a common sight on the dirt tracks and roads around there. When they got to the track leading to the wooden pier at Ekne Harbor, the men got off and went down the pier to Jorgen's boat.

'Any news?' shouted Jorgen as they climbed aboard.

'We've got news all right. She's there.'

'What? Really? Is she all right?'

'Never seen a kid look so healthy.'

'I can't believe it,' said Jorgen. 'We better get her home'

'The farmer's wife says it's not safe for Solveig to come out. So she asked us to get you.'

'Let's go,' said Jorgen, pulling his jacket on despite the heat. The men accompanied him to the cart and stared after it as it set off for the farm. They had not seen their boss look so happy since the last visit from his daughter months ago.

In a moment, the cart was back at the farm. A tall, white-haired man in a dark suit was helped off the cart by a stocky young man with a loose sweat-stained shirt and hefty brogues. They walked across the yard and entered the house. Fortunately, there were no guards around to witness the arrival of the stranger.

As soon as Jorgen had entered the kitchen, Solveig ran up to him, whooping for joy.

'My little Solveig, I can't believe you are here.'

'Grandpa!' she cried as she jumped up and down and hugged him. 'What are *you* doing here?'

'I've come to find you, of course,' said Jorgen with a laugh.

'But I didn't tell anyone I was coming here.'

'Ha! But we are really clever at detective work.'

'Have you found Papa?' said Solveig

'No, angel, I have only found you.'

'But there's no point coming here if we don't find Papa. He's in the prison. I sent a note to him. We have to go in and get him.'

'But Solveig, we can't just walk to a Nazi prison and ask them to let one of their prisoners out.'

'Why not? He hasn't done anything wrong.'

'Look, Solveig, we don't even know if he's here,' said Jorgen.

'He is here. I *know* he is,' shouted Solveig.

'How can you be so sure?'

'The policemen said they thought he had been arrested and taken to Falstad Prison. And that's why he hadn't come to see us.'

Jorgen put his head in his hands and sighed. He had never seen Solveig so agitated before and had no idea what to do with her.

'Come on, Solveig, it's dangerous here. You need to come home with me. You like sailing in my boat, don't you?'

'No!' cried Solveig as she ran out of the kitchen, across the yard, and into the barn where she had slept the night before. She curled up on her soft patch of straw and pulled the sweater that she had used as a pillow last night over her head.

Jorgen and Gerda ran after her and tried to get her to come out, but all she would say was 'Go away.'

Gerda took Jorgen's hand and led him away from the barn.

'Let her be,' she said. 'She is exhausted, scared, and desperate to see her father. She can stay here with us for as long as she likes, and you too. Come with me and I will show you our guest room.'

Jorgen nodded. He wiped his eyes and sighed.

'Poor little Solveig,' he said to Gerda. 'Thank you so much. I will never forget your kindness.'

CHAPTER 34

Gustav's Farm

Thursday

July 8th, 1943

That same morning Solveig's grandfather had arrived at Gustav's farm, Harald, one of Gustav's sons, chased after his dog, calling and calling him to come back. The dog had stopped over the unconscious student and kept barking. Swearing loudly, he ran to the dog, now whining and licking the student's face.

Harald bent over him and shook him gently. There was no response. He felt his forehead and put his hand on the student's chest. It was warm and he could feel a heartbeat.

'Good boy,' he said to his dog. He ran back to the field and whistled to the dog. He called for a couple of farmhands and in a moment, they were heading back across the field in their tractor with the dog chasing after them.

They took the student into the farmhouse after checking that the coast was clear. The prisoners had not arrived yet and there were no guards in sight. They called Gerda who took them to the end of the downstairs corridor and instructed them to push a heavy cupboard to one side. After much heaving, they uncovered a door leading to a small, bare room with just a bed and a couple of chairs. In the center of the room, a rag rug covered a trapdoor which led down to the cellar. In grander times it had been a larder, but it was now the room they used for escaped prisoners and fleeing resistance fighters.

They lay the student down on the bed and Gerda started to check him over. She asked her son to bring a jug of water, a glass, a basin of warm water, and some old towels from the airing cupboard. When she had these, she set about her task with brisk efficiency born of experience.

The student came to as Gerda bathed his face and upper body in the warm water. She managed to sit him up, get him to rinse some blood out of his mouth, and drink.

'Thank you,' he said, slurring his words. 'Where am I?'

'You're safe and among friends,' she replied. 'You must drink some more water.'

'Are the others here too?' he asked.

Gerda shook her head. 'What others?'

'There were three of us. The soldiers took us to the woods to kill us. There were a lot of shots.' He continued to force his words out in short bursts. 'I think the other two got killed . . . it was dark, I couldn't see anything. They might still be alive . . . they saved . . . my life,' he whispered.

'God in heaven,' said Gerda, 'I'll get my husband.' She put a glass of water into the student's hand. 'You must take small sips.'

Gerda walked across the farm to fetch her husband. Gustav was repairing a tractor, lying on his back with just his boots sticking out.

'Gustav, you've got to come.'

'I'm in the middle of repairing this old piece of scrap. It's the third time it's packed up this week.'

'Come on, it's urgent,' said Gerda, kneeling down beside him so she did not have to raise her voice.

'Damn it. What is it?'

'Please come now, Gustav.'

Gustav wriggled his way out and followed her back to the house. She told him about the student and the possibility of two other prisoners in Falstadskogen.

'We are not allowed in those woods. Let me see the boy.'

Gustav asked the student his name and the details of last night. He doubted if either of them could have survived, although he had seen prisoners crawl out of there before with similar stories. There were rumors of bodies buried in those woods. Local hunters told stories of guards moving prisoners to the woods at night, hearing shots and seeing the guards return unaccompanied. The woods were fenced-off and patrolled. Much as Gustav despised the German authorities, he had to appear to be on good terms with them as otherwise he would not be able to help the prisoners who worked on his farm and who could tell him about escapees.

When he asked if the student could give him any more information, the student described how they had gone quite a way from the road but could not have been too far from the edge of the field he had crawled to. He mentioned that one was a Norwegian policeman and the other a Polish man.

Gustav queried this, but the student said that he was quite sure. He had been in the same hut as Johannes, and had heard his stories. Gustav knew that this could not be a coincidence. This must be the same Johannes that the girl was looking for.

'We have to look for him, Gustav,' said Gerda.

'I know, but it's dangerous.'

'If you come across any guards, I am sure you can make up a good excuse for being there. You might have lost your dog, or be repairing the fence and looking for more wood. A farmer might need to go into the woods for all kinds of reasons.'

'I'll go. Get the lads to listen out, and if I whistle then I'll need assistance.' He called his dog, an older and more trustworthy dog than his son's, and strode at an apparently leisurely pace over the field toward Falstad Woods. His son came running up behind him and insisted on accompanying him as his dog ran to join them.

Harald was able to show him where he had found the student. They squeezed through the gap in the fence and found a few footsteps and several areas where the student must have fallen down. They continued in the direction suggested by the tracks, but these were unclear and they had to use guess work. Harald's dog was bounding everywhere and barking every time he saw a squirrel, much to Gustav's annoyance.

Gustav and Harald had been searching for an hour when they thought they heard something. They strained their ears. Barely discernable against the rustle of the trees was a coughing noise.

'Hello?' they called softly. They called the dogs and led them toward the sound. The dogs ran ahead and started whining and digging furiously. The men clambered down a slope to join them.

'There's someone down here,' yelled Gustav.

Soon the men had lifted a man out of the hollow and brushed all the mud and dried leaves off him. They saw another figure nearby and checked him out, but he was dead. Dead, but he could not have been dead long. A breeze came their way, bringing the smell of damp undergrowth, below which lurked the sickly odor of decay. Gustav and Harald knew what death smelled like, and realized that they were walking in a graveyard. They trod their way with great care as they carried the survivor up the slope.

They listened for footsteps and the voices of guards, but all was clear. There would be more danger when they left the cover of the woods. When they got to the fence, they widened the gap so they could drag their load through. Before bringing Johannes out on the field, Gustav whistled for the dogs and Harald set off toward the farm.

The man coughed but remained unconscious. His breathing was rapid and shallow, and his face was as pale as death—apart from purple bruises and congealed blood around his swollen lips. Gustav wondered if he would survive long. He had no idea if he even was one of the men described by the student.

After a while a tractor came over. Gustav hoped that no guards had observed them the previous day as two trips to the same part of an open field would seem odd. But the guards were not interested in the everyday working of the farm and were so used to the tractors going about their business that they would not have registered a redundant trip across a grass-covered field.

Gustav and his son carried the man into the house and into the special guest bedroom where the student had been taken. The student was already recovering and made way for his fellow guest. He looked at the man when he had been laid on the bed.

'Yes, it's him. He's alive. He's alive.' He jumped up and clapped his hands, then crossed himself and prayed. 'Thank you, God. Thank you for saving my life and for saving his life too.' While the student was in his reverie, Gustav turned around to face Gerda, who had followed them in.

'So, it is Johannes. He may be alive but he looks like a dying man to me.'

Gerda walked over to him and felt his forehead. 'He's cold, we need some blankets and extra pillows.' Gustav nodded to his son who ran off to get some. When her son returned, she took the pillows and asked for help to prop Johannes up. He coughed and stirred.

'Johannes,' said Gerda, 'you're safe. Solveig is here. She came to find you. You have to stay with us.'

Johannes opened his eyes. One of them was swollen but he could see out of the other. He coughed and made rasping noises as he inhaled. 'Solveig?'

'Yes,' said Gerda, 'it's true. It's a miracle you have survived. Maybe it was just meant to be.'

'It is a miracle, a true-life miracle,' said the student, going on his knees and putting his hands together.

Johannes closed his eyes and passed out again. Gerda covered him with blankets, making sure his arms and feet were well-covered. She asked the student to stop praying and do something useful. The student crossed his chest once more, walked over to Johannes, and stood by him while Gerda went out to get Johannes some water.

Gerda came into the kitchen and called Gustav.

'You must get the grandfather and tell him. I don't know if Solveig should see her father in such a state.' Gustav went to find Jorgen, who was sitting outside the sitting room in the adjoining garden.

CHAPTER 35

Gustav's Farm

Thursday

July 8ᵗʰ, 1943

'**M**r. Jorgensen,' said Gustav as he approached him, 'I have some good news. We've found Johannes. But I'm afraid he's very ill. We don't think he'll make it.'

'What? Is that really true?' Tears came into the old man's eyes. 'Solveig was right after all.'

'Where's your granddaughter?'

'Oh, still in the barn, I think. She was very upset earlier.'

'Let's get her.'

Jorgen and Gustav hurried to the barn and called Solveig. Just as she started telling them to go away, Jorgen shouted out that they had found her father and asked if she would like to see him. Solveig jumped out of her straw bed and ran out.

'Where? Where is he?'

'He's inside,' started Gustav, but Solveig was already running into the kitchen and he had to propel his considerable weight as fast as he could to keep up.

When they reached the kitchen, Gustav and Jorgen were out of breath and Solveig was jumping up and down with excitement. Jorgen told her to sit down.

'I want to see Papa now,' said Solveig.

'Sit down. Listen to me before you go rushing in.' Solveig heard a rare warning tone in his voice and stopped. She looked at his face, sat down, and bowed her head.

'They found him in the woods, but he's been wounded and he's very ill. We don't know if he's going to live.'

'No, I know he is going to be all right now. He won't die, I know he won't.' She had to be held back from running straight to him. Jorgen gripped her hand tightly.

'Solveig, you have to be very brave.'

'Everyone says that to me, but I *am* brave.'

Jorgen drew in his breath. She was not the only one who needed to be brave.

Solveig stopped just outside the door to the special guest bedroom and looked up at her grandfather.

'It's going to be okay,' she said with great solemnity. Then she reached up, kissed his cheek, and led him by the hand into the room.

As Solveig came in Johannes was falling slightly to one side on his pillows. Gerda pulled him back to an upright position. His breathing was still rapid and shallow and his face was swollen and bruised. Although he was barely recognizable, Solveig ran over to him and grabbed his hand.

'Papa, you're here. I love you, Papa. You are going to be all right now. I'm going to look after you.' She held his hand and kissed him on the top of his head. 'Papa, wake up.'

Johannes moved his hand and held on to hers. He opened his one good eye and looked at Solveig.

'Solveig, you, er, you are . . .' he stopped as he tried to speak. 'Thank you, it is so wonderful . . .' he could not go on. Tears ran down his cheeks and he fell back and closed his eyes.

'Come on,' said Gerda, 'he's exhausted and needs to rest. You can see him later.' She showed Solveig and Jorgen outside.

'Will he be all right?' said Solveig.

'Yes, God bless you, he will come through this even if I have to stay up with him all night,' said Gerda.

'I want to look after him too,' said Solveig as she flung her arms around her.

'You'll be my chief helper,' said Gerda, bending down to kiss her.

'Thank you.'

Gerda returned to the room and looked at Johannes. Maybe she should ask the student to start praying again. The student had been shown to a makeshift bed in one of the nearby barns and told to lay low until he could be taken to Levanger. This would be the first lap of many to transport him across Norway to the woods on the border with Sweden. The resistance network was widespread and insured the escape of many a refugee from the Nazi regime.

Gerda sat up with Johannes all night, wiping his forehead while he was shaking and sweating with fever, adjusting his blankets, giving him sips of water and aspirin, and leaning him forward and patting his back to help him cough. Solveig helped too. She ran backward and forward to get clean towels, warm water for bathing him, clean sheets torn into strips to use as bandages, and taking used cloths to the laundry room. In between assisting Gerda, she would sit in a chair near his bed and try not to fall asleep. As long as she stayed awake, he could not die. He was delirious most of the night but became calmer and slept peacefully as the morning approached.

As things were stirring across the farm, Gustav came down and asked about breakfast. Gerda asked Solveig if she would come and help her.

'What about Papa?'

'He's sleeping and his breathing is better. It won't take long and you can pop in and check on him.'

*　*　*　*

After breakfast Gerda went in to check on her patient with Solveig close behind. Johannes stirred.

'Papa, it's me,' said Solveig, taking hold of his hand.

Johannes opened his eyes. The swelling had subsided enough to allow both his eyes to open. He smiled and put his other hand over hers.

'Solveig, I can't believe you traveled all the way up here.'

'I *knew* you were here.'

'Thank you, Solveig. You know you saved my life. When I was in the sick bay I could feel myself floating away. I wanted to die . . . it seemed so blissful, but then I got your note. It brought me to my senses. When the guards left me for dead, I thought of how far you had traveled to find me and how much courage you had. It gave me the strength to climb out of my grave. And you, Gerda, and your husband, without you I would be dead. I will be in your debt forever. Thank you so much.' He smiled and then let his eyes close.

Gerda smiled at Solveig.

'You know what? He is going to get better. He survived the bout of fever last night, and now he will recover.'

Solveig kissed Gerda. 'I want to be with him forever.'

'Yes, but right now you need to sleep. He needs his sleep too. Why don't you rest?'

Solveig nodded and went into the sitting room to get some cushions. She took them back into the room, laid them on the floor, and curled up.

A few moments later Gerda looked in. Johannes was breathing more deeply and was smiling in his sleep. Solveig was asleep on the floor beside his bed on her best cushions. *Perfect,* thought Gerda.

CHAPTER 36

Oslo

Friday

July 9th

T he next morning Gustav gave Jorgen a lift to Levanger from where he sent a telegram to Old Vic Farmhouse.

```
TO RUTH JORGENSEN,

TELL MARIA SOLVEIG IS SAFE. JOHANNES ALSO FOUND.
WILL RETURN NEXT WEEK.

JORGEN.
```

The telegram arrived in the afternoon of the same day and even Ruth was pleased with the news. Maria and Eva were supposed to arrive the day before but instead she had had a phone call from Maria saying that they were delayed because Eva was in hospital.

Ruth went to the phone and called Maria.

'Oslo three-seven-six-nine, hello?

'Maria, it's your mother here.'

'Yes?'

'Your father sent a telegram. He has found Solveig and they found Johannes as well.'

'Really? Johannes? I can't believe it.' She paused. 'Is Solveig all right?'

'All I know is that he found her. I presume he would have told me if she wasn't.'

'Oh, thank you, Mama,' said Maria, who was crying and sniffing into the phone.

'How's Eva?'

'She has to stay in hospital for a few more days.'

'Why does she have to stay in hospital so long?'

'It's too complicated to explain on the phone. She's all right now, that's all.'

'Fine. I'm only her grandmother, why should I be told anything?' said Ruth in her softest voice.

'Alright, Mother, I'm sorry. I'll come and collect Solveig as soon as Eva is home safely, okay?'

'As you please, Maria. It's always your choice.'

'Goodbye,' said Maria as she slammed the receiver down.

Ruth put the receiver down, stared at the phone, and shook her head. After some minutes, she clutched her chest and called her maid. By the time Kari ran in, she was sitting upright gasping for air. Kari propped her up on the cushions on the settee, and fanned her with her apron.

Gradually Ruth's breathing settled and Kari helped her upstairs. Ruth would spend the rest of the day in bed, and Kari would make many journeys up and down stairs, fetching drinks, magazines, medication, and damp sponges to dab over her face.

★   ★   ★   ★

Eva was in hospital when Maria told her the good news and, despite the discomfort of her stitches and her fatigue, she had whooped for joy. Her mother looked happier than she had ever seen her and gave her such a warm hug that she found herself wondering if this was really her mother and not the same person who had visited her the night she had tried to get rid of her baby.

Eva was sent home from hospital after a few days, and told her mother she was perfectly able to look after herself, and that of course, she must go up to her parents' house to see Solveig and Papa. She had not been able to admit it to herself before, but she had been convinced that he was dead. The relief that he was still alive and that Solveig had not disappeared for good made her feel happy, despite her own problems.

She had a lot to reflect on; in saving her life the surgeon had had to remove her womb. She had never thought about having children and now she had been pregnant, lost her baby, and would never have another. She had only been four months pregnant. The nurses told her that it would have been a boy but refused to let her see it. She asked if she could have the body so she could give him a burial, but the doctor told her that they had procedures after miscarriages and would not allow her to keep what was nothing more than a by-product of a failed pregnancy. They told her that it was no bigger than her hand and was barely more than a blood clot.

Eva had no power against the insistence of the medical and nursing establishment. But he was still her baby. She imagined a perfectly formed baby in miniature and named him Leif, dearly beloved. He was her own beloved child, her first and only one. She cried for him, for herself, for Inger, for friends who had disappeared, and for all the grief of the war.

As she imagined a future without children, she saw something else. A vision of herself gowned up in an in an operating theater. She was the surgeon. This felt so right that she was not even sure if she had imagined it or if this was a true message from her future self.

Back on the Farm

Jorgen and Solveig stayed at the farm for the next week until Johannes had recovered enough to manage the journey home. Jorgen's fishermen had enjoyed their break and had made one of the bars in Levanger a second home. They had made friends with the locals and would give them lifts to various nearby islands in exchange for food and drinks.

After a tearful farewell between Solveig and Gerda and much handshaking and thanking, Jorgen, Solveig, and Johannes were given a lift down the road to the small harbor and, after helping Johannes onto the boat and Solveig hugging Gustav and his son, the fishermen started up the boat. They would be back at Old Vic Farmhouse tomorrow. Solveig was anxious that her mother would be angry, but Jorgen told her that she would be so pleased to see her that she would never be cross with her again. Solveig was not so sure but allowed her grandfather to convince her.

Maria traveled up to Trondheim, took the overnight ferry to Bronnoysund, and was collected by a couple of her father's men as arranged. Eva was safely recovered but too weak to travel.

When they arrived back at the farmhouse, they had a tearful and joyful reunion. Maria hugged Solveig so much that if she were not so happy she would have felt squeezed nearly to death.

Johannes had been carried to the downstairs guest bedroom and helped by the men and Kari to settle into bed. Kari fetched him some water and helped prop him up on the pillows.

She went down to Maria and Solveig, and told them that Johannes was comfortable. Solveig pulled her mother's arm.

'Don't be cross with Papa. He's been very ill. I'm going to look after him forever.'

'I'm not cross with him anymore. We can all look after him. But I need to speak to him on his own. Just for a moment, then you can go back to him.'

*　★　★　★*

When Maria saw Johannes, she ran up to him, kissed him, and cried all over him.

'You look terrible,' she said.

'And it's nice to see you too,' said Johannes, smiling lopsidedly.

'My god, what did they do to you?'

'I'm lucky to be alive. I nearly died twice. The first time I had pneumonia, and I could feel myself passing, but then I got the note from

Solveig.' He paused to catch his breath. 'It was like an electric shock which forced me back to life. The second time, I was tortured and shot at by the guards. They thought I was dead and left me in the woods. I was rescued by the farmer and nursed all night. They thought I was going to die. I could hear them whispering to each other but I couldn't let myself die after, after . . . and I wanted to see you again, Maria. I must be stronger than I thought.'

'Shush, you need to rest,' said Maria, stroking his hair. 'Have some water,' she added, passing a glass to him.

'I could do with something stronger.'

'Huh? Still the same old Johannes, I see.'

'Maria, I still love you. I know I have been no good, but there is only—has only ever been—one woman for me. I want to be with you again. Can you forgive me?'

'I know you love me. But,' she shook her head, 'do you think you can change?'

'I have changed, I promise.'

'I'd really like to believe you. But there's something I want to ask you,' Maria paused and stared hard at him. 'Can you forgive *me*?'

'You? What is there to forgive?'

'I am sorry for all those years when I shut you out. All the time I spent locked in darkness after Olaf died, I forgot I had anyone else in my life. I lost myself and had nothing to give. Can you forgive me for that?'

'I have always forgiven you. I was selfish and never tried to reach you. Maybe if I had, you would not have been so lost.'

Maria looked at him and smiled. She ran a hand over his forehead and touched his swollen cheek.

'We both need time. I shall stay here for a while and look after you. I'm sure my father will let us stay even if Mother objects. But then Solveig and I have to go back to Eva. Solveig has to go to school, Eva has to go back to work, and I have to find a job. You are an escaped prisoner, even if they believe you are dead. What will you do?'

'I'll either have to hide out here or go to Sweden.'

'It's too dangerous to escape to Sweden. Anyway, you won't be well for some time yet. Maybe you'll have to pretend you are a farmhand or something, but right now you need to get some sleep.'

'I'll get my strength back, don't worry. And I'll never stop trying to win you back.' Johannes fell back into the pillows, exhausted but smiling.

Maria walked slowly to the door and blew him a kiss.

The End

Lightning Source UK Ltd.
Milton Keynes UK
UKHW03f1538290318
320234UK00001B/35/P